TWIDDLEDUM TWADDLEDUM

also by Peter Spielberg

BEDROCK: A WORK OF FICTION COMPOSED
OF FIFTEEN SCENES FROM MY LIFE

TWADDLEDUM TWADDLEDUM

a novel

by

PETER SPIELBERG

FICTION COLLECTIVE   NEW YORK

Acknowledgments. Portions of this novel appeared, in somewhat different form, in the *Mad River Review, North Dakota Quarterly, New: American & Canadian Poetry, Quartet, TransPacific,* and *Zeitgeist.*

First Edition
Second Printing
November 1974

Copyright © 1974 by Peter Spielberg
All rights reserved
Library of Congress Catalog No. 74-77779
ISBN: 0-914590-05-7 (paperback)
ISBN: 0-914590-04-9 (hardcover)

Published by   *FICTION COLLECTIVE*
distributed by   *George Braziller, Inc.*
                    One Park Avenue
                    New York, N.Y. 10016

One-ery, two-ery, ziccary, zan,
Hollow bone, crackabone, ninery ten;
Spittery spot, it must be done;
Twiddledum, twaddledum, twenty one.

Hink spink, the puddings stink,
The fat begins to fry,
Nobody's at home, but jumping Joan,
Father, Mother and I.

Stick, stock, stone dead,
Blind men can't see,
Every knave will have a slave,
You or I must be He.

[*children's street song*]

to my parents

part i.

1. A MIGHTY TRAUMA IS OUR BEGINNING   3
2. SON OF TANTALUS   6
3. GROWING PAINS   15
4. THROUGH THE FIRST GATE   33
5. IN THE MARKET PLACE   49
6. A BED OF THORNS   68
7. THE WALLS OF DECEIT   77
8. THE TRANSFER   80

part ii.

9. FARE FORWARD, VOYAGERS   87
10. THE SOUND OF WOMEN   105
11. DISORDER & EARLY SORROW   123
12. AN OVERWHELMING QUESTION   131
13. DIE HEART & LIVE EASY   144
14. THE PROMISED LAND   157
15. THE BOOT   164
16. CERBERUS   171
17. FULL STOP   175
18. THE FINAL SOLUTION   185
19. UPPER BERTH   193

TWIDDLEDUM TWADDLEDUM

part i.

1. A MIGHTY TRAUMA IS OUR BEGINNING

It was a hard birth. The mother-to-be strained and pushed at the doctor's command, but the foetus would not be dislodged. The assisting surgeon cursed, "Stubborn, headstrong little bastard!" and gave a vicious twist to the accoucheur's forceps. The woman screamed again. Dozent Hecht shook his head and called for more ether.

When, many hours later, a male child had been delivered, the assisting surgeon, anesthetist, and nurses were completely exhausted. Only Dr. Hecht retained his professional calm, his bedside detachment, although he like the others was covered from head to foot with sweat and blood. He pushed the fagged-out assistants aside, ignoring the screaming newborn infant, and gave his attention to the mother's swollen belly.

Stamping his feet for silence, he bent over the strapped-down woman for a closer examination, his huge head almost disappearing completely between her spread-eagle thighs. He probed and grunted.

Then his great, bald, red head reappeared and barked rapid orders. A fresh contingent of assistants was called for. The dismissed group of aides made way for the new, but did not leave the operating theater. They watched with awe as the great doctor, one of the most experienced and most expensive in Vienna, grunting and puffing, yet doubtlessly in full control of the situation, seemingly inexhaustible, prepared for another birth.

The mother was allowed to return to consciousness from her ether sleep so that Dr. Hecht could inform her of the turn of events. Neither she nor the doctor had expected a double birth. Though the news was repeated half a dozen times, the poor woman did not fully comprehend. To help illustrate the point under discussion, a smiling nurse in an immaculately clean, starched, white uniform held the first-born up to its mother.

She did not understand, did not recognize her child. She was confused. The throes of labor held her in captivity; her attention was given to the baby yet to be delivered, not to the one already born.

This time Dr. Hecht proceeded as had originally been promised. No further anesthetic was administered, and, in accordance with his patient's request, a mirror was installed at the foot of the operating table to enable her to witness the miracle of birth. The second delivery was much easier, or at least it seemed to be so. The mother's eyes remained open during the entire operation, fixed unblinkingly on the mirror.

The second child was also a boy.

The good doctor handed the new infant to the smiling nurse who was holding the first-born, and then pinched his patient's cheek affectionately. At the doctor's nod, the nurse knelt close to the mother so that she could clearly see the fruits of her double labor.

The difference between the two was immediately noticeable. Although identical twins, the first-born was much larger than his brother. The second-born looked sickly, his skin grey, already a mere shadow.

The naming of the twins presented the parents with a problem. One, as planned beforehand, was duly named in honor of a favorite fictional character. But the other's was settled upon only after a long debate on the pros and cons of its unorthodoxy; finally and, alas, all too aptly, he was named after a Christian martyr.

It was no great surprise when, a few days later, the second infant succumbed to the respiratory disease that also for a time threatened the lives of his brother and mother. Dr. Hecht had expected as much. He offered comfort to the grief-stricken father by assuring him it was far better that the second child had not survived since he could not have lived long in any case. At best, he would have dragged on for a few years, his body wracked by continual pain, his mind tortured by his inadequacies. The autopsy showed that his inner organs were not fully developed. The surviving twin had somehow sucked up all his brother's nourishment in the womb, had shouldered him brutally aside. The unfortunate infant never had had a chance. Still, it was a great disappointment. All that wasted effort!

The father, on the advice of the doctor, kept the sad news from his wife until she had sufficiently recovered from her illness. The shock might have proven too much for her, especially since it was obvious that she was beginning to show a preference for her younger son—perhaps precisely because he was the weaker, the more sensitive, the one in greater need of care and love. She did not voice this preference; in fact, went out of her way to let it be known that she loved both equally. Yet her instinctive, almost unconscious, partiality was noticed by both her husband and her doctor. Perhaps even the surviving baby was aware of his mother's feelings.

He did not seem to let this bother him. He attacked the full breasts of his wet-nurse with a ferocious appetite, greedily sucking the warm milk, stuffing himself doubly now that his brother was out of the way, rushing from one breast to the other. The nurse complained to the kitchen maid about her charge, asking for some goose fat to smear on her sore nipples.

She said, "Pankraz eats enough for two, the little pig!"

And she also mourned the death of his brother, although the master of the house did not reduce her salary, as he might well have done since she had been contracted to feed two mouths.

2. SON OF TANTALUS

Usually I did not see my father except on Sunday, although early on weekday mornings he could be heard rushing through the house, tramping to and from the bathroom, blowing his nose, clearing his throat, trumpeting like an angry sea lion. The floorboards groaned under his heavy tread. If I listened carefully, I could hear the noises from the bathroom itself (even though my bedroom was at the other end of the apartment, down the corridor, through two sets of double doors, past the great living room, and my bed on the far side of the long narrow chamber).

I could hear the water splashing in the tub. He washed at the bathtub, using it as a sink, letting the water run full force, splashing, scooping up the water with cupped hands, flinging it at his hairy chest. Bending over the tub, he rinsed his face repeatedly, snorting for air, snorting with satisfaction.

He was an exceptionally clean man. He was also a very large man who found the basin too small for his needs and, therefore, made use of it only to wash his hands before dinner, a ritual that took at least half an hour. The morning cleaning lasted much longer. Besides scrubbing his hands, arms, face, chest and armpits, he disinfected his mouth and throat, gargling strenuously and thoroughly, a good five minutes for each side, with a potent antiseptic solution (half Odol, half Listerine—undiluted, straight from the bottle).

I could follow my father's progress from bed. Although I had witnessed the morning scouring only once, the memory of the naked, hairy giant was clear—bent over the tub, fiercely attacking his flesh with cold water, slapping himself with open palms. I could easily picture the scene by the sound, but I tried not to. I closed my eyes tightly. Yet now I saw another unpleasant scene. Another room, the toilet, in which my father had threatened to lock me if I didn't stop whimpering.

The toilet was a small high-ceilinged room, off by itself, next to the entrance of the apartment, beyond the kitchen, separated by a long tunnel-like hall from the other rooms. From it, a narrow window opened onto a grey air-shaft at the bottom of which the garbage was kept. The water tank was rusty, high up on the ceiling. When the chain was pulled, the water roared down to be sucked away in a gurgling whirlpool, down into the thick round sewer-pipe. From bed, I could not usually hear the roar of the water. Only in the middle of the night, on cold clear winter nights, was it sometimes possible to hear the faint rumbling of water in the tank above the toilet when someone had flushed and neglected to close the door in haste to get away, to get back to the warmth and safety of bed.

I remained in bed until after my father had left for business.

Then I ate breakfast with my grandmother who saw to it that I buttered the crescent-shaped roll instead of dipping it dry into my coffee as I preferred to do. The coffee was mostly malt and chicory, with a spoonful of real coffee thrown in for flavor. Since my appetite was poor, I had trouble finishing even this meager meal. Also the thought of the schoolday to come made me sick to my stomach.

This lack of appetite—actually more than lack of appetite—this general revulsion to food had not always plagued me. At birth I had been an extremely large baby, weighing over ten pounds, blessed with an appetite that amused the interns and gratified my parents but which was said to have irritated the wet-nurse. Up to my fourth year I remained above average in weight and size. Then, all at once, I lost my appetite. The transformation came about overnight. Every meal became a battle. I spat out my food, turned my plate over, and kicked at the table.

My mother's sweet coaxing changed to irritated pleading, and then to sharp invectives.

"Pankraz, hold still!" as she tried to force the spoon between my clamped tight lips.

"Disgusting child!" as she wiped up the regurgitated gruel.

And later, "Stop sniveling and drink your soup. Look at your sister. She is finishing her second bowlful."

I did not look at my sister. I kept my eyes on my own soup bowl. The thick soup filled the plate up to the brim. Web of veins, the skin spread thickly over dense soup clot, spotted with lumps of butter, melted and congealed again.

"Pankraz, eat your soup!"

"No, I won't." I pushed the bowl away, glaring at the cold curdled mass, threatening to throw up what I hadn't swallowed.

I was always ready to throw up. My mother opened her eyes wide with wonder, disbelief. She couldn't understand where the foul liquid I brought up came from since I hardly ate at all.

My sister teased me. She told me that I had better not go out on a windy day, especially with my umbrella (it was really a Japanese parasol given to me by one of Father's business acquaintances) or I might be blown up and away, umbrella and all, ribs showing through skin. And to underline the point, she referred me to our favorite picture-book, *Der Struwwelpeter*, which showed such a scene: a skinny boy who has refused to eat his soup, who has gone out on a stormy day with his umbrella open, and who is being carried up and away by the wind.

She laughed, I cried. She was merciless, always baiting me. And I believed her. I saw myself attacked by the wind, knocked off my feet, swept away, disappearing from view, above the bending trees, above the chimney tops, past the clouds.

The more I cried, the more my sister laughed. Our mother smiled, joining in the fun. They would probably tell the story to Father when he came home from work to have another laugh at my expense.

I had become morose. Nothing pleased me. I lost weight. I changed from a healthy child, plump, cheerful, a bouncing boy, into a sickly whining sulker, pale, underweight and nervous. My lips trembled. The dark terrified me. I woke up screaming. My nose was always running. I was suspected of being constipated. The physical deterioration worried my parents.

Dr. Hecht was called for consultation. It did not take him long to reach a verdict. I was to be put on a strict regime. The sugar cure (his favorite cure-all) as a start. Every morning before breakfast I was given a glass of warm sugar water. To begin with, the mixture was prepared with ten lumps of sugar to the glass. Each day thereafter another lump of sugar was added, until the water became too thick to drink without a spoon. After a month, a satisfactory bowel movement was finally obtained—the maid rushing to the doctor's office with the warm specimen to obtain his approval, his imprimature, and my release from the sugar sack.

But still my appetite did not improve. To prevent further loss of weight, I was fed raw egg yolks mixed with a small amount of dark beer and a large amount of unrefined brown sugar. In addition, I was forced to swallow two tablespoons of olive oil three times a day (mercifully followed by a bite on a piece of lemon to deaden the aftertaste).

With the loss of appetite, life became more difficult. My father ordained that I was to sit at the dinner table until I had finished all that was on my plate. When this method failed, the leftover food from my plate was saved, reheated, and dished up to me again at the next meal.

I soon fell into the depressing habit of playing with the food before me. I shovelled roads through my cream-of-wheat. I burrowed tunnels through mountains of cold mashed potatoes. When secretly given a piece of chocolate by my grandmother to help me get through a meal, I bit off small pieces and let them drop into the white mush, stirring it with my spoon until I had obtained a uniform mud color (betraying my benefactress in the process). But this play did not give me any pleasure. I did it out of desperation, to make the time pass. I had no illusion that such games would make the egg-barley and green peas disappear any faster. Even the promise of a glass of water if I finished half of what remained on my plate (we were not permitted to drink while eating) did not help. I knew there was no hope of swallowing the food. The lump in my mouth swelled as I pushed it from one cheek to the other. The longer I chewed the harder it became. I did my best to keep from throwing up, although this was the only way to end the meal.

More often than not, the little food I did manage to get down soon came out again (mostly undigested). I leaked from both ends.

But there were some advantages to being sick. The leftover food was not reheated. Instead, I was given zwieback spread thinly with butter, and tea with lemon; and when I was feeling a bit better, hot lemonade and thin slices of a homemade cake, appropriately called *Gesundheitskuchen*. My grandmother (who lived with us, or, rather, with whom we lived, the apartment being hers) sat by my bed to read me stories from the brothers Grimm. I was glad to be able to stay away from school.

I was often kept out of school even when I was not sick, when an epidemic threatened, when flu was in the air, when the pollen count exceeded the recommended norm, when the Danube was cresting, at the vernal equinox, on the day before All Martyrs' Eve, on major Jewish holidays—out of respect for my living (maternal) grandmother and to honor the memory of my other grandparents, deceased (the paternal ones by their own hand)—on election days, and at other times when the political or sanitary or general situation looked particularly ominous to my father.

There were also certain disadvantages to being sick. Dr. Hecht called, prodded, scolded, and invariably ordered that wet compresses be applied. We all knew what that meant! The patient was stripped, his naked chest tightly wrapped in an ice cold, wet sheet, secured by old diaper pins, next a dry sheet to pinion his arms, and then a layer of thick turkish bath towels. Covered with heavy blankets and all the quilts in the house, he was allowed to steam and sweat for an hour or so. To speed the process, the doctor's helpers—mother, grandmother, maid, cook, the washerwoman if it was her day—poured boiling tea down the patient's throat and sat on his feet to keep him from kicking the quilts off. When his face became lobster red, when the last drop of poisonous fluid had been sweated out, the process was repeated. From scratch. A fresh cold wet sheet, dry towels, and more blankets. And then, after another hour, another wet sheet.

In the evening my father looked in. If, in his opinion, I was still ailing, a camomile tea enema was administered to cleanse the body of any remaining traces of the toxin.

When I was considered strong enough, a visit to Dr. Hecht's office was mandatory. The doctor's office was not far away. It was right in the middle of one of the busiest business sections of the city. Yet the moment one entered the office building, the boisterous outside world was shut off. The heavy iron street-door swung shut by itself with a final click. A black glass sign in the form of a severed hand pointed across the courtyard. Another hand pointed up a broad flight of stairs. The stairs, which looked like ordinary stone stairs, were softer than stone and had much the same effect as a rug in sopping up all noises, especially footsteps. The building was too quiet.

An oversized double door led to the doctor's apartment, opening into a murky waiting room where the patients sat in a silent circle. Children cowered under their guardians' watchful eye and raised finger of warning. Coughs were stifled by gloved hands, sneezes by whispered reprimands.

We waited quietly. The only movement—our heads turning left and then right, watching the various doors which led into or out of the antichamber, for we never knew from which door Dr. Hecht might appear to summon us. There were so many doors that after a half-hour wait I was no longer sure which was the door we had entered by.

When our turn came, my father (and on rare occasions my mother) would first hurry off for a lengthy conference with the doctor. Only after this secret consultation was I taken into the inner office. The doors to the room were soundproofed, upholstered like a sofa, stuffed with wadding and covered with green plush. Like the outside doors they were double, with a space between the two sets of doors deep enough to accommodate a full-grown adult or to hide two or three children.

One half of the room, containing desk, filing cabinet, and book-cases, was almost blindingly light. The other half, separated by a wooden screen, was as dark as the waiting room. There the doctor's machines, medicine cabinets, and leather consultation couch were to be found, and there the doctor examined and prodded, cut and injected.

Dr. Hecht was a small man, but gave the appearance of being much larger because of the width of his stomach and the enormity of his head. He was bald, his face and scalp a dark reddish yellow. He grunted as he worked. His fingers were thick and warm. The sound of his breathing was labored and irregular. This snorting became louder and louder as he worked. It was the only sound. The padded doors sealed the office from any outside disturbances. They also prevented all sounds from reaching the waiting room. The patients bent over the examination table knew this only too well. Even the most cowardly soon learned to keep his mouth shut. Moans were useless. Cries of protest would be a waste of breath. If anything, they could only lead to worse. The doctor had no sympathy for squeamishness and would not tolerate any back talk, any interruption of his work.

When the examination was finally finished I was handed three pieces of chocolate candy to signal my dismissal. The doctor's gift was not meant to be taken as a sign of kindness or liking. It was an old habit, by now an empty gesture. Long before, before he had become famous, the doctor had hit upon the trick to pacify his wounded patients and had invested in a large supply of poor quality nonpareils. And now, although he no longer needed to please his patients, he continued to dispense the stale chocolates, without a smile, grunting with impatience, pushing the recipient out of his office. The candy was always the same kind and Dr. Hecht always gave three pieces which I always threw away the moment I was out of the office. I would no more have wanted to taste his nonpareils than I would have thought of drinking a bottle of iodine. For a visit to the doctor I was also given a small reward, called pain-money, by my parents. This I always spent immediately, running to the nearest fortune-telling-weighing-machine in sight. There was one in the shopping arcade around the corner which foretold my future in rhymed doggerel.

I hated Dr. Hecht. And it was obvious that Dr. Hecht disliked me as much, if not more. I am sure that the mutual animosity began the day I was born.

This is why:

Both doctor and mother had suffered much at the delivery. And for a long time before and an even longer time after the birth, the mother was totally confined to bed. Her recovery was slow and precarious, complicated by pneumonia and then by the great emotional shock of the second twin's death. Only Dr. Hecht's great skill and persistence had saved the mother's life. But throughout this struggle with life and death, the first-born had thrived, unconcerned, growing fat at his wet-nurse's breasts.

To make maters worse, the twins' mother never completely regained her health. She could have no more children. For the rest of her life she would have to suffer from a dropped stomach, incurable (and painful too—the fallen stomach pushing against the intestines, large and small, the intestines crushed against the liver, the liver against the kidneys, the kidneys against the bladder, and so on and so forth), a chronic condition which resisted all the doctor's talents, all the doctor's cures. She spent months in his sanitorium, lying in bed with her feet suspended way above the level of her head so that the dropped stomach might return to its normal position, slip back to its proper place. But to no avail. Dr. Hecht frankly admitted that there was little hope. The husband became hysterical and in a moment of panic dismissed Dr. Hecht (to the good doctor's great chagrin—it had never happened to him before and never would again). Other doctors were brought into the case—chiropractors, surgeons, faith healers, physical therapists, neurologists, alienists, acupuncturists, urologists, allergists, allopaths, podiatrists, gynecologists, stomatologists, pediatrists, geriatricians, pathologists, homeopaths, and nature doctors of all persuasions—but they also, one after the other, failed. Finally, the case came full circle. The husband begged Dr. Hecht to forgive and return. The doctor, still insulted but vindicated, consented to reaccept his old patient. He ordered one more lengthy stay at the sanitorium. The treatment, as expected, was not a complete success (incurable means incurable), but at the end of a year Dr. Hecht felt relatively satisfied and allowed the mother to return to her home provided that she avoid all excitement, all irritation whatsoever, and spend the greater part of each day in bed with her feet raised at the proper angle. Accordingly, the needed apparatus was installed in the bedroom of the apartment, and the bedroom door soundproofed with felt padding covered with American leather.

Meanwhile, the surviving son continued to prosper. When the mother returned to Vienna from her long stay at the sanitorium, she found that her baby was no longer a baby, not even an infant or a toddler, but a husky child, already more than three years old, large for his age, with a full set of teeth. Yet there he was, right out in the open, happily sucking at his nurse's teats.

The sight drained all the blood from the mother's already pale face. If the doctor had not been at her side to hold her up, she might have fallen down in a dead faint and done herself serious physical injury. She wanted to say something, but couldn't. The shock paralyzed her (though now her cheeks were turning red, flushed with shame).

Leaving his patient to be supported by her husband's arms, Dr. Hecht stepped forward, placing himself between the mother and child.

"Pfui!" he shouted, "What a disgraceful business, you shameless bloodsucker!"

He fired the nurse on the spot, insisting that she button up her blouse, pack her bags and leave the house that very day (showing no mercy toward the simple cowlike woman, refusing her pleas for severance pay or at least a letter of reference).

The child, interrupted in mid-meal, gnashed his teeth and began to scream like a stuck pig. He rejected his mother's arms, instinctively sensing that there was no sustenance to be gotten from that quarter. He spat at his father and bit Dr. Hecht's thumb.

The mother could not understand and took to her bed weeping. The father ran to the bathroom to scrub his hands.

Dr. Hecht was furious but managed to control himself better than the child. Yet from then on, the hatred between the doctor and the child was firmly established and mutually acknowledged.

End of explanation—(most of which I garnered from backstairs gossip, eavesdropping on the maid and washerwoman, and from obscure references darkly hinted at in my father's fulminations).

After the unexpected, though admittedly overdue, dismissal of my wet-nurse, I was handed over to the care of the maids and my grandmother. Later I was placed in the charge of a procession of blond governesses. Soon the memories of my first nurse became hazy. All that I could recall was a general feeling of comfort, a vague sensation of forbidden pleasure. For years after, whenever I misbehaved, the maids or my sister would threaten to recall the nurse so that I could be treated like the baby I was showing myself to be by my silly behavior. (The nurse would give me a good hard smack across my bare bottom, they promised, then wrap me up in a diaper and put me to bed with a pacifier in my mouth. Another squeal out of me and she would do worse!) I blushed. I hid my head. I was humiliated. Yet secretly I would have liked nothing better than to have had the nursemaid back. Her threatened return was the main subject of my childhood daydreams.

3. GROWING PAINS

I was sitting in the kitchen, my favorite room, watching the maid at the stove. Her clean apron swung neatly as she moved; starched and white, it reminded me of the freshly ironed sheet on my bed. I wanted to touch its hem, to run my fingers along its edge, to feel its crispness cut between the fingernails and the soft skin of my finger tips. I had done this once while sitting on her lap, but Anna had slapped my hand and told me to stop. When I tried again, she had pushed me off her lap.

It was Sunday morning, just before lunch and after the weekly bedbug hunt which I had as usual joined but not actively participated in.

For some reason, Anna, as well as the maids who had preceded her, thought that I should find these expeditions enjoyable. The maids went about the work with gusto, stripping the beds with one quick gesture, heedless of the flying feathers. The mattresses were turned over roughly to have their undersides examined. Every fold and crevice was opened and peered into. When they uncovered a nest of bedbugs, the battle was on. Speed was essential. Giving a hoot of satisfaction, the maids went to it. They speared the bugs on the points of their knitting needles, quickly and efficiently. The brown corpses and red blood were wiped off the needles with strips torn from old newspapers which were dropped into a half-filled chamber-pot in order to drown those vermin which, although mortally wounded, were still trying to escape. To finish, the breeding place was sprayed thoroughly with Flit. I was also provided with a knitting needle for a weapon although I never used it since the bugs frightened and disgusted me. Anna was amused by my squeamishness, but did not make fun of me.

The beds were made, the chamberpots emptied into the toilet, its foul contents flushed down, the needles and Flit put away for another week, and Anna had changed into a freshly laundered uniform and apron. Back in the kitchen, she busied herself at the stove, boiling the soiled sheets in preparation for the washerwoman, while I sat on a low bench, my back to the door, watching her stir the huge caldron with a long wooden stick, legs spread to give her leverage. Her movements were graceful yet powerful, like that of a country woman at a folk dance.

I offered to help, but she laughed at the idea.

"Anna!"

"Yes?"

"What are you going to do this afternoon?"

"Why do you want to know?"

"Just a question. You don't have to tell me."

She bent over to lower the flame under the caldron.

"Anna, where are you going?"

"To see my friend."

"Oh."

"Are you jealous?"

"No."

But I was. And Anna knew it and seemed pleased. She crossed the kitchen to stand close to me, wiping her hands on a dishtowel, purposely letting her apron brush against my bare knees.

I raised my legs to bring them closer.

"Better behave yourself, young man. Or I'll tell the master of the house on you for pinching me where I wasn't looking. He'll have you put away in a house for evil children."

She gave my knee a squeeze with hers. But all of a sudden she was gone. A second later, when the door sprang open, she was back at the stove, calmly stirring the boiling laundry. My father, clearing his throat, his head bobbing up and down politely, ushered a young woman into the kitchen.

"Aha! Here he is, Fräulein. Just as I thought, as usual in the kitchen bothering the maid. . . . Fräulein Müller, my son."

I had jumped to my feet the moment the door opened. My eyes met those of the young woman who held out her hand to me. I shook her hand and lowered my eyes, having seen very little but impressed by what had registered: her blue eyes, her blond hair, her piercing beauty. I felt her eyes still on me, waiting for me to respond to her greeting, but I found it impossible to say anything.

"Don't mind him." My father bridged the awkward silence, "He is an extraordinarily shy boy, as I have been telling you."

"I don't mind," she assured him. "Not at all. I'm sure we'll soon be getting along very nicely."

She dropped my hand and I was dismissed. Already my father was leading her away, down the corridor toward the living room, clearing his throat, repeating in his loud, high-pitched voice, "An extremely shy boy. . . ."

The kitchen door swung shut.

* * *

After the customary Sunday lunch of cold, boiled vegetables (arranged in a flower pattern on a round silver platter by the grandmother), after the dishes had been cleared and Anna had departed for her afternoon out, the gathered family—father, mother (who left her bed to join them for the meal), grandmother, daughter and son—remained silently seated at the oversized dining table. No one seemed ready to break the mealtime silence even though the meal was over and the law against talking while eating no longer applied. The elders sat quietly: the mother staring down at the tabletop; the grandmother, hands folded on her lap, thumbs circling each other, clockwise, counterclockwise, eyes partly closed; the father, hands in his trouser pockets, from time to time, slowly, almost imperceptibly, shaking his head in some unvoiced disappointment. The children did not look at each other. Their eyes were fixed on the afternoon mist that was settling first in the far corners of the room but gradually moving closer, threatening to cover the twelve ornately carved, high-backed chairs around the table. The boy's hands fidgeted with the napkin on his lap (overlooked by the maid in her rush to get out), fingering the stiff white cloth.

Finally, the father, with what seemed to be great effort, pushed his chair from the table and rose. The others watched as he made numerous trips between the sideboard and table, bringing back with him ruled and unruled paper, well-sharpened red and blue crayons, two lead pencils, a fountain pen, a bottle of ink, a ruler, a hard red rubber eraser, several notebooks, a ledger, a calendar, an armful of reference works. He lit the lamp over the table, adjusting it by raising and lowering the heavy brass counterweight till the circle of light was concentrated solely on the work area.

He cleared his throat, but before initiating the discussion of the coming week's menu for which the gathering was assembled, he explained the morning's visitor, ostensibly addressing himself to his wife and mother-in-law, although the information (and accompanying admonitions) was obviously intended for his son, since the mother, grandmother, and daughter, it now became apparent, had been present during the interview of Lotte Müller that morning. The father expressed the hope that the new governess would find her charge bearable, perhaps even acceptable, at the very least willing to cooperate—that was the important thing. He trusted that his son, now no longer a child but almost a young man, would know how to behave himself, to control himself, and not antagonize Fräulein Müller the way he had antagonized the previous governesses. (No, he was not going to review past failings and offenses, though that did not mean that he had forgotten or forgiven; but at present he had neither the time, nor the patience, nor the strong nerves needed for such a resumé.) To continue—Fräulein Müller was of superior intelligence, a student at the University, not your run-of-the-mill babysitter by any means. That should be apparent even to the dullest, thickest of ingrates. He further hoped that his son would appreciate the financial sacrifice involved. He paused.

On cue, the mother agreed, seconding the last point (—money was scarcer than ever, however . . .), adding her voice in praise of the new governess. The father nodded impatiently. The matter could then be considered settled.

After a final reminder to his son that it would be his duty to obey the new governess in all matters (she would be acting in loco parentis, so to speak) and delivering the oft-repeated warning that any further trouble for his invalid mother and nerve-strained father could prove fatal, he turned his attention to the weekly problem of the family's proper nourishment.

This was serious business. More often than not, the father worked himself into a frenzy during the discussion. The past was reviewed, scrutinized. Charges were leveled, infractions cited. Accusations, complaints, recriminations—one followed hard upon the other.

The meals of the last week had been too heavy as well as too greasy. He would not tolerate any more fried dishes. They were dangerous if not deadly.

"And can you offer me an explanation for the sauce on Wednesday's cauliflower?"

It had been far too rich. Also, cauliflower tends to bloat the intestines. He had not been able to sleep the whole night. It was a fact that he felt ill even at the moment.

"This I will not forget easily! The same holds true for the sauerkraut. Why do you insist on spoiling clean vegetables with thick sauces?"

No wonder his son looked so pale and underweight.

"We shall have carrots on Monday!"

The mother reluctantly disagreed with this since the washerwoman was coming on Monday and the standard meal on wash days was spinach with a fried egg in the middle. Anna had already cleaned the spinach so that she would be free to help the washerwoman.

"True. But why must the mistakes of the past be continued forever?" And had he not told her that fried foods were forbidden?

"What is a fried egg?" he demanded.

She tried to answer, but was not allowed to. He would tell her himself what a fried egg was.

"Fried!" he let her know. "Exactly."

He held up both hands for silence as he gathered his patience for the next question. "Are you deliberately trying to ruin my health?" He included his mother-in-law in his accusation.

Neither woman answered. But after a painful minute of silence, the older woman suggested that they postpone a decision on Monday's menu for the time being. For Tuesday night egg-barley and green peas were agreed to. The father noted the fact on one of the large sheets of ruled paper, underlining it twice with red crayon.

Wednesday was a problem. The mother suggested *Naturschnitzeln* but the father was not convinced.

"We have been eating altogether too much meat lately, and if we have meat on Wednesday when can we have meat again?—Saturday?" Staurday was a bad day because he worked late and the grandmother would go to synagogue. "Who is going to buy the meat? . . . Anna!"

He laughed with scorn. No, they would not have meat on Wednesday or on Saturday either. As far as he was concerned he could do without any meat at all. He pushed the loose pieces of paper aside, opened one of the books before him, turning the pages angrily until he found the marked passage he was looking for. After having reminded his family that the author of the work was a famous nature doctor, noted for his successful treatment of malformed children as well as for his investigation of longevity, he pointed to a pertinent passage with his pencil and read out loud the doctor's eulogy on hot or cold polenta cooked with prunes. An old Italian dish, the author explained, time proven (the father underlined this point by reading it twice), the main source of nourishment of the peasants in central Italy who were among the healthiest people the author had encountered in all his years of research and explorations of the eating habits of the world.

In his excitement the reader's voice had become louder, his face red, the same color as his huge deep-pink hands which appeared to be freshly scrubbed and still steaming from the hot water.

"We do not eat enough farinaceous food," he shouted and shoved the book across the table to his wife so that she could see the doctor's words with her own eyes.

"In black on white! ... Prunes and polenta ... strong peasants ... nourishment from the soil ... proven by research ... unbleached ... no chemicals added ... a world-acknowledged authority ... odorless white stool ... natural behavior ... unnatural behavior ... deliberate conspiracy ... criminal poisoners ..." The phrases spilled out, one after the other, punctuated by blows on the table, first with a pencil, and when that splintered, with the ruler. The mother's protests and tears were lost in the verbal deluge which continued unabated until his fury had spent itself, or rather, until his voice gave out.

The grandmother forestalled a further violent argument by suggesting that since he wished to cut down on meat eating, they should have it only once that week, on Wednesday. They could then have the polenta with prunes on Saturday, hot for dinner and cold for supper. Her son-in-law grudgingly accepted the compromise; sullenly entered the decisions on the appropriate sheets of paper. Thus, two other days could be scratched out. Still, there were four more to be taken care of, although Sunday was never a real problem. Lunch would consist of the usual platter of assorted cold vegetables without sauce or garnish; for supper, bread and butter and fruit.

The monotony of the day continued. The father finished the menu and withdrew to his reading room. The mother returned to bed. The grandmother put her eyeglasses on and took up her knitting. The children sat by the living room windows looking out on the street. The girl at one, the boy at another. It was Sunday outside also. People walked in pairs and family groups, visiting relatives or perhaps going to the movies. It would soon be dark. Already the grey stone apartment houses opposite were merging with the grey clouds behind them.

*   *   *

Lotte had many talents. She played the piano, had a good voice and a seemingly unlimited repertoire of folksongs, lovesongs, and marching songs, spoke fluent French and some English, told blood-curdling ghost stories, knew how to play chess and all kinds of word games and riddles, could fold paper into a variety of birds and beasts and boats, read poetry dramatically, recited Goethe by heart, did long division in her head, and made conversation effortlessly. She was also very beautiful, tall with smooth blond hair, cut at the shoulders, clinging to her head and neck, touching her face when she bent forward. Her clothes, like her hair, clung to her as she moved.

The first few months were wonderful. We understood each other. She accepted my shyness and seemed to enjoy having to take the initiative, glad to be making all the advances. She took me by the hand at exactly the right moment, at exactly the moment I needed to touch her hand. She talked to me as if we were old friends, not seeming to notice my awkward answers, skipping over gaps as if they were not there. She took me into her confidence, told me about her studies, imitating the most amusing of the professors, their tics and affectations, showed me her notebook, the margins of which were covered with caricatures of her schoolmates, admitted her dislike of winter vegetables (cabbage, rutabagas, and Brussels sprouts led the list), confessed her weakness for whipped cream and white wine and that she slept with a half a dozen goose feather pillows in her bed (three under her head, one at her feet, the other two in her arms), acknowledged her hatred for getting up early in the morning and her inability to go to sleep before midnight at the earliest (things might be going on which she wouldn't want to miss). Soon she had me talking also, eager to reveal myself, volunteering to tell her all.

At teatime my new governess and I were often joined by my sister and our grandmother. And again Lotte's charms had their magic effect. The cold living room, where tea, bread and butter, and homemade orange marmalade were served, became warm. The massive furniture became comfortable, its ugliness blurred in a soft haze. Our grandmother was persuaded to participate in the guessing games. Lotte kept score by drawing a gallows. For each mistake another limb was added to the condemned man. The player who was hanged first lost.

When it became too dark to continue with such games, Lotte recited ballads or told us horror stories. She told of the beautiful young princess who had been cursed by a witch and turned to a black corpse (or so it seemed). She was buried alive in the vault of a dark, deserted church. There she roamed about and screamed every night from midnight to dawn, suffering horrible tortures, beating against the locked doors in her agony, ringing the church bells wildly in a desperate call for help. No one dared come near the haunted church. The neighbors crossed themselves and closed their shutters. Tightly. But a young man who had secretly loved the princess came to rescue her. He stood in the highest pulpit of the church and drew a magic chalk circle three times around himself (to keep the living corpse away or she would have killed him, ripped his flesh away with her teeth). He kept his lonely vigil for twelve long nights. And every night the princess turned lighter, her screams less urgent, her moans softer, till finally she came back to life. But as the princess became whiter and whiter, her rescuer turned blacker and blacker. When dawn ended the last night of his vigil and the doors of the church sprang open, the beautiful princess ran out laughing into the bright sunshine. Her lover lay dead on a stone sepulchre, aged, wrinkled, black in death, a putrid corpse.

We preferred not to turn the lights on. In the darkness, the four square windows of the coal stove glowed bright orange. Our grandmother, usually silent, became talkative, told of her morning's shopping in the market and of her youth in Russia when she and our grandfather had ridden in a horsedrawn wagon from one country fair to another selling their wares in weather so cold that their nostrils were stuffed with ice, running from mountain bandits, passing through strange and dangerous places, and then at my request told Lotte the terrible story of the fire—long ago in the days before insurance companies existed—in which her husband had lost his fortune, his warehouse, wagons, horses, house, and even the dowry of three-hundred-and-sixty-five sheets and one thousand embroidered pillow cases which she had brought him. Lotte was a good listener, asking the right questions, laughing with pleasure, sighing with sympathy, shivering with fear, showing her understanding with a penetrating comment, illuminating an old story by a sudden insight.

When it came time for Lotte to go home, the spell was abruptly broken. The room became cold, the four windows of the stove dark. The electric light hurt my eyes, and the furniture seemed uglier than it had ever been before, bulky, overwhelming, somehow ominous, surrounding me, closing in—the oblong dining room table, the twelve high-backed chairs, the grand piano, the plush covered sofa, the leather couch, the armchairs, the sideboard, the tall cabinets, the clock, the round coal stove, the closed French windows, the black wood panelling, the flowered wallpaper—and yet at the same time the room gave the impression of being half empty, not completely furnished. I was frightened by the giant size of the room. It made me feel very small as if I were shrinking. I thought of hiding under the table.

But by the next afternoon when Lotte was with us again, my fears had vanished.

Then, abruptly, things changed.

Lotte turned against me. Although, at first, she did not voice her dislike, I sensed it. It was as if she had given me a chance, tested me, but I had failed the examination. She was disgusted with my awkwardness, annoyed by my timidity, by my cowardice. When we were alone she no longer bothered to hide her impatience.

Once I was aware of the change, I became even shyer and clumsier than I had ever been before. I garbled my words like a stutterer, muffed the simplest homework problems, tripped over doorsills, dropped my tea cup, laughed so hard at her jokes that I wet my pants. Or I hardly said a word all afternoon and then, just before she left for the night, blurted out something foolish, some inane nonsense, a jingle I had heard at school or a flip wisecrack, just to say something. At these moments she either chose to ignore me completely or pushed me from her as if I smelled bad.

Our day together began when my school ended. She waited for me outside the school gate. We walked over to Mariahilfer Strasse and down along it to the Volksgarten or the Burggarten, stopping on the way to look into the churches and cafés, and especially at the display windows of the shops that lined the avenue, bakeries, sweet shops, haberdasheries, leather-goods stores, merceres, fancy boutiques, corsetières, antique dealers, hardware stores, hesitating before the windows as if we were pricing the merchandise. Eager salesmen smiled, made way in the doorways of their shops, and then, disappointed, politely called after Lotte, "Perhaps another day, Fräulein."

Assistants on step ladders wearing white smocks were nailing red and white bunting above the entrance of a department store; others were raising a gilded wreath encircling the words:

40   JAHRE
GUTE WARE

The drivers at the taxi stands recognized us. They smiled and saluted. Although Lotte paid no attention to them, I was pleased. At these moments I forgot that Lotte was my governess and hoped that the cab drivers would mistake her for my girlfriend.

But that was another daydream. The walk was part of a game that ended as soon as we reached the park. There, Lotte reestablished her role clearly. She was my governess. I was a silly ungainly boy whose stupidity and impudence must be punished.

There were many ways of punishing. Sometimes she ignored me completely, did not answer me. She sat down on a bench, crossed her legs, adjusted her skirt, opened a book and did not look at me or say another word until it was time to leave. Or she made fun of me, ridiculing something I had done or told her. She was an expert at this, having an excellent memory as well as being a first-rate mimic. At times she became the strict disciplinarian. I was obliged to obey her command instantly. Hop to it! But I was not obedient enough.

"You are a sly, disrespectful child."

She spoke loudly so that the people nearby could hear every word. "Answer me. Are you?"

There was, of course, no right answer. I kept my mouth shut.

"All right, if you are going to act like a baby, I shall treat you as one. You'll go stand in the corner until you apologize."

The corner was the wall of the Kunsthistorisches Museum, where, in full view of the public, I received my punishment while Lotte sat on a bench close by and watched. Every half hour she came over to me to ask whether I was ready to beg her pardon. I wasn't. Standing in the corner, I pretended that I was there for a purpose. I was looking for fossils embedded in the stones of the museum.

A man with a cane who came strolling by stopped and asked me why I was standing there so straight and still like a soldier on guard duty. Before I could answer, Lotte's voice, clear and precise, answered for me.

"He is being punished."

"Aha!—really? He is a bad boy then?" The man turned to Lotte, lifting his cane to his hat in greeting.

"Yes, an insolent and disgusting child."

"I am sure he will learn to behave himself very quickly now, Fräulein. How can he not, being in such good hands? You strike me as being an excellent disciplinarian, kind but firm. Yes, very firm . . . and beautiful. Topnotch. The boy does not know how lucky he is."

He approached Lotte, smiling, "May I make a small suggestion?" Bending over to whisper in her ear.

She smiled also, but the gentleman's hopes were disappointed. She quickly dismissed him, and firmly too, judging by the speed of his retreat.

The punishment was repeated the next day and the day after. We walked home in silence.

My family was unaware of the trouble between us. After tea, Lotte, as usual, helped me with my school work, gave me a piano lesson, played compositions for four hands with me, suggested water-colors we could do together which she then brought to my mother in her bedroom to show her how well her son painted. Winter land-scapes of Alpine villages at dusk, mountains in the background, wooden houses with steeply pitched overhanging roofs, smoke rising from the chimneys, the tall spire of the church behind the houses, a curving road leading to the village on which a sled drawn by a single horse approaches, the driver's whip is raised to strike, the passengers huddle beneath thick rugs, their red faces unrecognizable, a copse of snowcovered pine trees in the right foreground, more snow is falling. I drew the mountains, houses, and trees; Lotte the horse and sled.

The few times my father bumped into Lotte, the effect of her charm was obvious. He blushed, asked her how she was, how her studies were coming along, how her family's health was, and was Pankraz behaving, not making too much of a nuisance of himself? And then he blushed more deeply, again asked her how she was feeling, smiled, excused himself, and went off to scrub his hands, locking the bathroom door behind him. Neither did my grandmother suspect Lotte's dislike for me. Perhaps my sister had noticed the change, but if so, it did not particularly interest her.

Lotte said nothing about it. And I would have died first. I did not want to acknowledge the rift which had developed, not even to myself. I still hoped that everything would suddenly change for the better, just as it had changed for the worse, suddenly, without warning or reason (oh, I had searched for the reason! dug up every word I had said to her, scrutinized everything we had done together, hoping that I could find my error and then a way to correct it, an apology, a promise never to let it happen again, an offer to make reparation, some heavy penance, to pay the penalty, anything to redeem myself, to be given another chance). For despite her scorn, despite her obvious enjoyment in humiliating me, despite her hard words and unvoiced disdain, I had the feeling, almost the premonition, that one day she would understand and forgive me, perhaps even fall in love with me.

I waited impatiently for the time to pass until I could see her again. I looked from the school window to see whether she was waiting for me. When I came to the gate and she was not there, my stomach turned. But it was only another part of the game. She had noticed my anxiety or maybe only smelled it, yet she was quick to turn it to her advantage. She deliberately came half an hour late. I pretended not to care, to be interested in the ballgame of the boys in the school yard. (Had I been asked to join in the game, my unconcern might have been more convincing; but my schoolfellows ignored me.)

My worst fright came when the maid was waiting for me instead of Lotte. Although this occurred rarely, when it did, I suspected the worst—that Lotte had decided to leave me. But, as it turned out, she had been delayed only for an hour and would call for me at the apartment instead. Sometimes the weather was so bad that my mother insisted on sending the maid in Lotte's place; we then spent the afternoon indoors. This did not happen often since my father strongly believed in the health-giving powers of fresh air and walking. No matter what the weather was like. He himself walked to and from business every day regardless of the condition of the streets or sky.

Sunday was the worst day of all. I did not see Lotte and had too much time to mull over the events of the past. I remembered her taunts; I also remembered her face and the scent of her body and clothes.

Sunday afternoons were long and empty. It was forbidden to make any noise or to play the piano because our father who had been away at work all week long needed his rest, desperately needed absolute silence in order to soothe his quivering nerves rubbed raw by the grating pressure of business. He withdrew to his room to wrap himself tightly in a compress of silence. The slightest sound, the click click of my grandmother's knitting needles, was intolerable to him. He screamed with pain and fury, and stormed into the living room, his voice rising higher and higher, shrill and piercing. He chased children and grandmother out of the room, barring the doors. But even there with the doors shut our father's scream cut through, continuing to echo and vibrate long after the screaming had ceased. In the dead silence that followed, I still heard his voice. I put my hands over my ears, but the screaming was inside, continuous, stretching on like the final high note held miraculously long by a strong-lunged coloratura soprano. Only another noise, the slamming of a door or the breaking of a window, could have cut the thread. But no one dared to make a sound. We sat without moving, waiting for the afternoon to pass, my eyes fixed, despite all efforts to avoid it, on the dark half of the long narrow room in which I knew our grandfather's empty bed stood. He had died in it before I was born and no one had slept in the bed since, yet there it remained, the bolster, the pillows and stained quilt naked, stripped of linen, the unshaken feathers settled to the bottom. The dead man's set of military hairbrushes, yellow bristles up, lay on the marble-top dressing table. As the musty odor which filled the room thickened, I listened to my grandmother's breathing and hoped that she had not fallen asleep. I could not see her face in the darkness. Her head was bent forward; her hands lying motionless on her lap.

When she was younger she had taken my sister and me to the park on Sunday afternoons. Now that she was over eighty and found walking difficult it was only on an exceptionally beautiful Sunday that we went to the park together, although she still insisted on making her daily morning shopping trip to the market.

I would have liked to go out by myself, to walk down to the river, perhaps to the amusement park across the Danube, or even just to sit on a park bench and pretend that I was waiting for someone. But my parents would not allow it; the streets were dangerous, the traffic wild. I would have to wait until Monday for Lotte. I waited impatiently; yet I dreaded her return. She would ask me what I had done all day Sunday, knowing very well that I had done nothing except to wait for the day to end. (I no longer found the bedbug hunt amusing, and had for some time refused to accompany Anna who, misinterpreting my decision as a loss of interest in her, had banished me from the kitchen.)

During the first year I had made the mistake of confiding far too much to Lotte. I had told her in great detail exactly what Sunday at home was like and how much I hated it, had always hated it since I could remember, even when I had been very young, when my father's depression had not been so obvious or as deep and when he had, on the rare occasions when he was in an especially good mood, walked about the apartment humming a tune from a Mozart opera, dressed in green striped pajamas, a shaving brush in his hand, lathering his face, now and then stopping to pat his children on the head. Once in a while I made an effort to lie to Lotte, telling her of the relatives who had come for a visit. But she was hard to fool. She knew that my father saw his relatives only once a year, a duty call, on the anniversary day of his parents' death. She knew that these two old ladies never returned the visit. The only other relative with whom we were in regular contact was a distant cousin who served as our family dentist until the day he committed suicide (strapped himself in the chair and give himself an overdose of laughing gas).

On Monday Lotte would ask her question and I would have nothing to answer. She would smile understandingly as if she sympathized and did not really blame me for the dull life I led. At the same time she would make it clear that she could have little interest in a person who led such a dreary life. She had spent Sunday afternoon drinking cool white wine with a new friend in a gay country inn on the outskirts of the city.

"Do you know, Pankraz," she confessed, leaning closer, "I feel a little giddy even now. Perhaps I drank a bit too much after all."

She shook her head, "We shouldn't have had the second bottle. . . . But it was *so* good!"

She stretched her arms wide to show how good. The motion pushed her round flesh forward, filling her white longsleeved blouse, straining against the smooth material, revealing in outline the pink flesh of her shoulders and the dark points of her breasts. Her face was so close to mine that her breath tickled.

I backed away, running my hands over my arms and chest, fingernails clawed to stop the tickling, but I couldn't stop myself from giggling despite all efforts to control it, to choke down the silly laughter. Lotte dropped her arms to her thighs and laughed also. Her laughter was cool and controlled.

"You are a little idiot," she said.

I took this as a judgment as well as a dismissal. Although she insisted on dropping the matter without another word, waving off my attempts to explain, we both were aware of what had happened. She did not mention the incident again, yet I could not forget my failure and knew that she would not forget either.

The next day Lotte was not waiting for me after school.

Instead someone who looked like Lotte and who pretended to be Lotte met me. Although her face, her figure, her voice, her walk, her gestures, all her mannerisms were the same as Lotte's, I recognized the imposture immediately. Yet I pretended to have seen nothing. I was frightened. I forced myself to behave normally, to be interested in the shop windows during our walk to the park, to wave to the taxi drivers, to keep my mind on the word games, for I feared that if I showed my recognition of the substitution the true Lotte would be lost to me forever. My only hope was to pretend not to have noticed. Although I did not fully understand the reason for the impersonation, although I could not be certain of its implications, it did seem clear to me that I was being tested. The exact purpose of the trial remained somewhat obscure, but its dangers were obvious. I was convinced that if I failed, as I had failed the other tests Lotte had put me through in the past—if I failed again, Lotte would never return. Her double would replace her permanently. And I realized that it would be no use to protest since neither my parents nor my grandmother nor my sister suspected the deception. They would not believe me.

At tea time Lotte's counterfeit volunteered to tell a story. She told my favorite one, the tale of the bewitched princess and her faithful lover. I listened closely, moving my lips to her words in case there was a hidden message woven into the story for me. The story was unchanged. But unlike the unfortunate lover I did not have to endure my ordeal for twelve nights.

Lotte returned the next Monday. I spotted her from the school window, leaning against the stone entrance post of the gate. I approached her slowly, carefully. She seemed tired, as if she had returned from a distant and strenuous journey. Although she offered no explanation for her absence, she knew that I had seen the difference.

"Did you miss me?"

I did not know whether I was expected to answer.

"Do you like my sister as much as me?"

"No."

She appeared to be pleased with the answer. She linked her arm through mine in full view of my schoolmates, a gesture she had not made before. I appreciated the change, but dared not hope for too much since I remembered the many instances in the past when Lotte's affection had turned to hatred without warning. Neither did I trust the warm pressure of her fingers. I suspected that Lotte herself might not be sure why her fingers tightened on my arm.

"It won't happen again. I promise."

We walked away from the school together; Lotte close to me, in step, her leg touching mine as we moved.

"You were splendid."

She continued to lean against me. I was not certain whether this was because she was tired or whether she wanted to reward me.

"Let's have some coffee with whipped cream to celebrate," she added. "You pick the café. But not too far away. I really am tired."

Because the weather had turned nasty we were no longer able to sit in the park. Instead, we walked. Lotte liked to look at the show-windows of the expensive stores along Kärntner Strasse. I preferred to walk along the Gürtel which at Christmas time was filled with tents and stands, transformed into a gigantic market, lit up by Chinese lanterns and strings of colored lights, overflowing with people, tradesmen, hawkers, shills, women with shopping bags, loiterers, policemen, and dirty children. Or we sat in a coffee house all afternoon long sipping raspberry extract mixed with soda water.

A cold fog had settled on the streets obscuring the rushing traffic along the boulevards. The streetcars slid by with hissing wheels like ghostly galleys over slick silent waters, the foreheads of the conductors pressed against the window glass, warning bells clanging continuously but muted by the thick fog. People hurried home, heads lowered, hands in pockets. By four o'clock in the afternoon it was already completely dark out.

For a moment, as Lotte and I stepped off the streetcar, we could see nothing. Although the conductor had called out our stop, we thought we were lost. Lotte turned back to ask directions. The streetcar had disappeared. Cautiously, holding hands, we moved forward, relying first on Lotte's memory, then guided by shards of martial music, and finally by the dim glow of light from the skating rink.

The ice was milky white, opaque. Our skates cut through it as if it were soft water, slurping as we turned sharply to avoid colliding with another couple. Then we were off again, circling expertly, smoothly, arms crossed behind, holding each other around the waist, completing one circuit after the other without interruption, without being aware of the revolving orbit, as if the path along which we sped were a winding river road leading to a desired destination. Although Lotte was a far better skater, I had the illusion that I was leading her, my legs providing the power for our flight.

Then we were no longer circling alone. Someone was moving with us, next to Lotte, keeping in step. The fog made it impossible to see who it was. I sensed the stranger's presence; I heard the drag of his skates on the ice. I tried to turn sharply but Lotte's arm around my waist stiffened and I was forced back easily but sternly. A hand touched my arm, moved across it to Lotte's wrist. The man's arm encircled Lotte, pinning my arm around her waist beneath his. The joining was accomplished effortlessly, quietly, the timing perfect. Not a step was lost. It seemed to me that we were now revolving even faster though I hardly moved my legs. The lights of the bandstand flashed by at more frequent intervals.

"It's only my friend, Hans Streicher."

They had changed positions without stopping: Hans on one side, Lotte on the other side, I between them; their arms crisscrossed behind my back, Hans' hand resting firmly on Lotte's haunch. They talked familiarly, exchanging gossip about people I did not know, laughing at allusions I could not follow yet whose implications I seemed to understand.

"I haven't seen your charming sister for a long time, Lotte. Has she been away?"

"Not really."

"I'd like to see her."

"I know you would."

"Well? . . ."

"When?"

"Tonight."

"Are you that anxious, Hans?"

"Of course. Can't you see?"

"The fog's too thick. But I'll take your word for it."

"Stop a while and I'll show you."

"Never mind. You can show me after."

We left the rink later than usual. Hans was extremely polite to me, addressing me formally which amused Lotte. He insisted on driving us home in his car. He was older than Lotte, of medium height, blond, his hair parted neatly to one side. On his left cheek he had a dark pink duelling scar which he touched continually, fingering it cautiously as if it still pained him. He wore a brown belted raincoat with a small shiny silver emblem in the lapel.

At the entrance of the apartment house he bade us good-night, expressing the hope that he would see us both soon again at the rink. But at the same time he took no trouble to be convincing in the lie. I was meant to know that he would wait for Lotte in the car. Lotte touched Hans' cheek. She whispered to him. On the way up to the apartment she asked me to do her a favor.

"Don't mention Hans to your parents—will you? They might not understand."

Without waiting for an answer she kissed me quickly on the mouth, stepped through the doorway, and ran down the stairs.

No one noticed my lateness. The apartment was dark. The only light, partially visible, seeped from behind the closed door of the kitchen where I could hear Anna washing the supper dishes. My grandmother had fallen asleep in an armchair in the living room.

I rushed to a window, opened it, and leaned out in time to see Lotte jump into the waiting car. Its headlights cut into the mist. The automobile moved away and was quickly out of sight. It was finally snowing.

The thin lace curtains moved uneasily, brushing against my face. The clock in the room ticked loudly. The gold colored pendulum swung back and forth. The polished wood floor creaked. I could hear the distant rattling and clanging of streetcars on Mariahilfer Strasse. The sounds were familiar, but they were night sounds. I had heard them before, when I awoke from a nightmare in the middle of the night and was unable to fall asleep again.

Someone had turned on the light over the dining room table. My father, mother, sister, and grandmother were sitting stiffly at the table. No one moved or talked, and it seemed as if the gargoyles who looked through the windows from the house across the street had stirred, shifted position, advanced into the room and settled on the faces of those who sat at the long table. Even the flowers on the wallpaper smiled the grin of the gargoyles.

4. THROUGH THE FIRST GATE

Is it a child's scream or a cat's? The boy crouched against the thick stone wall listens. Somewhere in another room a clock strikes the hour. It is the middle of the night. The boy moves from his cramped vigil, stepping out into the maze of arch-shaped hollow corridors. As he moves, the corridors lengthen, the walls recede, slowly crumbling. Without a sound. He stumbles forward, tripping in the darkness as the floor seems to collapse beneath his weight. Then he regains his balance. His right hand finds the banister of the staircase. The steps are steep. He descends rapidly using the railing as a crutch, hurrying onward eagerly, around the coiling spiral of the stairs, circling endlessly, flight after flight connecting one dark landing to another. The further he descends, the more familiar the staircase becomes. He knows that he has run down it before. He remembers the echo of his boots on the stone steps, the damp feel of the wooden railing, the rancid stench of rotting refuse rising from the bottom of the stairwell, sharp and bitter, mildewed, fleshy. And at the moment of recognition a vague awareness of purpose returns. He has come here to find someone. Someone is waiting for him. As if in response to his thoughts a shadow moves at the turning of the stairs; the darkness thickens. The shadowy form takes shape, revealing familiar features. It moves to meet him, deliberately like the hands of a clock, high leather boots creaking at each step. The boy tries to stop himself, but it is too late. He rushes, now trying to scream, eyes fixed in recognition, into the outstretched welcoming arms of the shrouded figure. They close about him with a cry of triumph; grinning, soft wormeaten flesh presses against his lips, his eyes, smothering him in a breathless embrace, covering him as with a heavy quilt.

*   *   *

I thought I awoke in a large room with a domed ceiling and high walls covered with flowered rugs, hot, stifling. The air was dusty, reeking of age. Something large and heavy held me down in the bed. Quilts choking, and a bloated body squashing me under its weight. I was far below it, small and getting smaller yet, fading away ... drifting ... falling ...

The weight receded. Suddenly it was no longer hot. A cool breeze came in through the open window. A storm was nearing. I heard the rumbling of distant thunder: one ... two ... three ... low and slow ... with long intervals between the heaves as if someone were breathing in the same room, close to me, panting. I thought that I could feel the warm touch of breath against my face. Although I was awake, I kept my eyes closed. The panting continued.

Finally the labored breathing became fainter and then ceased altogether. I opened my eyes and sat up, my back to the wall. The room was empty. My pajamas were wet with sweat. The blankets lay on the floor.

For more than a week the double windows had remained shut, the curtains drawn, the front door locked and bolted. From behind the curtains I had seen our neighbors leaning out of their windows, waving handkerchiefs and paper flags, tearing newspapers into shreds, tossing flowers and kisses to the troops in the street. I had listened to the music of the bands, the heavy shaking rumble of tanks, the beat of the drums, the stirring cadence of the marching troops, envious of the cheering crowds, resentful at not being allowed to join in the festivities. The noise of the celebration had continued throughout the nights making sleep impossible; until finally, after a week of ceaseless shouting, the city fell into an exhausted sleep. Even then an occasional shout could be heard in the distance, and the echoing heel-beat of marching men. On the morning after the week-long celebration of welcome to the new regime, the inhabitants of the city were asked to return to work. Yet a certain aura of gaiety and excitement remained. Sound trucks continued to move through the streets broadcasting martial tunes. The radio station played the same music, interrupted only by official announcements.

"Are you sure that you will find the way?" my father asked, and without waiting for an answer once again repeated explicit directions—when to cross, where to turn, and where not to.

I was not listening. I waited impatiently for my father to finish his instructions, automatically mumbling "yes" whenever I sensed a response seemed called for.

The school to which I had been transferred was within walking distance, but I had never been in that part of the city before. Because our maid had quit her job on the first day, and Lotte had not been heard from, I was to go to the new school by myself. My father was worried.

"Are you sure you will find the way?" he asked once more.

"You will be careful crossing Mariahilfer Strasse?" my mother added.

"Yes, I have crossed it before."

My father was not so easily reassured. He warned me of the dangers of the exceptionally heavy traffic, and cautioned me against speaking to anyone on the street.

"It's almost seven. You'd better go now."

I heard the door being double-locked behind me. Although I was not eager to return to school, I was glad to get away from the gloom of the sealed apartment. I reminded myself to walk slowly. I had an hour to reach the school, half an hour more than I should need.

The way to Hundsturm Platz was easy to find. Once I had gotten across Mariahilfer Strasse, passed by Esterhazy Park, and reached the footbridge over the canal, I discovered that all the streets ran downhill.

The main avenues were littered with multi-colored confetti and torn newspapers, the sidewalks smeared with white painted slogans and party emblems, the lampposts swathed in bright new flags. The grey buildings on both sides of the boulevards were wrapped in giant flags, long narrow banners, one next to the other, reaching from the roofs down to the sidewalk. Rectangular columns, almost as high as the buildings, covered with green vines and laurel leaves, crowned with huge silver emblems, had been erected on each side of Mariahilfer Strasse, uniformly spaced to form a seemingly endless arcade.

But away from the main avenues, across the canal, there were hardly any signs of the long celebration, only here and there a scrawl on the rolled down shutters of a store, an illegible slogan or an obscenity on the blind wall of a factory. Here the houses crowded against each other, walls bulging outward. The streets narrowed, twisted, and turned suddenly, all running steeply downhill, like rain-gutters emptying into the square.

The gutters were filled with students, approaching the school in single file from all directions, hurrying, half running, not because they wanted to or because they were late, but because the angle of the streets was now so steep that walking slowly would have been impossible. And even if one had attempted to slow up, the pressure of the students behind would certainly have prevented him from doing so. As it was, the boys, unintentionally, shoved each other along, forward, downward into the square and into the school.

Hundsturm Platz was like a deep valley paved with cobblestones. It lay encircled by walls of masonry, grey hills rising around it on all sides, houses pasted on top of houses, black chimneys, shuttered windows, crudely reinforced walls, stones heaped upon stones, clinging, heavy and thick, overlapping, threatening to crumble, to slide down into the square at any moment. But there was no room in the square. The squat school building at the center of the cavity almost touched the surrounding houses, separated from them by only a narrow belt of cobblestones. The school, an octagonal structure, looked ancient. An architectural monster of brown plaster, reddish brick, and dirty grey stone, it was patched together by arches and buttresses. On one of the sides, thick wooden beams propped up the outside wall. The windows were small, spaced at irregular intervals, without pattern. It was difficult to tell how many floors the school had since the original structure seemed to have been enlarged and built upon so many times that the accretions had become intergrown and hopelessly tangled. It was much larger than it first appeared to be. The low outside walls merged with higher inside walls and patches of roofs, and then more walls, building upward and inward. In the center of the building, a round tower rose high above the square. The tower appeared to be even older than the rest of the construction, almost medieval.

The inside of the school was as confusing as the outside. Corridors ran in all directions, crisscrossed by flights of narrow steps. In some places the corridors became so steep that they turned into staircases. Pale students swarmed through the corridors, no longer silent as they had been in the streets, but loud and aggressive, yelling to each other, pushing.

On the first day I had trouble finding my classroom. The boys in the halls paid no attention to my questions. I bumped into a rabbi, but he did not seem to understand. He was in a hurry and pushed me away. The classrooms into which I looked were in complete disorder, chairs and desks scattered about instead of being arranged in neat, fixed rows as they had been in the old school. In one room I found three rabbis talking excitedly to each other in a foreign language. When they saw me looking in at them, they rushed to the door and slammed it shut in my face.

I forced my way back to the entrance of the building where I had seen a group of school guards lounging about. I presented my notice of transfer to one of them who read it carefully and then motioned me to follow him. We moved easily since the students quickly stepped aside at the sight of the uniform. We climbed a flight of stairs, turned down a corridor, descended again, cut back along another corridor, made a sharp right turn. The guide counting the door numbers out loud, perhaps for my benefit, stopped at the third one from the corner and threw it open. The rabbi who had been sitting at a table in front of the room jumped up from his seat to bow to my escort.

"Another scholar for you, my friend," he nudged me forward.

"So I see."

"You'll soon have a full house here," he looked around the room.

"No matter. We can always squeeze in one more."

The guard shrugged his shoulders. He handed my transfer notice to the rabbi to sign, pocketed it before the ink had a chance to dry, turned smartly about and was already out of the classroom, slamming the door behind him, not giving me a chance to thank him for his help.

I waited to be told what to do, but my new teacher sat down again and busied himself with the papers before him, angrily shuffling through them, scribbling a word on one sheet, crossing one out on another. I cleared my throat to draw his attention; he was not interested. Another five minutes passed before he looked up. He was annoyed to see me still standing before him and waved me away, pointing vaguely to the other end of the room.

I found an empty chair near a window and sat down. The chairs and desks were better arranged than in the other classrooms I had seen in the school, but they were not in straight rows as I had expected them to be. The blackboard was cracked down the middle and dirty. It had been written on and then smudged, and something else written over it. I tried to read the words. They made no sense. The windows were closed. The glass in the one nearest me had been replaced by a piece of wood, yet I would not have been able to look

out in any case since the windows were too high up on
the wall.

The long narrow room filled rapidly. All the chairs were taken.
Some of the boys sat on top of the desks; others leaned against the
back wall of the classroom. A bell rang; it was eight o'clock. The
students paid no attention to the bell. They continued to talk loudly
and to scurry about, changing seats, kicking each other, spitting into
the empty inkwells. When the din became too loud, the rabbi looked
up from his papers and banged on his desk with a metal ruler. The
noise subsided for a moment, but after a while it was just as bad as
before. Screeches and hoots, the sound of fifty boys talking at once,
fighting, scraping chairs along the floor, pounding on their desks.
Again the rabbi rapped on his desk with the ruler. But soon again the
noise was unbearable.

At a signal from the rabbi, two students began to distribute the
books which were piled up in disorderly mounds near the blackboard.
The room quieted down somewhat. The rabbi got up from his desk
and walked around the room, ruler behind his back. The boys bent
over their books. They all had different ones. The student in the seat
in front of me was solving the problems in a mathematics text,
writing the answer in the book itself since he had no other paper. His
neighbor was studying what appeared to be an advanced anatomy
book. One boy was working his way through a dictionary. Another
was reading an outdated history of Austria-Hungary. I had been given
a geography book. I turned to a map of America and tried to locate
New York.

After lunch which we ate in our seats (everyone had his sandwich
wrapped in a brown paper bag, our teacher also), we exchanged
books. I received the math text. All the problems had been solved. I
checked them over carefully but could find no errors. The classroom
became darker. The small windows admitted little of the weak afternoon light. The room was still. The whole school was quiet. The
classroom looked even older and dirtier than it had before, the
plaster cracked and brown paint peeling off the walls. The students,
huddled over their texts, mirrored the sullen dreariness of the room.
Some were dozing, using their books as pillows. The rabbi, his black
hat pushed back on his head, followed the noisy flight of a fat fly
with sleepy interest. When it came near him he waved it away,
half-heartedly swiping at it.

I must have fallen asleep, for when I lifted my head I saw that the classroom was empty except for the rabbi who was sitting at his desk bent over his papers. It was after four. I closed my book and left the room quietly. The rabbi did not move.

On my way out of the school, I stopped off at the toilet in the basement of the building. It was such a low-ceilinged room that I had to stoop to enter. The urinals extended from floor to ceiling and were extremely wide, made of leprous white porcelain with brown stains like sores oozing down the middle. I stepped back and tried to finish as quickly as possible, but in the rush to get away from the oversized urinals I slipped on the wet floor. To save myself from falling in, I grabbed at the wall. Both hands touched the slimy porcelain. When I regained my balance, I fought my way out of the toilet, out of the school, eyes blinded by revulsion. I did not stop running until Hundsturm Platz was out of sight.

* * *

I knew it was raining before I opened my eyes. The wind drove waves of rainwater against the window panes. The windows shook with each impact. I lay in bed holding onto its warmth, postponing contact with the cold day until the last possible moment, prepared to plead with my father for an extra minute in bed. I dozed off, woke, dozed again but not completely, not letting myself sink too deep, keeping an ear cocked for the expected, now overdue, reprimand. But no one came to prod me. When I heard the clock strike half past, I threw the blankets aside and dressed quickly, not pausing to wash or to use the toilet.

I met no one on my way out. The living room was empty. The door to my grandmother's room stood open, yet she was neither there nor in the kitchen. Because it was so late I did not bother to look for my morning coffee. Probably none had been prepared. I could not even find my lunch bag. The kitchen table was bare and I did not have the key for the pantry.

I hurried to school, taking a short-cut across Esterhazy Park. On the way through the park, my curiosity was aroused by shouts and laughter coming from the public toilet. I had no intention of investigating the noise since I was late already and since I remembered my father's orders to keep away from crowds as well as his warning against stopping to talk to strangers. I did not mean to stop, even though (despite my father's injunction) I was interested. Perhaps, I thought, a group of workers has sought shelter from the rain. But then I clearly heard a woman laughing.

I hesitated. And before I had a chance to continue on my way, two schoolboys, probably also attracted by the noise, ran up behind me and grabbing my arms, one from each side, turned me around.

"Hey, let's have a look," they shouted.

"What's your hurry?"

I did not know the boys by name although they looked familiar. I thought that they might be students from my old school. They were about my age.

"Lay off!" I protested, trying to squirm out of their grasp.

They would not let go. Tightening their hold, they forced me forward between them. We entered the toilet three abreast.

"School can wait," the boy on the right snorted.

"See?" the boy on the left pointed.

At first I could not see. The round room was filled with people—both men and women. Many of them, especially the women, looked as if they had decided to come to the park on the spur of the moment and had hurriedly slipped coats over their housedresses. They did not want to miss the excitement. Some still wore hairnets. They jostled each other, vying for a better place, and would not let us through. Not even on tiptoe or by jumping up could we see above the heads of those in front of us.

"Give us a chance," my companions pleaded.

A tall man grudgingly moved aside. They squeezed through, dragging me along between them, arms linked, heads lowered, elbows out. When we reached the clearing, we were finally able to see the center of atrraction. A middle-aged woman and two men, one bearded, the other clean-shaven but with traces of soapy lather around his ears and the underside of his chin, were kneeling before the urinals. The men, both dressed in striped pajamas, were scrubbing the urinals with brushes and brown soap. The woman followed, mopping up the dirty water with a rag.

Standing over them, hands on hips, the female custodian of the toilets, shouted directions.

"A little more elbow grease, Herr Professor!"

The men in the front row of the ring roared their approval. They seemed to know both the janitress and the kneeling man whom she was addressing.

"You tell him how to do it properly!"

"Clean and shiny like a soup plate."

"He should lick the filth clean with his tongue," suggested a fat woman who had pushed her way forward behind us. She rested her hands on the shoulders of my comrades, her stomach and bosom pressing against me. The crowd moved forward with her, shoving even closer to the urinals.

"Do you need some help?" another of the spectators wanted to know.

The janitress yelled back in answer: "You can't help. You've got to belong to the trade union nowadays."

"Unless you are invited," a little man with steel-rimmed glasses corrected her.

"Very true."

"No volunteers."

"By invitation only."

The crowd thickened and took another step forward. Someone kicked a bucket of water over. As the kneeling woman moved to set it upright, her coat opened and before she could pull it closed I caught a glimpse of her body. She was naked beneath the coat, her large breasts hanging low, blue veins showing clearly through the white skin. My companions snickered. The poked me with their sharp elbows.

"Did you see what I saw?" the one on my left asked.

"Have you ever milked a pair like that?" the one on my right asked.

The janitress, who seemed to be in charge of the activities, tried in vain to make herself heard above the increasing noise. She waved her arms for silence. But each time the crowd quieted down, she could not get more than one word out without breaking into an uncontrollable fit of laughter.

"Gentlemen . . ." she began. "Listen . . ." she tried to continue. "We need . . ." But it was no use. She gave up trying to put her ideas into words. Instead she pointed to the half empty pail and then to the male spectators. Still, no one could understand her. She gestured; spreading her legs apart, she squatted down. The women screamed. The men whistled.

"You're a real pig!" a man yelled with admiration. He unbuttoned his fly and aimed a thin stream of urine in the direction of the pail. Other men pushed forward to do the same. The janitress collapsed completely. She sat on the floor, tears running down her face.

The stout woman behind us covered her mouth with both hands and hopped up and down. "I can't look! I can't look!" she squealed in my ear.

Then I realized that I was no longer linked to my companions. They had detached themselves in order to unbutton. Holding their penises upward, they aimed their urine not at the pail but directly at the kneeling woman.

Freed from their arms, I was able to get away. The crowd opened for me, glad to get at my place. When I was at a safe distance from the toilet, I stopped running and tried to adjust my dishevelled clothes. To my shame, I saw that my pants were wet through. I was not sure whether I had wet my pants out of fear or excitement.

The rain had not let up. I was glad of this. I walked slowly, letting the rain sink into my clothes. By the time I reached Hundsturm Platz, my coat and shirt were soaked through. The square was filled knee-high with water which continued to pour into the depression from the gutters of the surrounding streets. The water was filthy, more like sewage than rain-water, covered by a thick skinlike layer of grey scum. I waded through it, trying to avoid the floating lumps of garbage.

Although I was more than an hour late, no one reprimanded me. The classroom was dark and unusually quiet. The students did not look up when I entered. The rabbi, sitting at his desk, seemed to be asleep, but when I said good-morning, he lifted his hat in greeting and smiled knowingly. He looked me up and down taking note of my wet clothes with interest.

"The square is full of water," I explained.

The rabbi nodded his head in agreement, yet he looked skeptical and made a sucking noise with his mouth as if he were trying to dislodge a caraway seed stuck between his teeth.

"It's raining very hard," I felt impelled to add.

The rabbi continued to make the sucking noise, tilting his head back at an extreme angle, following my movements with his heavy-lidded eyes. I found an empty seat as far away from his desk as possible. After a while, though, he seemed to lose interest in me. Perhaps he was tired. His eyes closed, his head drooped, fingers playing with the fringes of a white silk prayer shawl that he wore wrapped around his neck. I wondered whether he was praying or trying to keep warm. The classroom was cold, as if it were still winter.

The room smelled of rotting, mouldy wood and dank, sweat-soaked clothes. I found it difficult to sit still. The wet clothes itched; my underwear stuck to me. I squirmed in the chair trying to detach the damp cloth from my skin. The palms of my hands were wet. When I cupped my hands over my face, the stench of urine made me gag. I could taste it.

He had no intention of stopping at the toilet, but in his hurry to get to school on time he left without using the toilet at home. The hiss of the rain splashing on the cobblestones mocks his need as he runs. By the time he reaches school he is desperate. He is surprised to hear shouts and laughter coming from the toilet in the basement. He wants to keep out, but has no choice since he is about to wet his pants. Although the toilet is filled with students, he cannot recognize any of them. At first they do not let him through. He pleads with them and pushes with his elbows, pressing his legs together to avoid an accident. When they see what he wants, they suddenly make way for him, shoving him through, urging him on. To save time, he unbuttons his fly on the way. The students cheer. The women scream. The men whistle.

"You're a real pig," squeals the janitress and slides to the floor, her backside fitting neatly into the concave niche of the first of the three giant urinals. She tries to speak again, but a fit of giggles prevents her. Instead she points to the next urinal before which his father kneels, dressed in green striped pajamas, half of his face covered with shaving lather, scrubbing at the brown slime which oozes down the center of the receptacle.

"Maybe he wants to help," one of the onlookers suggests.

"He can't," another argues.

"Why not?"

"You have to be circumcised to get a card from the toilet cleaners' union nowadays."

The janitress tries to speak, but she has still not regained her breath. So she points at his fly, at the same time making sucking noises with her mouth. The sound makes him shiver. He tries to cover his penis with his hands, but it keeps slipping out between his fingers.

"That boy doesn't want to help his father!" an elderly housewife who has pushed her way to the front of the crowd raises her voice to accuse him.

"I recognize the yellow louse now!"

He backs away, attempting to escape the rising anger of the spectators. He does not want to look at his father again. In his rush to get away he slips on the wet floor. To save himself from falling into the third oversized urinal, he grabs at the slimy procelain. When he has regained his balance he looks down at the woman who is kneeling before him sopping up the overflowing urine with a rag. Her coat is unbuttoned, revealing her nakedness. Her heavy sagging breasts swing as she works, blue veins swollen in the grey flesh, her fat brown nipples almost touching the floor.

He feels the blood in his penis throb. His flesh tingles and hardens. He frantically tries to hide the erection, but the crowd provoked by the spectacle, screaming with glee, steps forward towards him.

Without warning, the rabbi brought his ruler down sharply on my desk-top to signal the end of the school day. The students, as if awakened from a deep sleep, stumbled out of their chairs and shuffled from the classroom.

The rain had changed to a light, almost imperceptible, drizzle which wet my face softly as if I were walking through a maze of cobwebs. Clouds of fog drifted across the square, separating the school building from the city. It stood isolated like a medieval fortress, its tower disappearing and then reappearing in the haze. Forbidding, unreal, yet familiar. I walked through the twisting streets away from Hundsturm Platz, not looking back, but the brooding fear followed. I was shadowed by it, haunted by it, expecting at any moment to be pounced upon and devoured by it. I could not remember when it had begun. Perhaps it had always been with me, lurking in the dark niches of hallways, reaching out at me as I ran by.

I walked along aimlessly, not wanting to return to the apartment where the family was gathered waiting in the dusk, the lamps unlit, curtains drawn. The mother lying on the couch, feet propped up, a silk kerchief tied around her forehead and over her eyes to keep even the dim light out. The grandmother in the green plush armchair, hands folded on her lap, head nodding, yet so slightly that the movement is hardly discernible, following the swing of the clock's pendulum. The father unshaven, his pajamas wrinkled, sitting at the oversized dining room table, a pot of tea before him, elbows on the table, hands pressed to his temples. The daughter sitting at the piano, her fingers running through the scales but producing no sound for all her effort. The son squatting by the window, tracing the faint outline of last winter's ice flowers on the window glass. The rabbi bent over his desk, fingers playing with his prayer shawl. The large flowers on the wallpaper dumbly staring at the occupants of the room. All listening expectantly to each sound, the creaking of the parquet, a gust of rain driven against the windows, the roar of a motorcycle, the rattle of streetcars, the hollow echo of footsteps on the stone stairs—descending, a shout in the courtyard, the scraping of a garbage can, a door slammed, footsteps on the stairs—ascending, a knock, repeated, knuckles rapping on the front door. All looking up, waiting, eyes fixed on the door, but not surprised, recognizing the moment, as if it had all happened before, as if they had all dreamed it before, sharing the same recurring dream.

I walked aimlessly, neither toward the apartment nor away from it, unwittingly walking a ring around it. Although I paid no attention to the street signs, I did not lose my way. Now and then the fog lifted to reveal a landmark which I recognized, a six-cornered cross-road, the terminus of a streetcar line, a leather-goods store, a bridge, a dead-end street, the entrance to the park, a church, an underpass, a statue, a gilt-tipped iron fence, the lamp-lit entrance to a glass-covered arcade, the brick wall of a factory. Near the railroad yards the fog thickened, mixed with the smoke of the steam locomotives. When I reached the middle of the footbridge which crossed the network of tracks, I leaned far over the side hoping to be able to see the passengers looking out of the windows of a departing train. Instead, a locomotive steamed by directly below me, spewing chunks of brown smoke from its large black funnel. The smoke clung to the bridge, hiding the chain of cars which the engine pulled, couplings clattering, wheels gathering momentum as the train rolled out of the city.

Away from the railroad tracks the fog lifted again, only to hover just above the heads of the pedestrians. The streets were crowded; the shop windows lit up to attract customers. Shopkeepers stood in the doorways of their stores calling to the passers-by, inviting them to buy their wares.

Two helmeted soldiers walking leisurely arm-in-arm with two young girls momentarily blocked the sidewalk. A maid, her starched white apron flapping, bumped into them and almost spilled the beer mug full of whipped cream she was holding. The soldiers' girls were angry; they shook their butter-colored heads. The soldiers were willing to forgive and called after the maid.

"Give us a taste, sweetheart!"

Appetites aroused, they stopped before a bakery to look at the fancy pastry displayed in its showcase. They argued loudly but good-naturedly with each other before deciding to buy two giant-sized cream tarts which they shared with their girls, starting from opposite ends, eating their way to the middle. The girls competed gamely, opening their red mouths wide, sucking the soft cream, biting into the shell with small sharp teeth, swallowing quickly, pink tongues flickering in and out to catch the crumbs. The couples finished at the same instant, lips of the soldiers meeting the lips of the girls with one loud wet smack. The evening shoppers forgot their hurry and paused to watch, forming a ring around the tart eaters. The soldiers wanted more. They bought two new cream tarts from the pleased bakery woman and again the couples faced each other in friendly competition; lips to cream, steel helmets approaching blond heads. The onlookers clapped, cheering them on.

Finding the way blocked by the crowd, I turned around and headed back toward the railroad yards, over the footbridge, through the glass-covered arcade, past the locked gates of the park.

As suddenly as it had lifted, the fog descended, and by the time I reached Mariahilfer Strasse, the rain was coming down heavily, soaking through my jacket and shirt. The staircase of the apartment house was dark. Although afraid of the dark, I did not push the light button and forced myself to walk up the black stairs slowly.

                            *   *   *

The living room was all lit up; the open door a blinding rectangle at the end of the dark corridor. My father was talking to a woman, his high-pitched voice shrill, suddenly rising and then abruptly breaking off. Then the two voices broke the silence simultaneously, but stopped again immediately. The woman laughed. For a moment I thought it was Lotte.

I entered the room blinking, half blinded by the lights, unable to see the woman's face clearly, only the featureless outline. But I knew at once that it was not Lotte. The woman sitting on the couch was an impostor. She greeted me with a cry of welcome, rushing to me, taking me by the shoulders, embracing me, then holding me away at arm's length to examine me from head to toe.

"My God, it's unbelievable. I hardly recognize him. How he has grown! Why, he is almost a man. Isn't he?" looking at me but addressing my father.

She slipped her arm around my waist and walked me over to the couch, forcing me to sit down next to her, her arm still around me. I could feel her breathing. My shoulder touched her left breast. She did not take her eyes off me and squeezed even closer.

"Could it be that he was always this big and I just didn't notice before?" She cocked her head sideways and playfully rubbed her forehead against mine. "Maybe it's I who have changed," she challenged.

"Do you notice the difference?" she finally addressed me directly. "I was just telling your father: I'm engaged to be married—to Hans Streicher. You met him at the ice skating rink. Do you remember, Pankraz?"

I did not have to answer since my father repeatedly offered congratulations, echoed by the voices of my mother, grandmother, and sister who, as I now noticed, were standing in the shadows beyond the lights at the other end of the large room. Lotte's sister accepted the congratulations with poise, blushing faintly, self-satisfied, smiling.

"Hans and Lotte. Lotte and Hans Streicher . . ." she chanted gaily and crossed her legs smoothly, pleased with the rich sound of her silk-sheathed thighs rubbing together. And aware of the effect, she moved her blond head closer to mine so that her hair touched my face.

Soon though, she let go of me and got up, straightening her skirt and pulling her sweater down.

"Don't look so sad, Pankraz. I won't forget you."

We walked to the front door together, my parents following a step behind. My father helped her into her raincoat and offered to find her a taxi.

But she did not need one. "No, really. It's quite all right. Hans is waiting downstairs in his car."

She shook his hand briefly and turned to me. Hugging me tightly to her, she kissed me on the forehead and once quickly but hard on the lips. Her coat was open and I felt her breasts pushing against me. Then she stepped back.

"Enough of this hugging and kissing. You'll have me crying in a moment. Be a good boy and don't forget me. . . . I promise I'll try to come and see you again soon. Maybe we can spend a whole afternoon together as we used to."

She hurried through the doorway and ran down the dark stairs. As she brushed past me, I noticed that she was having great trouble holding back her laughter.

My father methodically locked and bolted the front door and shut off all the lights but one in the living room. I was about to tell him of the imposture, but on thinking it over I changed my mind, realizing the triviality of the discovery. It really did not matter. At best, the masquerade was a poor joke. I sat down by a closed window and listened to the rain. The window glass was dusty and I could see the faint outline where it had frozen over during the winter, where the ice flowers had grown. When my father shut off the last light, the reflection of the room disappeared; in its place appeared the faces of the leering gargoyles on the house across the way. The rain, running over their cheeks, distorted them. Their features disintegrated, melting together as if the stone flesh had turned into a soft jellied mass. My clothes were almost dry, but the strong sweet smell of urine persisted. It mingled with the spicy scent of Lotte's perfume which clung to me, especially to those portions of my clothes with which the impostor's body had come in contact. I breathed deeply, savoring the odor with open mouth.

5. IN THE MARKET PLACE

The dark of night lifts. The color of the sky changes to a sickly grey—the first squint of dawn. The market is already in full swing. Dead meat hangs in rows, skinned and quartered, disemboweled. Stout butchers, aproned and well armed, work with precision, not wasting a movement, expertly cutting the flesh from the bone. Now and then they pause to sharpen their knives or to shake hands with an early buyer.

". . . gets the worm." Butchers' jokes. They pitch balls of cut-away fat at each other. Whisper in the ear of the shrewd housewife, "Wanna give the old man a real treat tonight? Take home a pound of raw liver. He'll never know the difference."

Butchers' tricks. Behind the poultry stall an apprentice inflates chickens with a bicycle pump, then displays them plump and head-less, the dead birds hanging by a string around the neck, fat as balloons. Another turns a rabbit inside out with one quick pull. Shiny pink meat. The aisles are crowded with animals and vendors. Hawkers block the way, force free samples on the shoppers, suggest menus. "Today's gourmet special, Coddled Breasts of Goose: Choke a fleshy young gosling to death and immediately pluck the feathers from the breast so the blood will rush to it . . ." They confide secret formulas—de luxe, homemade beauty soap rendered according to a traditional middle-European recipe: "Plunge twelve pounds of fat into ten quarts of boiling water, gradually adding eight ounces of caustic soda to a pound. Boil for two to three hours, stirring frequently . . ."

Butchers' world. Beheaded pigs, rosy-fleshed, their throats sealed with cardboard bottletops, trademarked with green ink in the shape of a leaf, lie piled high on marble counters. Everywhere the same preparations. Meat hooks gleam in the abattoirs. This morning's killing for our daily bread. Dawn. The sun rising form a pool of early blood.

*   *   *

I was careful to watch my feet so that I would not step on anyone else's, or worse, into a basket of eggs. I was jostled, pushed aside by determined women who used their shopping baskets like battering rams.

The merchants were busy setting up their stalls, unpacking and arranging the food, chalking prices on chipped pieces of slate while their helpers ran back and forth bringing more supplies. The butchers were the busiest, cutting and chopping, beating the flesh into the desired shape and thickness. The tradesmen yelled with the gravel voices of newspaper vendors, shrill, excited, almost incoherent. According to them everything was fresh, ripe, juicy, wonderful, good, better, the best! Everything was cheap yet top grade, a guaranteed bargain. The chickens plump, hand-fed on the choicest grain, waiting, eager to be taken away—dead or alive, as the customers wished—the lambs still warm, the rabbits jumping in their cages, the apples just picked, the radishes fresh from the garden, even the fish were swimming merrily in large tin vats which looked like the tubs in which washerwomen boil dirty clothes.

The crush of the shoppers forced me against one of the fish stands. The owner was stuffing a huge fish which he had stunned with one swipe of the side of his cleaver into a net shopping bag a woman held open for him. Although half dead, the fish twitched violently, twisting out of the net bag to the chagrin of the fish-monger who had to deal the culprit a second blow. When he realized that his professional ineptness had not gone unnoticed, he turned his annoyance from the fish to the witness. He gave me a vicious look and buried the cleaver deep in the wooden chopping block.

"Hey you!" he screamed. "What are you staring at? Snotnose! Do you want a good knock on the head? Or is it a taste you're after?"

He reached into the nearest tub, brought out a squirming eel and waved it in front of my face.

"Have a bite!" he roared.

I wriggled away, looking for a way out of the market but could not get through. The crowd held me, forcing me to move with it at its own slow shuffling pace. The forward movement stopped at the next stand, then started again, dragging me along. An impatient shopper stepped on the back of my heel. My shoe came off. When I tried to drag it after me, I stumbled and fell to the ground. The mob of eager shoppers kept moving, inching along. They stepped over me. Some stepped on me. They would not take time out to look down. Filling their shopping lists was all important. The hawkers called to them, warned them that there were not many bargains left. They had to eat. Their stomachs were empty and growling, and there were more hungry mouths waiting to be fed at home.

I could not get the shoe back on; and since it was painful as well as dangerous to remain sitting on the market floor, I fought my way up and, with the shoe in hand, hobbled along as best I could. Cursing the shoppers under my breath, I tried to avoid stepping down hard on my bare foot. The ground was littered with all sorts of refuse, soiled pieces of newspaper, chicken skin, banana peels, fish heads, rotting fruit, and the wet, green tops of carrots which the vegetable women had torn off with one motion as if they were twisting the neck of a chicken.

Having finally pushed my way to an exit, I untied the knotted shoelace and slipped into the shoe. I was sweating from exhaustion and lack of oxygen. The stench from the inside of the market was so strong that it polluted the outside air. The hot sun acted like an oven; it broiled the food while it was being sold. My hands were sticky as though smeared with gravy.

Yet, all in all, I was pleased by my new unrestricted way of life. I thrived on it, growing tall overnight, feeling the surge of strength in my muscles.

The memory of the old, strictly ordered routine was already shadowy, separated from the present by dark gaps. I could hardly believe in the reality of the time when my father had gone to his business every morning, when I had trembled at the sound of his heavy footsteps, when I had sat on my hands all Sunday afternoon like a dummy afraid even to whisper to my sister, when the weekly menu was fixed by paternal fiat and no deviation whatsoever was tolerated, when our Sunday dinner had consisted of a platter of cold boiled vegetables prepared by Anna before her afternoon off, when I had had to wait for my grandmother to cut and bless the first slice from a fresh loaf of bread, when the biggest thrill of the week had been to go ice-skating, when I had been escorted to and from school,

taken by Anna in the morning, picked up by Lotte in the afternoon.

I often thought of Lotte. I could no longer believe that there had
been any trouble between us, that she had enjoyed humiliating me.
Instead I remembered the texture of her hair and her perfume and
the way she moved, the swing of her skirt. Whenever I saw a
well-dressed woman strolling down the street or a pretty nursemaid
bending over her carriage in the park, I compared her to Lotte. None
of them was as beautiful or as desirable. Yet I tried not to put too
much faith in her promise to visit me again.

When climbing the stairs on my return home in the evening, I
would not let myself think of her, superstitious that my hopes would
spoil my chances. I knocked on the locked apartment door,
expectant despite my resolution. When my grandmother cautiously
opened the door, I hid my disappointment.

The apartment was dark—my sister at the muted piano; my
mother lying on the couch in the living room, her eyes closed; my
father sitting at the long table drinking tea, fully dressed with a
packed knapsack next to him. My father who had always smelled of
strong soap, his skin pink, freshly scrubbed, was almost unrecognizable, his clothes wrinkled, unshaven, hands streaked with dirt,
fingernails black. Even his once brilliant white teeth were now a
brownish color. It was as if he had grown another layer of skin.
Sunken deep into the wrinkled greyish flesh, his wary eyes peered
out at me with a look somewhere between dread and doubt. I
avoided looking at him.

In the morning I left the house very early, sneaking past my
dozing parents in the living room as silently as possible; but never
silently enough, for my father's head snapped up, his eyes opened,
blinking, dazed. Then they focused on me, narrowing with mistrust,
as if he suspected me of wanting to rob him. His hands moved to the
knapsack, to the pockets of his suit jacket, patting them, checking
their contents.

*   *   *

As predicted, it turned out to be a hot humid summer. The heat
was especially thick in the low-lying sections of the city. The water
in the canal did not seem to be moving at all, its surface covered by
brown slime. The brief thunderstorms which occasionally brought

relief to the sweltering city passed over the valley in which the school was situated, barely wetting the roof of its tower. The accompanying winds could not penetrate the heat-filled pocket. The little rain water which did seep downhill into the breathless square from the surrounding streets was promptly sucked up by the greedy sun. The cobblestones steamed. The damp heat bred flies which soon became so numerous that their buzzing threatened to drown out the voices of the schoolboys. The flies swarmed over the pale sweating students, attacking the backs of their necks and the exposed flesh of their arms. No matter how many they killed there were always more. Those which could find no naked flesh to feed on settled on the students' trousers and shirts. Only in the early morning were the occupants of the school free of the pests. When the sun had sufficiently baked the walls of the building, the old flies woke up, the new ones crawled out of their eggs, leaving the warm wet corners of the classroom which provided even better nesting grounds than the muddy banks of the canals, their appetites enraged by the pungent smell of sweat.

The teachers were not as displeased by the heat and the flies as they might have been since they discovered that the discomfort was partially offset by the better behavior of the students. The heat tired the boys out. They became relatively quiet and docile, especially so when they realized that the best way to get along with the flies was to keep as still as possible, for a sudden movement or a loud noise caused the flies to swarm about wildly. In any case, it had been promised that the overcrowded building would be closed down soon.

At the end of July the authorities ordered the school at Hundsturm Platz to be vacated and the students to prepare themselves to be transferred to a newly constructed institution in the country. The transfer was rumored to be a permanent one. The boys were told to include winter clothing in the one valise each would be allowed to take along.

But the days passed. August was almost over and still the expected move to the country had not been carried through. In the meantime, the boys were free to do as they wished. Those who were not kept at home by their parents roamed idle through the streets and parks glad of their unexpected freedom. When they met, they pretended not to know each other as if they hoped that by keeping apart and trying to mingle with the other youngsters the authorities might forget about them. But these attempts were foolish, doomed to failure. The citizens readily recognized the intruders and chased them away, giving those whom they caught a thorough thrashing. Thereafter, many more of the ex-students from Hundsturm Platz stayed home. Those who continued to come out had learned their lesson and were more careful. They also soon discovered that the apparent lethargy of the administration was deceptive. Plans for the removal of the students and their families were proceeding as scheduled. By the end of the summer a number of adult transports had left Vienna. The students were to follow on a special train.

*   *   *

The day started poorly. Although I had intended to get out early, I overslept. My mother had to wake me by shaking me repeatedly—I was so sound asleep. She pulled frantically at my sheet. Even then I had trouble returning to consciousness and understanding what she was trying to say. I was furious with myself for having overslept and with my mother for having woken me up. Besides, I could not understand a word she was saying. She mumbled. She had to start all over again. Still I could make no sense of her babbling. The third time round I was finally able to get the drift of her message: the student train was scheduled to leave Vienna the next morning. I would have to be at the railroad station at dawn.

Then my father rushed in. He read the telegram out loud, his shrill voice breaking. He started to read it again, but interrupted his reading to admonish me for my laziness.

"Get dressed! Get dressed immediately! Do you want to be dragged through the streets in your pajamas?" he wanted to know (even though, because of the awful heat, I was not wearing any pajamas).

An argument followed on how I should spend the day. I wanted to go out as usual, but both my parents insisted that I stay home. My valise had to be packed, my room put in order.

"When will I see you again?" my mother asked, trying to embrace me. She wept.

I was unimpressed and continued to dress calmly, at my own pace. I carefully laced my shoes, finishing with a double knot.

My father became angrier, "Look what you have done. You selfish brat!" He trembled with fury. "Unnatural child! Good-for-nothing loafer! Greedy, callous egotist! ... Nothing moves him, not even the sight of his own mother's grief. Look at him! He doesn't care. Growing fat at our expense. Bloodsucker! Spendthrift! Traitor! Changeling! ... This I will always remember!" he threatened and running out of words raised his hand to strike me.

I easily evaded the slap, grabbed two apples and a half a loaf of bread from the pantry, and ran out of the apartment, not in the least bothered by my mother's tears nor by my father's threats and curses.

But the last curse did strike home. "Changeling!" he had called me, reaching out blindly for verbal flatirons to throw at me and coming up with one that hit the mark. Not that it floored me, but it did come uncomfortably close to the truth and I didn't particularly like the idea of having that which I was proud of distorted, maligned.

Of course I had changed. But that was nothing to be ashamed of. It was remarkable.

I who had always been shy, afraid of my father, afraid of the dark, of thunderstorms, of being alone, of strangers, of school, afraid of talking back—of talking at all, had undergone a radical transformation of personality. Overnight, I had become aggressive and tough.

I pushed to the head of the line shouldering the others aside, grabbed for the largest portions (or the best seat) and then tried to get my neighbor's share as well. I talked back to my elders, snickered indecently, found double meanings in the most innocent conversations, laughed scornfully at my so-called betters, picked fights with weaker boys, and, elated with success, insulted the stronger ones as well who were so surprised at my audacity that they let me get away with it. No longer fearful of being hurt myself, I found that it did not upset me to see others insulted or injured. Not even my father's violent temper (which had become worse now that his business was lost and he spent all his time at home) bothered me. I had no sympathy for my mother's invalid helplessness and felt impatient with my grandmother's wide-eyed sensitivity. (Already having forgotten that only a short time ago I, like my grandmother, had retreated to the shelter of the kitchen, hands over ears, in order to avoid witnessing the full wrath and thunder of a family storm. I did not like to be reminded of my past cowardice.) I looked with contempt at my sister's quiet obedience. I thought her a fool not to have emancipated herself when the opportunity arose.

I turned my back on the whole family, disassociating myself both from the tensions and the gloom of the household, keeping away from the apartment as long as I could, making a new life for myself on the streets.

Just the day before, I had approached a pretty nursemaid in the park and brazenly asked her for a match to light my cigarette, all the while ogling her well-filled blouse with unconcealed interest. And after she had given me the match I had sat down close by to watch her playing skip-rope with her charges. When it came to her turn to jump, she had lifted the blue skirt of her uniform, holding it above her knees—for my benefit, I was convinced. She waved to me when she left the park and I followed her until she disappeared through the doorway of an elegant apartment house. I was sure that we would meet in the park again soon and that I could initiate a more intimate acquaintance with her then.

My flirtation with the nursemaid was in part carried out at the instigation of a friend I had made at Hundsturm Platz and whom I later frequently met on my walks through the city. Red, who was a couple of years older than I, was always bragging of his adventures with women. According to him, he had slept with every maid his family had employed since the age of nine. But when he saw the deep impression his confession had made on me (I, in my inexperience, was so obviously awed and envious), he felt that it was his duty to add a word of caution: It wasn't wise to overdo it either.

To illustrate the warning he told me the tragic story of his older brother who starting from infanthood had had an exaggerated, if not unnatural, inclination for venery and who had ended up having a disastrous affair with a farm-girl in Poland one summer. The girl demanded so much of him that he was soon worn out. They sneaked to the barn ten times a day. His brother became pale and thin, although he had been as strong as an ox before. He lost his appetite and could not sleep at night. Finally, his parents became worried. Suspecting that something was not right, they kept a close watch on their son's comings and goings until they caught him with the girl. They pounced on them, tore them apart (with great difficulty, they were so tightly yoked), and gave them both a sound beating. They sent the girl away, forbidding her ever to bother their son again, and immediately called in the best doctor of the province to examine the afflicted youth. The doctor shook his head sadly, yet he hoped (though he promised nothing) that it was not too late. He prescribed good rich food, plenty of red meat, wine with meals, sour cream at bed-time, and lots of rest. Gradually, Red's brother seemed to be recovering his health. But, although his cheeks regained their color and he again looked as strong as an ox, the internal damage was irreparable and he did not live through the winter.

The warning fell on deaf ears. Instead of being impressed by the moral of the story, I became excited by the salacious portions of the tale and pestered my friend for greater details.—What was the color of the girl's hair? Was she older than his brother? How much older? Were her breasts full? Did she wear a brassiere? Were her nipples so big—or *so* big? Did she take her dress off or just hike it up? When the parents caught them in the barn, did they allow them to finish?

The extent of the turnabout in my character was most dramatically illustrated by my new attitude toward eating. I who had dreaded each meal, who had fought against every bite of food, now approached the table with the eagerness of a lover at the sight of his sweetheart's naked breasts. I threw myself at the food, stuffing my mouth with bread, greedily slurping the soup, rushing from one course to the next. On the rare occasions when meat was offered, I cast fork and knife aside impatiently and tore into the meat with my bare hands and teeth, lovingly sucking up the juices. I ate every bit of it, the fat as well as the lean, the gristle as well as the skin (the mere sight of which had made me gag before). Even the hated noodles and polenta were shoveled down with gusto.

My father was too preoccupied to notice, but when my mother called the change to his attention, he was appalled, seeing it as another example of my general moral corruption. Gluttony going hand in hand with sloth, covetousness and lechery.

"He's doing this deliberately," he postulated, "to make life harder for us. On purpose. He smells that we're helpless, that we can't stop him. . . . Wait, this is only the beginning! He'll suck us dry. I know him now for what he really is. Let me warn you: be prepared for anything . . . anything. For the worst."

My mother was confused. For years she had struggled to force food down her son's gullet without success, and now when she had given up, when she no longer expected an improvement, her prayers had been answered without warning and without reason. The success seemed a mockery of what she had wanted. It came at the wrong time. My appetite was not only ferocious but insatiable. The food supply in the store-room would not be enough; getting more was not easy. My grandmother had to do the shopping all by herself and the local shopkeepers were none too friendly.

After a full discussion of the problem, my parents concluded that their only course of action was to ignore their son's bad table manners and appetite. The strategy worked. Due to an obscure but, to them, welcome quirk of character, I was sheepish about my new-found appetite. Although I gobbled up all that was placed before me and licked the serving spoon clean, I would not (much to the relief of my parents) ask for more.

My grandmother who had not been consulted by the parents in their private discussion inadvertently aided the success of the conspiracy. Realizing that something was amiss and believing that my strange conduct was more due to the pains of puberty and to the strain of the times than to a deterioration of my moral fiber, she tried to find a way to make things easier for me. Remembering that as a child I had had a predilection for chocolates (a craving she had secretly fed by supplying me with the forbidden bon-bons) she squeezed a banknote into my hand every morning, slipping it to me on my way out, so that I could buy myself all the sweets I wanted during my diurnal wanderings around the city. The money went a good way toward slaking my appetite.

I also found that cigarettes helped. These I was able to steal from my father who kept a supply in the bottom drawer of his desk to be used medicinally at moments of exceptionally great tension when out of desperation and with an *apres moi le deluge* attitude of bravado he quickly took a puff or two and just as quickly spat it out before the nicotine could permanently damage his lungs.

Once shown the power of money, I was not long satisfied with the sums given me by my grandmother. I looked elsewhere for funds and found them in my mother's pocketbook. But I restrained my greed, limiting myself to amounts I hoped would not readily be missed. They weren't. (Rather, I thought they weren't. It's possible that my mother knew what was going on but for some reason of her own pretended not to have noticed, choosing not to give me away in order to shield her husband from further pain or because she did not have the heart to turn me in or because she felt partially responsible for my crime. Perhaps she purposely left her purse unguarded in places where it was easily accessible to me. In any case, I was never caught.)

Swollen with the success of my petty domestic thefts, I tried my luck in the public markets, only to discover that the shopkeepers were ready for me. They saw everything. They stared at me as if they knew what I was up to. They stood in front of their stands, arms folded across chests, looking at me with suspicion, ready to protect their merchandise. Even the egg-woman who seemed to be all engrossed in checking each egg before the light of a candle kept one sharp eye open for thieves.

"What are you doing here?" she accused me. "Do you want to buy anything or are you waiting for me to turn my back? . . . Don't try any of those tricks on me! I'm warning you—"

Her anger aroused the other shopkeepers. There was no use protesting. I backed away, but the egg-woman's accusation had awakened the market men. They reached for their cudgels and stepped forward. I did not know what to do to prove my honesty or to distract their attention long enough to make my escape. Luckily, I stumbled on an old woman who was selling freshly baked rolls. I bought two. This transaction seemed to appease the other merchants and they returned to their work. I hurried on, careful not to linger before any of the stands. My experience with the egg-woman had made me realize the danger of arousing the suspicion of the vendors. They would not hesitate to whistle for a policeman. It would give them pleasure to see the thief dragged off. I left the market halls empty-handed. My morning's work had been highly unprofitable.

Discouraged, my self-esteem hurt, my stomach growling with hunger-pains, I retreated to the park, planning to find a vacant chair near the nursemaids and to eat my lunch—even though I knew it was too early and that it was imprudent to squander my meager supply of food all at once (two freshly baked rolls, two apples, and what was left of the half loaf of bread). But the park was full, not a chair or bench empty. The trees were encircled by baby carriages; the old men made themselves comfortable to read their newspapers, spreading their fat thighs wide on the benches; the women had moved the chairs into a semicircle; towheaded, red-cheeked children in leather pants raced around on two-wheeled scooters; soldiers walked up and down flirting with the nursemaids.

When I saw a group of boys playing ball, kicking it across the park, I took advantage of the opportunity and ran through the park with them. Safe on the other side, I detached myself from the players and headed toward the center of town. The boys, confused by my conduct, stopped their game. They scraped their shoes on the gravel and looked at each other dumbly, but hostile. Then, the leader shrugged his shoulders and gave the ball a good hard kick. And off they charged, back across the park.

I was upset by what was happening. I had hoped to spend my last free day pleasantly, but my plans were going wrong; everyone was belligerent, everything seemed threatening. At the same time I was angry with myself for letting myself be frightened. It was as if I had suffered a relapse and were childish and insecure again.

To take my mind off such thoughts I ate an apple and the remainder of the bread. Immediately I felt better. And before I was aware of what I was doing, I had also devoured one of the rolls. Then, realizing the foolishness of my gluttony, I fought for control and restrained myself from wolfing down the last of the food. This left me with the other roll and an apple for later. Although still hungry, I now felt proud of my self-discipline and somewhat reassured that the day would, after all, turn out all right.

But no. Five minutes later I met with a further setback. Turning a corner without first looking, I found myself face to face with a brawny, fierce-looking tough and his two companions. Although I stopped in time, did not actually bump into them, they blocked my path.

"Sorry." The word of apology was already out of my mouth.

The trio snickered and spat into the gutter as one man.

I panicked. Disregarding the heavy traffic, I made a dash for the other side of the street. I was almost across when my foot caught on a loose cobblestone. As I went down, the apple popped out of my pocket and rolled into the gutter.

Before I could recover, the trio was standing over me. One of them pulled me to my feet.

"What's the matter with you, boy. Did you rob a candy store?"

"Not that little milksop. More likely he's running away from his mommy. Or did you lose your nursemaid? Speak up, friend!"

He turned to his grinning comrades. "This one's still asleep."

"Wake up! Watch your feet, not the sky."

I waited, not daring to move, not even to brush the mud from my clothes.

"What do you want now? A good kick in the ass?"'

"Move along, you're blocking the sidewalk."

I had barely taken a few steps when I was called back.

"You, boy! Is this your apple?" he pointed to the apple in the gutter.

I shook my head.

"You're sure?" he insisted.

Receiving no answer he shrugged, drew back his boot, and kicked the apple down the street.

His friend cheered, "Good shot!"

The other lit a cigarette. "You really scared the brat."

"Do you think so?"

"Shit, I know it. That was his apple. I saw it fall from his pocket."

And they were laughing again.

I sneaked away.

When I had recovered my breath and the worst of the fright had passed, I first began to assess the extent of my stupidity. Not only had the accident publicly demonstrated my cowardice, but the clumsiness had cost me dear. Half of my food supply had been needlessly squandered. If only I had picked the apple up! My panic was inexcusable. Or if I had at least eaten the second apple when I had wanted to instead of smugly saving it for later. I bit my lip in anger and dug my nails into my thighs through the cloth of my trouser pockets. But this did not bring the juicy apple back. I graoned when I recalled the sound of the boot meeting the red skin and cutting into the ripe flesh of the fruit.

To add to my troubles, people were stopping to look at me. My muddy pants, torn shirt, and dirt-smeared face invited their disapproval. Mothers pulled their daughters out of my path.

"Keep away from the dirty swine!" they scolded.

* * *

Although the sun lay hidden behind layers of mist, its fire crept through the haze and enveloped the city, swathing it in a blanket of heat. The mid-afternoon traffic was noisier than usual. Irritated drivers honked their horns. Bells clanging, streetcars pushed along, one after the other. Sweating teamsters rolled beer barrels into the cool cellars of restaurants, but, despite their efforts, fell behind in deliveries, unable to satisfy the city's thirst. At the curb, exhausted dray horses snorted, saliva foaming, heads bent as low as the harness allowed, straining to reach a puddle of water. One of them raised a hairy leg and kicked at the puddle so that the water splashed upwards.

A prosperous looking middle-aged gentleman, highly polished walking stick in hand, watched. Now and again he cautiously patted his ears with gloved fingertips. The gesture called attention to his unusually prominent ears which were stuffed with cotton soaked through with yellow earwax. When a youth approached him to ask for the time, he reluctantly unbuttoned his dark blue suit-jacket to take a gold watch from his vest pocket. He showed the face of the watch. The youth thanked him but did not leave. When the well-dressed man moved on, he followed, walking along with him. Although the man said nothing, he obviously did not welcome the intrusion. He cleared his throat loudly, pulled at his earlobe, and, using his cane expertly, speared the small pieces of paper that littered the sidewalk, flicking them out of his path to indicate his displeasure. He stopped in front of a watch repair shop and took his timepiece out to check its accuracy. Satisfied, he wound it carefully and gave his uninvited companion a quick sideglance. The rebuke had no effect. The youth continued to walk next to him. But just as suddenly as the boy had attached himself so he parted company, veering to the right and halting at the pedestrian crossing. The gentleman with the sore ears was relieved, but puzzled when he noticed that the youth was now walking suspiciously close to a decidedly attractive lady, crossing the boulevard with her in the direction of the public gardens.

The woman soon became aware of what was happening. When she slowed down, so did her escort, staying in step with her, but at the same time keeping a proper distance apart. Only once did he accidentally brush against her. He mumbled an apology and carefully avoided bumping into her again, slightly widening the space between them. Although she pretended to ignore him, she became interested in his persistence, wondering what she had done to attract him and whether he would eventually gather enough courage to speak to her. For the moment he seemed satisfied with just walking next to her and being mistaken for her acknowledged companion. She was amused, but when she had the opportunity to take a closer (yet guarded) look at her escort she became angry. The youth was younger than she had first thought and filthy besides; sweat ran down his dirt-stained face. When she saw a policeman, she headed toward him. The stratagem worked better than she had expected.

On her way back home for the bakery, the old woman stopped to rest for a moment in the sheltered entranceway of a small curio shop. Although she was very old she had never been so tired before. The thought of the long flights of stairs which she would have to climb made her feel helpless. Without realizing it, she had been leaning against the glass pane of the shop's only display window which was covered with such thick dust that she had thought the store was deserted. When she looked closer she saw that a light was burning behind the door. The dirty showcase was filled with an odd assortment of wares: rusty statues, candleholders, leatherbound books, ivory carvings, umbrellas, a pyramid of canned goods, cracked dishes, and miniature oil paintings in gilded frames, so old that the paint was hanging from them in shreds. What attracted the old woman's attention the most was the center display (the other objects in the showcase had been cramped closely together to give it ample room). One high leather baby shoe lay on a purple velvet cushion and next to it a tiny yellow skeleton. The bones looked like those of an underdeveloped, crippled child or dwarf, amazingly delicate and twisted. The old woman's curiosity had not gone unnoticed. The wrinkled face of an ancient white-beared man, wearing a high stiff black hat, pressed against the grating-covered window of the door. He cleaned a spot on the glass with his sleeve so that he could see her better and tapped on the window to draw her attention, motioning for her to enter. Frightened by the invitation, she backed out of the doorway and hurried away from the shop.

Despite the heat, the citizens enjoyed a parade. Even a minor troop movement without music or banners attracted them. They ran out of stores and office buildings, jumped off streetcars, left their chairs in the park. Windows opened. Everywhere heads appeared to admire the soldiers who marched with absolute precision, each step as sharp as a drum beat. The women and children especially continued to be thrilled by the sight of the uniforms. The housewives, were always ready to drop their sewing. The maids listened hopefully, glad of the chance to stop peeling potatoes. The children willingly let their hoops roll away—all anxious to run, to wave, to take part in the commotion.

The children wanted to go closer. They whined and pulled at their mothers' skirts; but the women kept them back at a safe distance, forbidding them to accept the fat man's invitation to share the excrement-covered stone bench or to sit on his enormous thighs. Sweat oozed down his white neck, gathered in the crevices of fat, overflowing, soaking into the handkerchief he had stuffed into the collar of his open shirt. The grossly obese man was oblivious to the flow of sweat; he ignored his audience which as on every other weekday had gathered nearby to watch him feed the pigeons. His attention was given exclusively to the birds that swarmed around him, sitting on his shoulders, on his lap, on his cap, eating from both his hands. The pigeons surrounded him, beating their wings, fighting to get closer, waddling over his wide lap on their naked pink feet. The fat man cooed to the birds and put a piece of bread between his ripe lips. One of the pigeons perched on his cap responded: it flapped its wings, beating the air, and plucked the morsel from his puckered mouth.

The silence was interrupted by a sharp rap on the front door. No one moved to answer it. The wife lying on the sofa opened her eyes; the husband carefully put his teacup down on its saucer; the old woman raised her head to listen. When the knock was repeated, louder and more insistent, the old woman reluctantly rose from her armchair and slowly walked down the dark corridor to unlock the door.

Though the youth had washed himself thoroughly in the tepid water of the park fountain, the foul smell of refuse and sweat persisted. It clung to him. He did his best to rub the dirt off his clothes and then sat down on the stone steps of the museum to eat the roll which he had carried about with him since morning. It was soggy and spotted with shreds of tobacco from his pocket; nevertheless, he enjoyed it, savoring the aftertaste, sucking at his teeth in search of the last crumb. When he had finished his sparse meal, he surreptitiously lit a cigarette, hiding it from view in his cupped hands, and blew the smoke down the open collar of his shirt, hoping that the smell of tobacco would overpower the rancid odor which clung stubbornly to his body and clothes.

Owing to an extremely heavy load of traffic and the record hot spell which caused the main roadbed to give way, all trains entering and leaving Vienna were delayed. The crush at the station was chaotic. Finally a long train pulled out of the yard, only to be shunted to a side-track where it stood broiling for hours in the height of the late afternoon heat.

The houses looked rotted and neglected as if they would crumble in a bad storm. Although it was late, scrofulous children played games out in the middle of the road, yelled and fought. Only an occasional automobile interrupted them. They did not let it pass until the driver leaned on his horn and threatened to run them over. When the children heard the approaching rattle of a junk man's cart, they scattered, disappearing among the shadows. He called up to the windows of the tenements, his words unintelligible, but the singsong sound familiar. The windows, like blank holes in the faces of the buildings, remained vacant. No one leaned out in response to the call. The junk man did not seem to have expected any business. He pushed on and repeated the cry. Even when he was out of sight his moaning could be heard through the dusk, echoing from another street.

Unseen, covered by low-hanging, bulging storm clouds, the sun sank with deadly precision, ending the day. The sky darkened, blending with the city's soot grey walls of masonry, merging.

* * *

It was late, later than I usually stayed out. The Burggarten, emptied of its daytime inhabitants, was quiet, almost completely deserted. The lovers who should have replaced the children after dark had not arrived. (Probably the black clouds and the threatening rumble of onrushing thunder were keeping them indoors. Or the heat had spoiled their appetites.) Only here and there a solitary figure paced back and forth, faithfully committed to an uncancellable assignation.

I remained seated, angry with myself and with my run of ill luck. To stop from once again rehashing the day's misfortunes and senselessly upbraiding myself, I attempted to take my mind away from my troubles by indulging my weakness for Lotte (yet prudently allowing only one short daydream). I stood up, lit one of my two remaining cigarettes and began, like the other faithful lovers, to pace back and forth, pretending that I had a rendezvous with her.

Soon the game lost its appeal; it seemed silly. Hunger relegated all other desires to second place. Not even the cigarette appeased it. I flung the butt into the bushes. It was senseless to delay further my return home. Sooner or later I would have to face the reproachful sighs of my parents. Yet I hoped that the gloom which awaited me would be outweighed by the special supper my grandmother was sure to have prepared. Spurred on by visions of thick slices of bread and butter, I hurried up Mariahilfer Strasse, any sense of foreboding overruled by the dictates of gastric juices.

Although I knocked repeatedly, beating my fists against the door, no one answered. I waited and then tried again, spacing the knocks between crashes of thunder. (The rain had overtaken me before I reached the house.) I stepped back to give the door a kick. It sprang open.

The hallway was dark, but lights shone brightly from the living room. I called out. No one answered. I felt my way cautiously down the corridor, eyes blinded by the light ahead. The apartment seemed to be empty, Yet every lamp in the living room was lit. The dining tables was set for supper—clean napkins, gleaming silver, large plates, soup bowls, a soup tureen. Two of the twelve chairs around the table were turned over, lying legs up on the floor. The green sofa was pushed into the middle of the room. The drawers of the sideboard were pulled out; one of them lay upside down on the carpet. The glass covering the pictures of my father's parents was smashed. The windows stood wide open. The curtains soaked by the rain flapped noisily, slapping against the window panes. A glance into my grandmother's room showed the same disorder: the open doors of the wardrobe, clothes scattered on the floor, the mirror over the marble-top washstand cracked. Our room, my sister's and mine, was a picture in contrasts—as if someone had strictly adhered to the imaginary line that separated her half from mine. The mattress had been dragged off her bed, the pillows disemboweled. White feathers spilling out of the slit ticking. But my half of the room was untouched, the bed freshly made, the windows closed. My packed suitcase stood ready by the foot of the bed securely tied with leather straps, my name painted as instructed on its metal surface in large white letters.

Although it was pointless to protest, I slammed the door of the room behind me. I rushed to the dinner table and raised the cover of the soup tureen. Empty! Furious, I kicked another of the chairs over.

Lightning gashed the sky and thunder followed at once. The storm surrounded the city. Lightning bolts clashed together, crossed, meeting from all directions. Standing by an open window I fought back tears of disappointment. Soon, though, I recovered my equilibrium and began to take stock of the situation. Most likely, my position was not as hopeless as I had first thought. There was bound to be some food in the larder. Perhaps a pot of soup was waiting on the stove. Temporarily consoled I retraced my way through the dark hallway toward the kitchen (deliberately refraining from turning on the hall lights to convince myself that I had recovered my nerve). However, before I could get to the kitchen, the door of my parents' bedroom swung open.

6. A BED OF THORNS

Lotte stood framed in the doorway. A dim light shone behind her, casting a glow around her blond head.

"Come in, Pankraz."

She closed the door and leaned against it, dressed only in a short white slip, her arms and shoulders bare.

"I thought you would never come home." She opened her arms wide, holding them out stiffly, then brought them forward and around my neck. She wet her lips with her tongue, leaning so close to me that her breath caressed my face, tickled, raising goose flesh. The tip of her tongue almost touched my lips; but she pushed me back.

"Still ticklish?"

Finding my dream threatened at the moment of its fulfillment, I denied the accusation vehemently. "No. No! Never!" I stammered.

And to my great relief, Lotte was not angry. She laughed and pushed me into my father's easy chair, kneeling down on a hassock next to me.

"But I like you to be ticklish." To convince me she proceeded to tickle me mercilessly. Finding the most sensitive spot between the ribs, fighting off my protests, she attacked till I lay squirming on the floor, out of breath, my torn shirt unbuttoned, pulled out of my pants, my heaving chest and belly naked. Gasping, I begged her to stop.

"Do you admit it?" she demanded.

"Yes. Yes!" I admitted.

She relented. Exhausted, we rested. She on hands and knees, leaning over me, pinning my arms down, her hair falling over her face, eyes hidden. I spread-eagle, looking up at her, slowly recovering, reawakening to the beauty of my adversary, aware of her closeness.

Her breasts leaned outwards, towards me. They filled the top of her low-cut slip. I could see the brassiere beneath stretched taut, the straps straining to hold the rich flesh. I tried to free my hands, but she tightened her grip.

"Wait."

I shifted my legs so that they touched her bare thighs and struggled to raise my head to find her lips. She turned her face away breaking the spell.

"Wait! I'm too hot."

Chastened, I lay back.

"Promise to behave yourself if I let you go?"

"Yes."

"Promise?"

"Yes!"

She let go. Pulling her slip down, she tossed back her hair. "Pankraz, be a dear and don't spoil things by sulking. All right? . . . Don't look so sad. We'll have a good time together. You'll see."

Unsure of what my reaction should be, I did not answer but following Lotte's example stood up and adjusted my clothes, tucking shirt back into pants.

"Don't," she said. "It's too hot." And then added: "I like you better without it."

I hesitated.

"Take your shirt off. Go on."

I did as she asked, folding the shirt neatly. Not knowing what to do next, I sat down in my father's chair again, holding the shirt on my lap.

"You're such a funny boy."

She moved toward me as if to embrace me; then changed her mind. "But I completely forgot! You must be starving. Have you had supper?"

"No."

"Are you hungry?"

"Yes."

"Thirsty?"

"Yes."

"Good!" she smiled happily. "I'll fix something nice. Wait. Stay here and I'll bring things. We'll have a feast."

As she moved, the shiny satin slip clung to her thighs; her back gleamed and her flesh seemed liquid, the strong dividing path of her spinal column leading down to the deep groove of her buttocks showing clearly through the white material.

Because she left the double doors of the bedroom ajar, I could hear her moving around in the kitchen, clattering dishes and opening cupboards.

"I'll be right back," she called.

Yet she took her time and I began to worry. At any moment my parents might return. My father would be beside himself if he found me trespassing. He would never tolerate such an intrusion. To add to my uneasiness, I now noticed that my parents' double bed had been stripped of its bedspread. It lay in a wrinkled heap on the floor, heedlessly tossed aside. And even worse, the sheets were rumpled, the pillows crushed, as if someone had made rough use of the bed. My mother's dressing table was in complete disarray, powder scattered over its glass top, perfume bottles unstoppered. Windows stood carelessly open, rain soaking into the rug.

I thought of running out the side door which led to my room and hiding there, jumping into bed, pulling the sheet over my head, pretending to be asleep, ready to disclaim all responsibility when my parents questioned me. But obviously this would not be believed. My father would be sure to blame me. Perhaps it would be wiser to try to straighten up the room before they returned. I would have to hurry, though, for if they found me in the midst of the work they would unhesitatingly condemn me. My very concern would be proof of culpability. But I had not considered the enormity of the task before me. Not only would I have to put my parents' room in order but also the living room and my grandmother's bedroom and my sister's half of our room, and most likely those parts of the apartment I had not had a chance to inspect: the kitchen, the maid's room, the storeroom, the bathroom, the toilet. Furthermore, the lack of disorder in my section of the bedroom told damningly against me.

On the other hand, wasn't it extremely unlikely that my parents would return that night? The disarray of the apartment seemed to indicate this. Most likely they had left in a hurry. Or had been forced to leave. Some time before supper. By the soup tureen on the dining room table, I placed the incident in the late afternoon. Perhaps they had been arrested and would not be coming back for days, if at all. Perhaps I was all on my own now. That seemed to be the most likely explanation. I remembered the unlocked front door and the broken glass of my grandparents' pictures. So my fears were needless, groundless.

I moved from the armchair to my parents' bed, flopped down on it, folded my hands on the back of my neck, stretched myself out fully, making myself comfortable. I tried to relax.

Yet I was not completely convinced. I re-examined the situation. Actually, the vandalism was limited. Nothing of real value had been smashed. The rugs could be cleaned, the clock repaired, the chairs set back on their feet, the mirror replaced, the pillow cases sewn up, the clothes brushed and put back on their hangers. It was always possible that the raid had simply been a warning, that my family was only being questioned, that they would be released in an hour or two, or sooner, that they were already on their way.

I did not know what to wish for. In either case, any case, I felt certain that I would be held responsible. Sooner or later I would have to pay for the outrage.

When Lotte returned from the kitchen with a tray filled with food, she found me folding the bedspread, attempting to smooth the wrinkles in the material.

"Lord, I never knew you were such a neat one," she exclaimed.

I blushed, "My mother will be angry."

Lotte shook her head.

"It's her best bedspread and if she finds us . . ." I tried to explain, but stopped, made aware of the silliness of my statement by the expression of scorn on Lotte's face. "You don't think so?"

"I know so."

"Oh."

"You needn't worry."

"Are you sure?"

"Absolutely. Don't be such a simpleton!"

She put the tray down in the middle of the bed. "Look what I found!"

Feeble with hunger I looked and my apprehensions were overcome. Besides three different kinds of cheese, homemade marmalade, goose fat with liver, and a can of Portuguese sardines, the tray held fresh bread, a bowl of preserved plums, and a tin of chocolate wafers.

"I brought the bread," she admitted. "And this!" revealing half of a Hungarian salami for which she knew I had a particular weakness. "That's not all."

She ran out and returned almost at once with two bottles of white wine. "That's to make you drunk and merry. Now dig in!"

Needing no further invitation, I attacked the food, swallowing mouthful after mouthful of the delicacies, uninhibited in the taking of my pleasure. Lotte curled up on the bed to watch, smiling at the speed with which I devoured the contents of the tray. She nodded encouragingly and filled my glass with cool wine whenever it was empty.

"You really have changed, haven't you?"

I couldn't answer because my mouth was still full, and before I had a chance to swallow she kissed me full on the lips. I tried to put my arms around her, but she slipped away easily.

"Finish your food first and then wipe your hands. You're all greasy."

I swallowed and pushed the tray away, dried my mouth with the back of my hand. Then, not knowing what to do with my hands, I put them into my trouser pockets, but took them out again quickly. Lotte, looking very much like a governess enjoying her pupil's embarrassment, refrained (for the time being) from coming to my assistance. When, to end the silence, I offered her my last cigarette, she broke into loud laughter. She laughed until the tears ran.

"Oh, you're sweet!" she cried and put her arms around me, hugging me tightly to her.

She took a full box of cigarettes from my father's desk and put one in my mouth. But for herself she preferred the squashed and dirty cigarette.

"It tastes better. Because it's yours."

We smoked in silence and drank more wine, like lovers, listening the storm and to the distorted strains of a waltz which the wind carried up to us from a neighborhood café. I looked at Lotte as much as I dared. Although disturbed by her nearness, I felt happy and proud of myself. An aura of well-being enveloped me as I contemplated my success—sprawled luxuriously on my parents' soft bed, half drunk with food and wine, about to indulge in further forbidden pleasure.

"Can I stay here with you?" I whispered.

She took my head between both cool hands and forced me to look into her eyes. "Idiot! I've locked and bolted the door and put the chain on as well. I wouldn't let you leave even if you wanted to."

"I love you, Lotte. I always have."

"Then take your pants off."

When I hesitated, she understood. "Are you still bashful? I can turn the light off if you like."

She left the bed to pull the lamp cord. The room became completely dark, the faint light from the window hardly discernible.

"Take your underwear off also. The sheets will feel nice and cool when you're naked."

I did as she asked and waited for her to return. I could hear her moving toward me and the smooth sound of her slip as she slipped out of it.

"Move over, silly."

She lay down on the bed beside me, found my hands and drew them to her, pressing them to her breasts. Although she had taken her slip off she still wore her brassiere. I moved my hands over her breasts, stroking them lightly, fingers circling their sharply defined contours. They felt hot and alive through the cool silk cloth, round and hard like smoothly polished stone, slippery, silk skinned, their points razor sharp threatening to cut through the undergarment.

"Do you want me to take my bra off?" she asked. "Then let go of them for a second. I won't run away."

She kneeled on the bed and unhooked her brassiere, letting it fall to the floor. Released from their confinement her naked breasts quivered.

For an agonizing minute she kept her distance. Arms bent backwards, hands resting on haunches, arching her back, she stretched and sighed until I called out with impatience begging her to return. Only then did she relent. She threw herself on top of me, breasts pressed to my face, their nipples heavy, lead tipped, scraping against my lips. Her fingers dug into my sides, moving down to my groin where she found my organ ready. Gripping it with one hand, she wet its swollen tip with spittle which she conveyed to it from her mouth with the fingertips of her other hand.

"Hold still!" she cautioned and straddling my loins with one leap (twisting expertly so as not to dislodge her breast from my mouth) she guided me smoothly past moist nether lips up into the soft core.

"Oh, that's so good, *so* good," she sang, while I swooned with joy under her and rushed madly from breast to breast, biting first one nipple and then the other, trying to stuff both into my mouth at the same time.

* * *

The silence wakes him. No wind, no rain. Not a sound from the black streets, nor in the room. Only the rasp of his own breathing; and between breaths nothing, vast silence and bottomless darkness. Then a door clicks shut somewhere in the apartment. And now he clearly hears the sound of high heels approaching from the direction of his bedroom (rather than from the hallway). Instinctively, he gropes for the sheet and covers his nakedness.

Even before the door opens, before the woman enters, he suspects that his visitor is not Lotte. When she speaks he is convinced that a switch has been made.

"Are you asleep?" she asks.

So as not to have to answer, he turns away from her and breathes deeply, pretending to be asleep. He pulls the sheet up further over his head, hoping that the impostor, snubbed, will leave him alone. But the woman has other ideas. She plops down on the bed and kicks her high-heeled slippers off—one in this direction, the other in that. Then she deliberately bounces up and down on the mattress, so hard that the springs jangle (so hard that he fears the bed will collapse).

"Wake up, you swindler!" she screeches and yanks the sheet away. "Don't pretend to be asleep. I know better."

She finds his head and pulls him up by the hair. Squatting, forehead to forehead, knee to knee, lips almost meeting, they face each other.

"I can imagine what you've been up to in your parents' bed. You little monster! And don't lie. I always knew you were a sly, dirty brat. Aren't you ashamed? Oh, how I'd fix you! I'm just itching to do it. I'd teach you. A good thrashing is what you deserve, smack across the bum. ... And then I'd lock you up and feed you nothing but bread and water, and after each meal I'd pull your pants down and give you another good going over. Yes! Till you learned to respect your governess. How would you like that?"

He is not allowed to answer. The pretender shoves him off the bed and stands threateningly over him.

"Kneel down and keep quiet!" she orders. "You dirty, perverted beast, I know very well what you'd like to do to me. I've seen it in your eyes. Pfui! I know what you do with yourself while you think about me at night in bed. Well, if that's the way you are, I'm going to give you a taste of it. But we'll do it my way, boy!"

And she pushes his head between her spread-apart legs. "Go ahead, you vile thing. Start licking!" she instructs him, holding his head in position. "Lummox! No, no, not like that. Clumsy! Don't be in such a hurry—gently, gently. Put your tongue all the way in. That's better."

"Thllp lmmn, thllp lmmn," he mouths, lips glued to her lips, tongue darting in and out, sucking the flowing juice avidly; at first only anxious to do the right thing, eager to please, afraid to offend, but soon overcome with excitement, he wallows in ecstasy, overjoyed with the delectable feast, hands kneading the double hillocks of her rump, fingering the deep valley between, gleefully rubbing his stiff tool against her bare legs.

"Ah, you filthy, filthy brute! You're getting me all sticky," she protests. Nails clawed, she pushes him away.

"More, please!" the depraved boy begs.

But she holds him off. "What's my name?" she demands.

"Lotte."

"Are you sure!"

"Lotte."

"Again!"

"Lotte!"

*　*　*

It was still night, but the rain had stopped. The windows were wide open, the curtains pushed aside. A cool wind swept through the room. The storm was over, the sky a deep dark blue, the moon brilliant, almost blinding. The few remaining clouds raced across the moon, casting long shadows. Her nude body lay exposed in the moonlight, her breasts pointed, finely hung like clinging drops of water, wet and full as if ready to burst. Her face was in the shadows, but I felt the heat of her eyes. I called her name again and suddenly she was in my arms. The terror and confusion of the nightmare was silenced.

"Were you scared?"

"Yes. Why did you leave me, Lotte? I don't want you to ever leave me again."

"I won't! Oh Pankraz, you're such a silly. But you're mine! You are in my bed and I'll never let you go. I won't."

Her words soothed me. Her wet tongue moved over my dry lips, insistently, back and forth, and then slipped between my lips to stab repeatedly, fiercely, forcing me to forget. The sound of her body moving on the smooth, starched sheet awoke my hunger. She heightened my desire deliberately, whispering to me, promising me everything; but holding me at bay, tantalizingly squirming and twisting, her turning thighs closing, slipping out of my grasp—. Then she opened her legs and pulled me down to her, carrying me with her to oblivion.

The moon had moved out of sight. The bedroom was dark, filled with shifting overlapping shadows. I fell asleep in Lotte's arms, her legs wound around me, covered by her flesh, my head buried between her breasts. The music from the dance hall floated up through the open window, mellow and slow, music for lovers, as if it came from far away and were played only for us, to soothe and to charm, to rock us to sleep.

7. THE WALLS OF DECEIT

My dreams turned blind and caked with dust. I tried to hold on to them, but they slipped out of reach, out of sight. . . . Sharp-edged, bright light banished the dreams and I awoke.

The naked sun showed herself, brazen, intruding through the open windows. The rays pierced, scattered drowsy thoughts, cut into the sour smell of sleep that hung like a canopy over the morning bed. The cool of the night was vanquished, making way before the hot rush of the oncoming puffing day.

I was alone. Lotte was not in bed with me. But I heard her moving about in another room. She called to me; her voice carried clear and strong.

"Pankraz! Get dressed. It's late!"

Her voice seemed sharp, irritated. "Hurry!"

I found my clothes lying scattered on the floor, crumpled and dirty in the clear sunlight. I dressed quickly. Before I was finished, Lotte entered the bedroom. She was fully dressed in a navy blue skirt and light blue blouse.

"It's about time. Hans will be here any minute."

"Hans Streicher?"

She looked at me coldly. "Do you know any other Hans?"

"No. But why is he coming here?"

"To help me get rid of you. Don't you think it's time?"

"How does he know that I'm here?"

"I phoned him this morning while you were asleep. When he heard that you were still here, he offered to drive you to the railroad station. . . . Now get out of my way. I've got things to do."

Lotte gave her attention to the bed. She pounded the mattress, smoothed the sheet, and slapped the pillows into shape. I watched her silently.

"Pankraz!"

She turned away from the bed and faced me, her voice painfully patient yet strict, as if she were talking to a child. It was the voice of the governess, filled with contempt.

"We had better get something else clear. I told Herr Streicher that I arrived here early this morning. Don't try to make a liar out of me. Last night never happened. Do you understand! If you say anything about it, it won't go well for you because I'll be forced to tell Hans how you assaulted me. I'll have to tell him all the filthy things you did to me. ... Hans can be very violent. Very. It's for your own good. If he finds out what you did, he'll rip your tongue out. Cut you to pieces. Don't make me tell him."

She looked at me closely to see the effect of her words. "Do you understand?"

I nodded, too mortified to speak. Yet I was not entirely surprised at her turnabout. I had half expected it. Neither did I feel that the punishment which was now to follow would be unjustified. It also was to be expected. I deserved it and almost welcomed it.

"You don't have to worry. I'll keep my word as long as you keep your moth shut," she added, softening her tone for the moment.

"But get away from the bed. And don't look at me like that ... like a moonstruck dog. For Christ's sake, close your mouth! You're drooling. Out of the bedroom, you evilminded pig! Wait in the living room."

She chased me away with a clap of her hands. I obeyed, the docile, obedient student, and settled with bowed head by a window in the living room, keeping out of her way.

When Lotte passed within my range of vision, I looked elsewhere, ashamed, for her clothes no longer shielded her from my knowing eyes. Through her pastel blue blouse, I clearly saw the naked breasts, and, beneath the cloth of her skirt, the hairy mount. I tried not to think of what I had done, yet I could think of nothing else. I remembered every lewd gesture, every obscene cry, every forbidden act. And just as I could not erase the scenes of our debauchery from my mind, so was I unable to detach my skin from hers. My bruised lips clung to hers, my fingers clutched her. The warm stench of the befouled bed enveloped me, adhering to my damp, slimy garments. The taste of her flesh clung to my tongue, sirupy, cloying. I closed my eyes and forced myself to swallow the curdled sour liquid which suddenly filled my mouth.

To avoid soiling the apartment I leaned far out of the window and took deep breaths. The nausea passed but not the disgust. Sickened by my own depravity, I bit the inside of my mouth hard. Yet I knew that the self-inflicted pain was insufficient reparation for the sins I had committed—neither for my carnality nor for the callousness I had shown toward my family. And even at the very moment of self-reproof, I doubted the sincerity of my mortification since I sensed that my anguish was caused solely by a concern for my own distress. If Lotte had not turned against me, I would still be lying in bed, wallowing in the slough, puffed up with the success of the conquest, indifferent to the fate of my family. My father had been right in reproaching me for my egoism and in foreseeing my disloyalty.

Sure enough! When half an hour later Lotte joined me at the window, I promptly forgot my heartache and disregarded my conscience pangs (despite the recognition of my culpability and despite my knowing that Lotte had enjoyed betraying me). The nausea was already gone. I found her nearness exciting. When she crossed her legs, the sound of her silk stockings aroused my desire.

Lotte slid closer, allowing her skirt to climb further up. She leaned out of the window, her head next to mine, her hair blowing against my face, and chanted coquettishly:

> *Einmal aus Liebe*
> *Einmal aus Zorn*
> *Einmal von hinten*
> *Einmal von vorn*

But it was too late. In the sunlit street below Hans Streicher's touring car pulled to the curb. He jumped out, slammed the car door shut and hurried across the sidewalk into the apartment building—the sound of his boots clear and precise, angry.

8. THE TRANSFER

The railroad cars were already filled to capacity by the time they arrived at the station. It took the combined efforts and threats of the young woman, her male companion, and two guards to push the youth aboard. The boys in the carriage refused to make way for him. When the door was forced shut, they pressed against him, squashing him against the door as if they hated him. He tried to raise his arms to protect himself from their attack, but found that this was impossible since his arms were pinioned. Soon though his fellow passengers calmed down. Although he was unable to move to better his position, the intense pressure which forced him against the door lessened. The shuffling feet, the muted protests ceased. Somehow, he had been assimilated by the group, become an inseparable part of its body, yoked, fused.

Although he feared that they intended to gang up on him, he now saw that this was not the case. They did not mean to harm him. The true reason for their apparent hostile action was that there was not enough room for them all in the railroad car. When the door was unlocked in order to shove a newcomer into the compartment, the schoolboys refused to move back and make room. Instead they pushed against the door, not to keep him out but rather to take advantage of the additional space offered by the partly opened door. It took the joint strength of three adults to prevent them from spilling out onto the platform. Only with great difficulty (and with the assistance of another guard) was the late arrival forced into the wagon and the door secured behind him. There simply was not sufficient room for the number of schoolchildren that had been packed into the train. Because the loading had begun the evening before, most of the students had spent the night in the same cramped position. They were forced to remain on their feet, held upright by the crush of their neighbors, body against body, soldered into one entangled sweating mass.

Compared to the noise and frenzied activity on the platform, the boys within the train were remarkably quiet and subdued. They did not even protest when the doors were opened and late-comers unceremoniously forced in (although they blindly pressed against the opening in a vain attempt to alleviate their discomfort). On the platform, the guards talked loudly with the conductors, arguing and joking. They hurried back and forth from one end of the long train to the other checking doors and searching for compartments where a passenger could still be squeezed in. The departure of the train was once more postponed when another truckload of students arrived. The ensuing confusion was quickly squelched as space for them was found in one of the partially filled baggage cars. The loading platform was suddenly cleared of all passengers. A loudspeaker counted down the time. Yet the signal for the departure was not given, even though the engineer sounded his whistle impatiently a number of times.

Crowded against the door, his face in profile against the glass pane, he retained the privileged position which enabled him to look out onto the station platform. (The sealed door was not opened again and he was able to use it to brace himself against the crushing weight of the bodies which surrounded him on three sides. Although at first he had mistaken the pushing and jabbing of his companions as antagonism, he soon realized his error. When the disturbance caused by his arrival subsided, the pressure against him diminished noticeably. The students quieted down. Because all movement was painful, they kept as still as possible.) Even though the loading platform was cleared of all passengers, the train did not get under way. The engineer sounded his whistle repeatedly, releasing clouds of grey steam. The long standards, which had been hanging limply from the rounded sides of the locomotive, suddenly bulged; filling with smoke, they appeared to be bloated. The signalman seemed unconcerned, his back to the train, his flag rolled up under his armpit.

The youth watched his escorts walking up and down by the side of the train. When they moved out of sight, he strained against the weight that held him captive, but it was impossible. At best, he could only move his head an inch or two, and, even then, he bumped against the heads of the others. Irritated by his attempt, they responded in kind, knocking their heads against his. The couple on the platform had come back. They returned to his field of vision.

Walking arm in arm, they approached the door and peered in through its soot-covered window. The young woman's lips moved, but he could not understand what she was saying. She repeated her remark, stepping even closer. Her companion seemed annoyed and pulled her away. Yet they did not go far. They stopped by the next pillar. Leaning against it, they embraced.

The people on the platform were becoming impatient. There seemed to be no reason for the delay. The train remained motionless. Guards stood around idly, thumbs hooked around their belts. The head of a rabbi appeared in the window of the locomotive, his white beard spotted with coal dust. He leaned far out of the cab and looked inquisitively at the signalman who paid no attention to him. Once again the engineer sounded his whistle. The rabbi smiled broadly as his head disappeared from view, covered by a hissing cloud of steam which enveloped the engine.

Waiting made the spectators irritable. To pass the time they paced up and down or walked in circles around the supporting columns of the high-domed station. A young woman strolling arm in arm with her fiancé persuaded him to let her take another look at the youth they had escorted to the train. They walked right up to the train, and, despite the protests of an official, her friend helped her up so that she could get a closer view of the inside of the compartment. She pressed her face to the glass.

The students in the railway carriage were so tightly knotted together that she had difficulty in telling one dirty face from another. Many of them seemed to be asleep, heads resting against heads, eyes closed. She rapped on the glass with her knuckles. Although his eyes were open, he looked stupified and did not seem to understand her parting words. Before the passengers or spectators realized it, the train was moving out of the station. The signalman cut across the tracks away from the moving train, meticulously rewinding his flag around its worn wooden staff. The network of gleaming steel rails reflected the brilliant morning sun. In the distance the rails curved, ablaze with the blinding fire of the mirrored sun.

Leaning against the iron pillar, she puckered up, standing on the toes of her high-heeled shoes, arms around her fiancé's neck, swollen breasts raised, their thick cocoa-colored points showing through the translucent, pastel blue blouse, Disengaging one arm from his neck, she waved. Without warning the train lurched forward. The domed station slid away. At first slowly, then rapidly, disappearing from view. His face glued to the glass pane, he strove to keep the couple on the platform in sight. He had not understood her parting words. He tried to move his head, but couldn't. The pressure of his sweating classmates increased; it tightened around him. As the station moved away, he saw her lift one arm to wave.

Supported by the pillar, they embraced. The man with his back to the train; the woman facing it, her head thrown back, eyes open wide, looking over her lover's shoulder at the soot-covered train window; coupled, arms wound around each other, breast to breast, pelvis grinding against pelvis, she strained on tiptoes to keep in position, her legs spread apart, her tight, navy blue skirt rucked up. Suddenly the huge wheels of the locomotive turned, piston rods clicking, pumping. And before the passengers fully realized it, the train was under way. For a while it ran parallel to the station platform; then, all at once, it moved away from the platform, sharply yet smoothly as if sliding sidewards. The rails greased, the run all down hill.

Instead of turning to the right, the train veered to the left, heading west, not east. The change in direction and destination appeared to have been a last minute decision. This would account for the unusual delay. Just before the train's departure a runner from the stationmaster's office informed the engineer of the decision. The conductors barely had enough time to change the plaques on the sides of the carriages. Here and there the old signs remained, pointing to the original terminus, an unpronounceable Slavic placename. The new plaques read: *Through-Train-Special* / *Le Havre—Amerika* / *Non-Stop-Express*. A second locomotive backed into position to help move the long chain of cars out of the station. The clashing of the couplings making contact covered the words of the public address system. The announcer repeated the message. But before the spectators on the loading platform had grasped his words, the train was rolling out of the station, lurching into full speed as if trying to make up for lost time. It was doubtful that the students on the train were aware of the change of plans. Most of them seemed to have fallen asleep, heads drooping, eyes closed. In any case, they could not see the plaques from the inside of the wagons. The voice of the announcer, distorted by mechanical flaws in the amplifier, was barely understandable in the great hall of the station. Garbled echoes bounced off the arched ceiling. The train was already moving at full speed, veering away from the city at a sharp angle.

part ii.

9. FARE FORWARD, VOYAGERS

A train roared out of the tunnel, climbed the steep, curved grade, and ground to a stop in the elevated station above the Bronx streets. Couplings clashed. Doors hissed open, then slammed shut. The train started up with a jerk, lurching clumsily, as each car in turn was yanked back into motion. When the train had gathered momentum, the movement of the swaying cars became somewhat smoother although the steel wheels screamed louder. Another train rolling in from the opposite direction crashed into hearing.

It was a good sound. Every click of the wheels carried him farther away from childhood, from the old landlocked city. Although fast asleep, burrowing deeply into the soft mattress, he could hear the count of the clicks. Five-thousand-two-hundred-and-eighty to make a mile.

* * *

The wheels kept clicking, the crossties flashing by like the markings on a tape measure, the telegraph poles every hundred meters. We sensed that we were better off on the moving train, better to be in mid-journey, still on the way, than to have arrived at the destination. Although no one knew that the train had turned around, that it was hurtling through the countryside (thick pine woods, patchwork quilt fields, dried-up river banks, shuttered villages) on a due westerly course, knowing would not have made much difference. The significance of compass directions was no longer clear. As long as the train did not stop. That was all that mattered. Not here, not yet.

When the train slowed down we leaned forward, all straining in the effort to push the wheels forward, fighting the brake. When the train halted (it was shunted to a siding to let the regularly scheduled cross-continental express by) we held our breath, waiting for the comforting motion to resume. Those at the windows were afraid to look out, as if by looking we would be accepting the fact that the journey had ended. And while the train stood there in the hot sun immobile as a house, no one would admit that it had stopped. Convinced that we could hear the puffing engine, we felt the movement and swayed unsteadily like sailors fresh off their ship who have not as yet found their landlegs.

Even when the train reached the harbor, the end of the line (the tracks led right to the water's edge), we continued to hope that the ride was not over. They had to pull us out of the wagons. In the dockyard shed we stood clumped together like so many sausage links, keeping to the groupings we had formed on the train, to the railway carriage molds into which we had been pressed.

Probably we were so stubborn because we had been pushed out of the train once before. At the border the train had pulled into a freight inspection center and all passengers had been ordered off so it could be steam-cleaned, outside and inside, in compliance with American immigration laws. We spent the night lined up before a row of customs sheds manned jointly by the refugee agency and representatives of the local government.

It was a warm night. We should have been glad of the fresh air but after an hour of waiting we had had enough. The concrete floor hurt our feet. And just as we were accustoming ourselves to the position, learning to sleep standing up like horses, the gates of the sheds were thrown open and the line began to move. Slowly, a few steps every minute, but enough to keep us awake. The processing was simple and efficient—perhaps a bit crude by modern industrial standards, but being ignorant in such matters we were impressed and did as we were told without hesitation. Actually, we weren't told anything—gestures sufficed. And even these were unnecessary. We simply followed in the footsteps of the person ahead.

We entered the first shed two abreast and handed our papers to the seated officials on both sides of the line in an alternating pattern, first left, second right, third left, fourth right, and so on: ticket, passport, traveling orders, genealogy, exit permit, tax clearance, report card, affidavit, vaccination certificate, transit visa, letters of reference. In the second shed we stripped, dropping our clothes onto a conveyer belt which carried them to a team of washerwomen who stood before a row of tin washtubs. Identically dressed in ankle-length black rubber aprons and kerchiefs which covered their heads and foreheads from the eyebrows up, they dealt with the clothes in short order: shoes and hats into one tub, pants and jackets into a second, body linen into a third, miscellaneous, such as socks and handerchiefs, into a fourth. The tubs were so large that five or six of the women worked at each at the same time. They pushed the clothes under with wooden paddles, stirred them around like dumplings in a soup, added lye and brown soap to the mixture, tossed some more wood on the fire under the pots to keep the water boiling. The next group fished the clothes out to give them a thorough going over on their scrubboards. A hard slap against the metal side of the tub and into the rinsing trough, then off to the wringer, and out through the window to the crew at the clothes lines. The work proceeded at such a breakneck pace that the washerwomen couldn't spare a moment to give us a second look although we stood there naked as the day we were born. Those of us who were particularly shy clutched our genitals. There was no need to cover up. One noisy fellow in line ahead of me whistled through his teeth to catch the women's attention and shook his organ at them, but he might as well have been waving a red flag at a blind bull. The line moved on, single file, to a bathhouse of sorts, something like a sheep dip. At the deepest part, the water came up to my chin. Bath attendants steered us through, prodding with wooden poles (they looked like the pronged cues used in shuffleboard), making sure that each of us was completely immersed in the chemical bath. Recalcitrant students and even those who simply hesitated for an instant were caught by the back of the neck with the scooped out ends of the poles and forced under before being allowed to step out of the trough. When we had run the gauntlet, we were herded into a shower room where the caustic solution of the bath was hosed off. Before we had a chance to dry we found ourselves sitting in barber chairs, six in a row, operated by men in white smocks who wielded shears and clippers with such expertise that our skulls were shaved before anyone had a chance to protest. Next a medical examination. The doctors' teamwork was even sharper than the washerwomen's. While one shoved a rubber-capped finger up my rectum, another cried "Cough!" and stuck a tongue depressor down my throat. A third wrapped a tube around my bicep, pumping air into me with one hand and knocking on my chest with the knuckles of the other. At the same time a male nurse handed me a jar and told me to piss in it.

I had barely squeezed out a few drops when someone plunged a needle into me from behind. I jumped forward into the arms of the next specialist who ordered me to look at the silver disk strapped to his forehead while he shone an electric torch into my eyes. "Good enough," the cyclops grunted and slapped my bare back, sending me flying, still half blinded, toward one of the two exits. Rejects were hustled off through the other one. The disinfected clothes were waiting in a wicker basket. Everything was in order, although a bit damp in the crotch and under the arms and reeking like a hospital corridor. The only damage done was to my shoes; one had its tongue ripped out and both were without laces. In the last shed papers were returned, exit and entry permits stamped, encased in an oilskin pouch and hung around our necks by a wire. Through a turnstile and the line was back on the loading platform.

At dawn we were reloaded for the last leg of the journey to the embarkation port.

The departure of the ship was delayed—by exceptionally high seas, one rumor had it; because of the crew's demand for extra pay for transporting potential job competitors, so another ran; by a snare in the red tape of immigration; because we were to be placed in quarantine, a suspected case of the pox; because the government had demanded our return; because war had been declared; because there were too many of us to fit on one ship and only one out of every three would be taken on board, the winners to be determined by lottery or by a contest of strength, indian wrestling—whispered hearsay. The stories became wilder the longer we waited. There was little else to do. During the day we stood on line, still keeping to the order of our position on the train. At night we sat around campfires burning in empty oil drums and sang songs: "Frère Jacques" in the round, "Bruder Martin," "Wir sind die Moor Soldaten," "London's burning, London's burning, Look yonder, look yonder!" "Die Gedanken sind frei. . . ."

At least a week or two must have passed like that. Time enough for a faint bluish fuzz to have appeared on the skulls of most of the boys, though not on mine. I didn't know why. I could feel the stubble, but nothing showed. Perhaps the barber who had shaved my head had done a more thorough job or my hair grew in slower. Or something had gone wrong with me—a blockage of the glands, a malfunctioning of the apparatus that governs secondary sexual characteristics. The girls, a trainload of them arrived the next day, had had their hair cut short and washed in kerosene. They said it was to prevent the spread of infection. And against lice. Yet I couldn't see why the lice would keep out of the girls' hair since their hair after cropping was now the length mine had been before they shaved my head.

Someone gave me a hat, a khaki baseball cap. I didn't ask for it; one of the relief agency people singled me out to give me the cap. A stroke of unexpected luck. I pulled it down over my forehead till the visor covered my eyes. The others didn't seem to mind. They grinned like monkeys, dutifully acting the fool, and bumped their shiny heads together, making believe they were playing soccer. The girls laughed. The suntanned counselors cheered and blew their whistles when the game became too rough (but not before a couple of skulls were cracked open).

There is a photograph of me with the baseball cap. I am squinting in the sun. I wear brown shorts which look very much like girls' bloomers, the material puckered by the elastic at the waist and legs. My arms are folded in front of me, hands cupped over my groin as if I were trying to cover up. It is a group picture of the family. My foster-sister stands next to me, my new parents behind. Compared to them I look like an albino. I am squirming (if one can say that of a still photo) like a fish on a hook. I look like a naked rat, big round head, bald skull, not even any eyebrows, large pink ears sticking out, eyeslits closing against the sun. I seem to have no eyes. Hardly any features, only ears and mouth, the rest is blank. Perhaps the photograph is overdeveloped or underdeveloped or overexposed. It is the earliest surviving picture. It must have been taken on the day of my arrival in America or a few days after.

* * *

It was a long trip, a rough crossing. Not only the weather—though that was bad enough, rolling through sickeningly deep swells, the tail end of a hurricane, and no ballast in the hold to keep the screw in the water—but a boatful of pallid landlubbers who started vomiting at the first sight of the ocean while their feet were still on solid ground and never stopped until they staggered down the gangplank ten days later each with a slop pail hung around his neck like horses deep in their nosebags.

The city came up out of nowhere. The only warning a swarm of dirt-grey gulls diving at the decks screaming with hunger, and at the same time a call over the public address system for all eyes to look larboard and starboard for the ship was passing between the legs of the Colossus (but no one could spot her, though some pointed knowingly to a thickening in the mist, while others craned their necks to look straight up, straining for a forbidden view of the giantess's private parts). Then the mist lifted and the towers of the city were dead ahead, jutting straight up out of the water, no sign of solid earth beneath them, no shore visible, no beach or land, hills, trees. The city floated toward them, building clusters rising from the water's edge. No breakwater or buoys, not even the machinery of a harbor, the cranes and hoists, cogs, weights, and levers, wheels, cranks, chains, the tugs, creaking, barnacle-encrusted piles, corrugated metal sheds. All of a sudden the ship was moving between vertical walls of masonry, slicing through the city streets like a giant trolley car. Yet looking down over the railing one could see the brown water, flat as a road, the prow of the ship making no ripples in the waterway, cutting through it as shears through a piece of silk. A light jolt, hardly more than a minor tremor, and the ship was docked. The watertight doors swung open and the ship corridors merged with the corridors of the buildings on either side.

His foster parents met him at the dock. They waved to him from the other side of the customs barrier. The mother used her white handkerchief both as a signal flag and to wipe tears from her eyes.

It may have been sweat. The heat was worse than he had expected, even though he had heard stories about the great number of people who died from heat prostration every day in the city (especially foreigners who were overcome by the change in climate). He could hear the ambulance sirens out in the streets. The temperature was higher down in the subway where the central heating was still, always, in full operation. (One of the deckhands had told him about this: "Oh sure, didn't you know? It's a true fact that it's more economical to keep the fires going all year round than to shut them down and start them up every time the seasons change. The temperature has been known to drop forty degrees in an hour. And rise just as fast. Nothing unusual about that over here. You'll see." And the fog which covered the city was really steam.)

A high-speed elevator plunged them to an underground ramp leading directly to the loading platform of the subway. Someone gave him a handfull of pennies to feed into a gum machine. The man had to bang the machine with his fist before it worked. The gum snapped back when he pulled on it. The woman rubbed his mouth with her handkerchief, wetting it with spittle to help remove the gum that stuck to his upper lip.

He could not understand a word. Even if he had known the language, the din of the train was so intense that conversation was not possible. The other passengers sat mute, strong jaws set, mouths opening and closing as they chewed. Two long rows of straw-covered benches facing each other. When the train pulled into a station they looked up and words spilled out of their mouths, a deluge, shouts of advice, questions, reprimands, snatches of song, advertisement jingles, battle cries, curses, babel, a glut of confused tongues. When the doors snapped shut, the clattering wheels roared them to silence. Then they were out of the tunnel, above ground, snaking between rows of buildings.

He could look straight into people's apartments, right from the train window. Double rows of houses standing shoulder to shoulder on both sides of the right-of-way, flat-roofed tenements with weathered brick fronts and narrow soot-encrusted windows, framing the way like the sides of a tunnel. Children's faces pressed against the grey windowglass, larger faces on top of smaller faces, their eyes alert, jumping from side to side as if they were reading, back and forth, racing across the page. They were lined up to watch the trains that sped by in both directions, two tracks this way, two tracks that way. The near lane of traffic so close that the features of the passengers dissolved into a continuous blur, an elongated smear like strands of pinkish chewing gum. But the occupants of the train in the far lane could differentiate among the heads at the windows, count them if they wished, although the high speed prevented them from identifying the individual faces. At night the children's faces were replaced by those of their elders (thick necks, goiters, glassy eyes, gaping dentures, yawning mouths, hair in curlers, black kerchiefs, skull caps). There was no need to turn the lights on in the rooms since the elevated roadway was lit as brightly as daytime by ranks of overhead mercury lamps suspended from stanchions anchored on the roofs of the buildings, necks bent over as if peering down on the rails. In the summer the windows were raised so that the inhabitants could rest their elbows on the pillow-padded window sills while they watched.

The windows of the apartment to which he was taken did not face the tracks. They looked out at a narrow back alley, the blind wall of the duplicate five-story apartment house barely a dozen feet away. No movement to watch here (only the snail-slow spread of a whitish calcium stain inching down the pitted bricks over the years). While waiting, he searched the graphpaper surface of the wall for other shapes. Faces, eyes and mouths, rows of teeth, snouts of gargoyles, hunchback humps and claws, omphali, papillae, eyesockets, skulls, fossils, ferns, footprints, spores, swirls, eyes staring back. It was not easy to find them, only by squinting or at dusk; even then the regular linear lines, a grey cement frame around each brick, prevailed —insisting, forcing the eye to focus on the unadorned reality of right angles, vertical and horizontal bars, geometric planes, sharp edges, ruled order.

After dinner the family sat around the kitchen table listening to the radio until bedtime. The father dragged his chair away from the table, right up to the window, turning his back to the others to read the evening paper. The volume of the radio was turned down so that the listeners had to lean forward, their heads bunched together like a group of conspirators. The father read his newspaper methodically, column by column, page by page, from front to back, slowly, not missing a word. By the time he reached the back page box scores, it was bedtime. He shut the radio off in mid-sentence. But the sound continued, now coming through the walls from the kitchen next door and from the kitchen upstairs. Later, while waiting to fall asleep in the bedroom he shared with his foster sister, he could still hear it, the frenzied falsetto voice of a comic, followed by spurts of laughter like static, drumrolls of applause, theme music up, chimes identifying the station, a beep signaling the hour.

A week after his arrival, his name was changed officially, first and last. The court clerk thought that "Paul" would come closest to his old name. He had no objections. The mother seemed pleased with the choice. The father repeated it out loud a number of times so that the youth would not forget it. He had him write it fifty times on the first page of his new notebook. Also their home address, the name of his teacher, class and school number. He started school on the afternoon of the same day. A month later, the mother bought him a pair of corduroy knickers at Klein's ("always on the square"). Paul left his old short pants in the dressing room of the store. The knickers made school life a bit easier, although not that much.

He was not liked at school. Right from the start. When the boys chose sides for a ballgame, he was the last to be selected. Actually he was not selected; he fell to the side that lost the toss for first choice. Paul resented this and did not attempt to catch the ball when it was hit in his direction. At his turn at bat, he swung wildly at the first two pitches to get it over with as quickly as possible. When, despite himself, he connected and drove the ball between the outfielders, he let himself be caught in a run-down or failed to touch second on his way around the bases. Or he missed his turn at bat completely, deliberately allowing the next batter to push ahead of him. The gym teacher, looking the other way, did not interfere.

Things did not go much better in the classroom. It was not that he was a foreigner. The language had opened to him with ease, even though he had not bothered to try. (One day it was a complete mystery, the doors locked, the dam unbreachable; the next morning the floodgates were unsealed. English phrases poured out of his mouth, a tidal wave, a veritable stampede of words: droves of nouns, packs of verbs, herds of adverbs, flights of adjectives, routs of reflexives, gangs of pronouns, prides of antecedents, bevies of expletives, sords of articles, coverts of absolutes, sounders of substantives, musters of prepositions, litters of objects, watches of conjunctives, shrewdnesses of infinitives, wisps of comparatives, exaltations of superlatives, springs of declensions, casts of modifiers, flocks of participles (past and present), skeins of copulatives, warrens of predicates, gaggles of interjections, drifts of substantives, troops of vocatives, gams of gerunds, sloths of infinitives, coveys of complements, skulks of subjunctives, broods of moods, falls of principal parts, pods of clauses, swarms of idioms, shoals of clichés. Just like that, like a miracle.) His classmates had probably already forgotten that he was not a native. Still he did not fit in, or would not.

Although he did his homework, turned it in on time, learned his multiplication tables and his common denominators, moved the decimal point in the right direction, recited the doggerel spelling rules and the required number of lines of poetry by heart, wrote two-hundred-and-fifty-word and five-hundred-word compositions on the assigned topics, memorized historical dates, battles, and heroes, the freezing point of water, the boiling point of alcohol, heights of mountains, names of navigable rivers, the capitals of all the states in the Union, the principal products, industries, exports and imports, and per capita income of the South American republics, the names of the seven seas, of the six continents, and of the first sixteen presidents, the number of days in each month, the number of pounds in a

ton, pints in a gallon, dozen in a gross, pecks in a bushel, feet in a
mile, square inches in a square yard; although he knew the six
immediate and eight underlying causes of the American Revolution,
could parse an diagram simple, compound, and complex sentences,
measure obtuse angles with his metal protractor, correctly differentiate between Sinding's "Rustle of Spring" and Schubert's
Unfinished Symphony, and had mastered all the words of the fourth
stanza of "America, America," his teachers were not satisfied.

They objected to his attitude. They thought he was sullen,
grudging in his answers. They accused him of mumbling, of not
opening his mouth wide enough. They suspected him of purposely
spoiling his dictation work with ink blots. His penmanship was too
sloppy and slanted in the wrong direction. He was not attentive
enough, did not really listen when spoken to. He never volunteered
to do work for extra credit. He made no friends among his classmates. He had no worthwhile hobbies, did not collect stamps or
coins, was not interested in making model airplanes or magazine racks
or pump-shaped table lamps in the shop class, showed no enthusiasm
for photography or butterfly collections, made no effort to help the
war effort by studying the Morse code or enrolling in an after school
first-aid class. His compositions on "My Favorite Hobby" and "My
Second-Best Friend" were obviously not sincere. Although he was not
openly disrespectful, although his responses to questions were usually
correct, the tone of his replies was wrong, almost sarcastic. One
teacher sent him down to the principal who reprimanded him on his
general lack of cooperation. Another teacher, suspecting that he was
secretly laughing at her and underhandedly snickering, sent for his
father to complain about the lad's shifty eyes and tendency to sulk.

The father was not surprised. He fully agreed with the teacher and
confirmed her suspicions by, in his turn, recounting instances of
Paul's recusant behavior at home. Mrs. Maloney, the teacher, really
being a kind woman at heart, was pleased with the father's attitude
and tried to deal more leniently with Paul once she understood his
hostility to be a general one, not directed at her in particular. But
the youth would not be reconciled. He refused to give an inch. He
turned his nose up at a chance to help color the Thanksgiving Day
class mural. He insisted on keeping the desk which had been assigned
to him at the rear of the room (according to the rule of seating
students by size-places) even though his benefactress offered him a
better seat, close to her desk with an unobstructed view of the

blackboard. When made a safety monitor at the insistence of Mrs. Maloney, he betrayed her confidence in him and the responsibility of the position by throwing ice-covered snowballs at the girls instead of guarding the dangerous streetcrossing to which he was assigned. Mrs. Maloney's attempts to rehabilitate her pupil finally came to an end when he defaced a geography textbook. The principal on a surprise inspection of the classroom caught him in the act, crayon in hand. Yet the boy refused to admit his guilt, refused to apologize or to pay for the ruined book. Mrs. Maloney, stunned and deeply hurt, paid for the book with her own money, but thereafter made no further attempts to cure him. Paul did not even thank Mrs. Maloney for her generosity, nor for her kindness.

He withdrew further into his shell of resentment, blaming his isolation on others. He acted as if the world had done him an injustice in expecting him to adhere to its moral, social, and natural laws. He had not been there when the laws were proposed, when the contract was originally signed. He had not been consulted. He categorically refused to accept the rules, would not be bound by them, not because he necessarily disagreed with them but because he had inherited them and had not been given a chance to say yes or no. His youth was soured by his indignation and by his stubbornness. He stamped his feet, shouted, blasphemed, tore up his notebooks, spat at mother, scratched sister, refused, at the last moment, to go to the longed for movies on Saturday afternoon, let the ice-cream melt untasted on his plate, waited for the fizz to escape from his Pepsi-Cola, and stuck pins deep into the palms of his hands.

Such a morose, negative attitude toward life was, not surprisingly, accompanied by a noticeably physical deterioration, no doubt aggravated by, hastened by, or resulting in, if not the result of (it was hard to tell which was the cause and which the effect) a general loss of appetite—shrinking away from chicken soup, averting meat and potatoes, rejecting all vegetables, green and brown, refusing all solid nourishment, recoiling from the national minimum requirement of one quart of milk per day. He ate nothing at mealtime, subsisting on dry hunks of bread and secretly procured chocolate bars.

The relapse was not pleasant to witness. The parents had thought that given a good dose of rich American food, three standard balanced meals supplemented by one-a-day vitamin pills in the winter, the boy would fill out. But his unwillingness to cooperate kept him as thin as a stick, his chest concave. A middling strong gust of wind would have been enough to knock him off his feet. He listed already, the right shoulder drooping, head inclined to the same side, leaning into the air at a dangerous angle, wearing his heels down in no time at all by his lopsided gait. The father was ashamed to be seen with him. Neighbors shook their heads. The school doctor had a look, but found no organic causes for the trouble.

"Nothing to worry about," he tapped the patient's chest with the rubber end of his pencil. "I've seen worse specimens in my day, believe you me. It's the age. Just don't spoil him with too much attention. That's what he's looking for. . . . Of course, see to it that he gets lots of fresh air. Push him out of the house if he won't go. Plenty of exercise. Keep him running. Wholesome food, no sweets (they constipate). If he won't eat, let him go hungry for a few days. It works like magic. At least six glasses of water a day and enough sleep. Early to bed, up at dawn. That's the ticket. He'll come around, you'll see."

Paul did not sleep well. He tossed from side to side all night long as if he were having convulsions, thrashing about, kicking at the blankets till they fell to the floor. He beat the pillow and turned it over and over, searching for a cool spot for his head. The springs of the bed squeaked under the attack, the legs creaked in protest. He mistreated the bed as if he had a personal grudge against it.

He hated his new bed because it wasn't new. It had been his foster sister's bed before his arrival. She had slept comfortably in it for years, peacefully, untroubled by the fact that it was secondhand, bought in a thrift shop for a pittance. It had not bothered her that the head and footboards were scarred with the toothmarks of countless unknown predecessors or that the yellow enamel was chipped in many places, exposing the raw black iron beneath. The father had originally intended to repaint it, but had never gotten round to it because he was too busy earning a living and because his daughter did not seem to care. Paul did not like the bed at all. He stared at the black bite marks for hours, kicked at the footboard, glowered at his roommate in her new large bed, and in his rage added a goodly number of chips to the already battered enamel.

The same pettiness showed itself at other times. Once when his foster sister had bronchitis and could not sleep because of her violent coughing, the mother asked Paul to give Sister his pillow so that her head could be propped up higher to make it possible for her to breathe more easily.

Paul refused. Absolutely.

"Just for tonight. Give Martha your pillow like a good brother."

"No."

"Please!"

"No."

"She only wants to borrow it. You'll get it back tomorrow."

No, he would not part with his pillow, even when Martha begged him herself, not even when she cried. He lay awake all night long listening to her cough, the contested pillow hot beneath his head. Toward morning he tossed the pillow out of bed. The mother found it on the floor when she came into the room to see how Martha had spent the night. She picked the pillow up and gave it back to Paul without a word. He threw it away, and again the mother picked it up from the floor and returned it to him. He began to cry. Soon his eyes were red with weeping, and between sobs he begged the mother to give Martha the pillow. The mother refused. He could keep his old pillow; no one wanted it any more. It was too late. Paul cried louder, screaming and biting the pillow. Finally, the angered father, disturbed in the midst of shaving, one cheek covered with white lather, the other red with irritation, was forced to intercede. He pushed the screaming boy from the bedroom so that Martha could rest quietly. Paul crawled out on the fire escape where he sat sulking the whole day, refusing to eat or to answer his elders.

Although Paul frequently fought with Martha, pinching, biting and scratching her, he liked her well enough. He stopped biting her when the mother told him that it would cause cancer. And when Martha threatened to pack a suitcase and run away to Mexico to throw herself into the fiery depth of Popocatepetl, he pleaded with her on his knees to pardon him. He offered to give her everything, do anything, if only she would not jump into the volcano. But she continued to pack her suitcase. Once she went as far as the entrance of the el before his sobs persuaded her to forgive him.

Martha, in her turn, seemed to have been extremely fond of her new brother (despite her tendency to tease him—he was such a ready and willing victim). On the day of his joining the family she stayed up through the entire night while he slept (turning and turning, groaning in the grip of a nightmare, blindly fighting against the confines of the sleeping-container, eyelids flickering as if struggling to open), standing guard, afraid that someone would come to take him away if she closed her eyes even for a minute.

The parents still liked to tell the story to company at Sunday afternoon tea, although the relationship between the children had long since reached a plateau of mutual indifference. Martha going her way (rolling bandages for the Red Cross, scheming for ways to get to the Paramount to see Sinatra, preparing for proms, practicing the latest dance step, preening before the full-length mirror, reading miles and miles of Whitman), Paul his way (scavenging in empty lots, pilfering the local candy store, filching quarters from the mother's purse, setting up pins at the bowling alley, trading baseball cards for French postcards, reading forbidden pulp fiction, *Operator 5, The Spider, Doc Savage*). They saw each other only at the evening meal, although they still shared the same bedroom—a constant source of disquietude to the father who clearly saw the handwriting on the wall but could do nothing about the danger inherent in the situation because of financial limitations (they could not afford a larger apartment) except to make sure, to insist, that the door to the bedroom always remained ajar.

*   *   *

The bedroom door was shut. (The wind had blown it closed.) Everyone was asleep, the parents on the Castro Convertible in the living room, Martha in her bed by the window, separated from his half of the room by a rice-paper screen. But Paul could not fall asleep. He felt hot and itchy. He kicked at the covers and shifted his weight cautiously, turning on his back. The springs creaked. He cursed the old bed and listened to Martha's breathing. It was steady; she had not woken up. Carefully folding his pillow double, he propped it under his head. It didn't help much. He couldn't quiet himself down.

"Fallasleep, fallasleep . . ." he ordered, but he didn't. He closed his eyes and jammed a finger in each ear. His thoughts returned to the same dead end.

There was none to be had. He looked everywhere. In the hallway, around the corner, behind the stairwell, out in the back alley, the fire escape, in the closet, under the bed, in the dumbwaiter, the refrigerator. None. He turned the lights off, squeezed his eyes shut and concentrated on seeing absolute, total, pure blackness. He was almost there, almost asleep, but they wouldn't let him.

They jump out of their hiding places. Arrogantly, they strut before him, pushing their breasts ahead of them, pointing them at him. Deliberately. Putting on a show for him.

Struck dumb with admiration he watches the parading women with greedy eyes, like a child with his nose pressed against the windowglass of a sweet shop, mouth watering. They come closer. Lewd, wanton, they stretch their luxuriant limbs, hold out ripe tempting breasts to him—thick nipples erect like stuck-out tongues —lean over him, offering themselves. They lie down on the bed, sunny side up, spread their legs wide. And he reaches

—but *foosh*, they are gone! Vanished.

And with every day it became worse (all those delectable sugar-plum girls wrapped in pastel-colored wrinkle-free cloth, straight legs and high breasts sticking out like a shelf, gleaming teeth and polished knees). Every day he became more resentful, hating the women who excited him but who had no intention of fulfilling the desires that they aroused. And even if he were to find one who was willing, how could she make up for the nights of torment which he had already endured?

Suddenly a miracle. The bedroom door swings open. She stands before him naked, head thrown back, cupping her breasts in both hands, lips wet, beckoning, laughing. She approaches and finally he touches her. He kisses her neck with open mouth, kisses her harden-ing breasts, tongue circling her nipple, sucking at the pulsating blood, the cool milk beneath the smooth skin. She lies on the bed moaning, bare ass on starched white sheets. His hands slide over her flanks, rounding the curve of her hips, pushing underneath her, fingers clutching, squeezing. His throbbing flesh finds the hot center of her body. He lifts himself to thrust forward

—when *bang*! The balloon explodes.

Paul sat up, eyes open. The room was empty. The bedroom door closed.

*　*　*

As soon as sticky fingered dawn had ignited the hot sky, he stirred from deep sleep, disturbed by a sequence of repetitious rancid dreams. Still entangled in the hairy roots of sleep he wanders through a shaded pine forest by the side of the ocean. Slim trees, yet when he looks closer distorted by bloated bulbous breasts which hang from the tree trunks, sprouting big where branches had once grown.

Suddenly, in the same breath, lust raises itself between his thighs, leaps and chokes him beneath its fleshy weight.

Thrust to the wall, she yields to him, all abandoned, her body impaled, opened and closed about him. Her feet no longer touching the ground, she pushes down, rubs against him with trembling hip action. Her weight centered on the burning point. Pierced, breath caught, she sways delicately balanced; her thighs clamped around his legs; his hands cradling her buttocks. And then (in slow motion) the tree behind her falls away and her arched torso bends supply backwards from the waist, arms curved, long hair tumbling to the earth, meeting the grass, breasts face skyward. The usual breasts, no different from the rest. The wild grass coils over his ankles and knots the flesh to the bedstead.

The craving rises from his groin, twists him. He writhes against the silken bonds. Her flowing hair whispers. It whispers as it encircles him, inflames as her breath. Soft hair and breath move downward to his loins. Her warm mouth touches. Her breasts press against his legs. Round, liquid breasts, slippery as ripe grapes beneath translucent skin, the usual breasts, no different from the rest . . .

His hand between the material and her cool skin sweeps the last undergarment past opulent protrusions, the fine lace torn, flung aside. He falls on her with rabid hunger. Feasts piecemeal. Enraged, he takes his fill repeatedly. His teeth rake the white skin, till beads of blood streak a breast with broken lace of red sea foam (the usual breast, no different from the rest).

Exhausted, but his appetite unslaked, he lies riveted to the boundless bed. The want aches. The swish of her naked body brushing against the stiffly starched sheets cuts into him. Her curved tongue and breasts (the usual breasts) sway, swing wildly. Grasping his pulsing flesh in her hand, she tears at him, beating it to her breasts. A rush of blood storms the onion-skin wall of desire. The thick liquid presses for release. The blister bursts.

The juice flows from the tip—slow continuous painful ejaculation —thick as crawling worms. He squeezes on, unable to stop. The discharge pours from him in an endless stream, dense as cold soup, yellow as glue, rich foam, coagulating pus. Semen mixed with blood and marrow drops from him, pulling his intestines along, until all that remains is a drained, shrunken sack of limp skin.

*   *   *

Night was waning. Dawn stretched herself in her creaking bed. Sickly pale morning light penetrated into the bedroom through the drawn curtains. The bed creaked with each breath. The mattress was warped; it sagged on broken springs. The covers had slipped from the bed. Wrinkled sheets drooped to the floor like overflowing drainpipes.

He tossed about trying to return to sleep, trying to bury his thoughts, his head beneath the pillow. The dreams waited unfinished He did not want to wake up. He shut his eyes and let his thoughts drift, but the excitement did not come back. Visions of pointed breasts and rounded buttocks would not take shape. Daylight had interrupted. It was impossible to return. His flesh felt empty and numb, the skin stuck to the night. (It became smaller and smaller, falling away, unhinged, collapsing, shrinking . . .)

Disgusted with himself, Paul bit hard into the pillow, sinking his teeth in deeply. Although he had known all along that it was wrong, that it would lead to his ruin (remembering his foster father's warning about the grave consequences of unclean practices and the even greater danger to mind and body brought on by contact with willing and therefore diseased members of the opposite sex), he could not stop himself until it was too late. Afterwards he was miserable.

But no matter how he tried, what he tried, common sense, logic, prayer, exercize, diets, punishment, bribes, threats, curses ("Smutty pig!" he cried with self-abuse), he could not manage to curb his habit. Seemingly unconsciously, automatically (yet with the dedication of a fanatic, with the compulsive skill of an addict), he gathered raw materials during the daytime for his nocturnal sport (his eyes recording with the accuracy of a high-speed camera, his mind filing the pictures for later use, misuse). He fed not only on the overtly erotic (the sight of the exposed white flesh above the dark-rimmed stocking tops of a young mother bending over to wipe her infant's nose, or the geometry teacher's prominent breasts bouncing against her beige jersey blouse, or the brassiere and girdle ads in the Sunday papers, or the inviting sound of the school nurse's plump thighs rubbing against each other as she hurried down the corridor in her crisp white uniform) but also on the innocent or, for that matter, even the sacred, twisting, polluting—cramming all that he found into his mill to be ground and kneaded into the dough of lust.

He stumbled through the routine of the day as if stunned, painfully dragging himself out of bed, barely making it to school, sitting through the required classes like a catatonic somehow finding his way back home, blindly reading the assigned chapters, disconsolately picking at his supper—performing his tasks by rote while his thoughts

remained stuck in the same frustrating rut. They circled and
deepened the groove until there was nothing else. No way out.
Dazed, he repeated his dull-witted cry of desire over and over. Ob-
sessed, mouthing obscenities, almost without variation: "I'd like to
you need a   just let me   the size of   the best pair of
piece of   just lift your   show you something   your big   all
the way up   tonight   let me   Jesus, I'd like to   when did
you last get   I'm the man to   have us a good time   you're
all night long   what a pair of   let me   good taste of   put it
between your   give it to you   take you on   the juice running
out   do you want   I've got a   way up   like that   top to
bottom   the size of them   give you a taste of it   just for you
right between them   saving it up   all the way in   never
enough   just lift your   up   you'll see   I'll   let me   anyway
you want   do it to you   like this   you need a good   hard as
the biggest you ever   spread juiciest piece of   can't wait   just
a touch   shove it   won't stop   in and out   won't stop till you
just for you   I'm going to   never stop   up your   bitch
what a   you need a   I'd like to . . ."

The need became stronger each day. The wait to get to the
privacy of the bed seemed endless. Darkness was long in coming. He
held on impatiently waiting for the relief, even though he must have
known that night would bring only temporary relief, inadequate
solace. His sleep though deep was not restful. At dawn he awoke
tired and pale.

Awoke to the same thoughts, the same words forming in his mind,
the same scenes, the same desire. But now it was a mockery, for his
flesh did not respond properly. Although the thoughts fell into their
familiar sordid pattern, the want was anesthetized, covered by a
rubber skin, insensitive, thick as the dead rind of calluses.

The day had really just begun. Time moved slowly, heavily.
Between nights there was still a whole day. Abject, but not cured by
any means, Paul sat up, swung his legs over the side of the bed and
strove to disentangle himself from the sheets. They were hot and
sticky, stained with yellow spots—the mark of his shame, the seal of
his sorrow.

10. THE SOUND OF WOMEN

A train crashed into hearing. The wooden slats of the elevated station clattered under its weight. Brakes screeched, steel grating against steel. Loose couplings clashed. A moment of silence; then the wheels turned, straining to jerk the cars along. The noise no longer bothered the inhabitants of the adjacent apartment houses. Those who were asleep slept on undisturbed. Those who were awake went about their business without glancing up.

An indigenous Saturday-morning lethargy prevailed. The voices from the streets and backyards were muted. The lazy drone of a high-flying airplane merged with the still distant but now slowly approaching whine of garbage trucks making their morning rounds. Radios were tuned to children's programs instead of the weekday soap operas. Yet the lull in activity was deceptive. A steady procession of women climbed the stairs of the el on their way to the downtown department stores. Trains, bound for the city, rattled by more and more frequently.

It wasn't the trains that woke Paul, but the sound of a woman's high heels, pacing overhead. Somewhere close by, the insistent, nagging voice of a young child called repeatedly to its mother. The lid of a garbage can dropped to the sidewalk.

In the apartment above, the woman continued to walk back and forth on high-heeled slippers. The sharp sound was not unpleasant, yet it disturbed Paul. He gave up any hope of returning to sleep. It was senseless to remain in bed any longer.

Instead he followed the housewives and their daughters, the receptionists, the file clerks, and the secretaries off on their weekly bargain hunt. He followed them up the stairs, through the turnstile, onto the platform, into the train, crowding closely behind them in the rush to find seats, almost touching them but side-stepping at the last moment, stopping short just in time.

He hesitated before choosing a seat. The train was already moving and now it was too late to sit down next to them. He took a seat across the way, a corner seat by the partition that separated the entranceway from the main section of the carriage. The straw covered bench to his right was only partly occupied, the space next to him empty.

At the following stop more women entered. Almost all the seats were taken, except the slot directly to his right which remained vacant. When the door leading to the next car slid open, Paul looked up expectantly. Two women passed through, unsteady on their high heels, holding on to each other for support. A thin young man followed them. When he saw the empty seat, he sat down and adjusted his newspaper by folding it in half the long way. He thumbed through the large sheets with habitual dexterity. The paper partially blocked Paul's field of vision. He moved further into his corner in order to see around the obstruction.

All' about him (except to his immediate right) women were standing and seated in a variety of enticing positions: legs crossed, blouses open, leaning against the doors, backsides turned to three-quarter view, arms raised to the overhead straps, leaning over the seated passengers or squirming in their seats, uncrossing and crossing their legs with a silky sound. All shapes and sizes. Some returned his look; others glanced away. Getting on and off the train, they proudly maneuvered their perfectly shaped whitewashed hindquarters, freshly scrubbed clean with a stiff long-handled brush (twice a day, in the morning and at night), patted dry with an extra-absorbent towel, sprinkled with talcum powder, encased in triple wrappings of lace, rubber, and polished cloth, upswept here, downgraded there —enticingly packaged for display.

Watching the display of puckered flesh, so expertly revealed through the clinging spring fabrics, Paul found it expedient to cover his lap with a book (with which he had wisely provided himself for such occasions). Although he was sure that no one had noticed his difficulty, he felt embarrassed. To add to his predicament, a buxom woman had moved into the space directly in front of him. Holding on to the strap over his head, she swayed with the rhythm of the train. When the car lurched sideways, she moved closer. The edge of her skirt, lifted above her knees by her efforts to hold on to the strap, brushed against the book on Paul's lap and then against his hands which held the book. Her knees touched the seat between his legs. Her leg met his. When she pressed closer—she was all but kneeling on his lap—Paul considered offering her his seat, but didn't dare lift his head, for even now his face was only inches from her bulging blouse. Any sudden movement might be misinterpreted. He tried to catch her eye without shifting his head, but she seemed engrossed in the overhead advertisements. She continued to ignore him even when his hand beneath her skirt accidentally caressed her thigh.

The train dipped and gathered speed as it entered the maze of tunnels which encircled the roots of the city. It switched tracks and crashed by dimly lit stations. Announcing its arrival by the shrill blast of its whistle, trumpeting around a corner, it finally pulled to a halt in an express station.

The woman who had almost covered him disappeared in the scramble for the doors and vacant seats. When the subway train got under way again, it was comparatively empty. Everyone had a seat. The man next to Paul had been replaced by a woman who held a large patent leather purse on her lap.

As she sat down in the seat next to him, she primly crossed her legs and tucked her skirt around her knees. But the material stretched tightly across her thighs as if her flesh strained to escape the tensed cloth of her skirt. When Paul turned his head slightly to the right to take a quick look at her full breasts lifted in sharp profile, she uncrossed her legs. Her bare flesh touched his trouser leg. Putting his weight on his toes, he flexed his calf muscle. Legs pressed closer. She responded, rocking in time with the up and down motion of the train, but still looking straight ahead at the people in the opposite row as if nothing were happening. Paul stroked the edges of the dustjacket of his book, not knowing what to do next. As if in answer, she also played with her hands, opening and closing her patent leather purse. Paul felt the rushing flush of excitement, yet he was afraid to approach her more openly even though he knew that he might not have much time to act since she might change trains at the next stop. The pressure of her leg against his increased. Her skirt had climbed higher, revealing her smooth knees. If he moved his right hand just a little to the right, he would be able to touch her thigh. He turned his head to look at her again. She chewed gum neatly. She opened her mouth and pushed the gum forward with her tongue until it protruded a fraction of an inch between her fuchsia lips. Encouraged, he made his move. He dropped his right hand from the edge of his book so that the back of his right hand now rested against her left thigh, just below the dip which marked the nether end of her prominent buttock. Since she made no objection, he became bolder. He inched his hand further beneath her, raising and lowering his fingers, stroking the curve of her flank with the side of his thumb.

Yet his advances ended there. He did not have the courage to talk to her. And before he could overcome his bashfulness it was too late. At the next stop, she walked out of the train without once glancing back, wriggling in her tight skirt, her legs squeezed closely together above the knees as if she were trying to keep the juice from running out.

Across the aisle, a man with rimless glasses nudged his wife. Both looked at Paul. The man laughed; the woman clicked her tongue angrily. Other passengers looked up from their newspapers, fixed their gaze on him. They pointed. They shook their heads. Some raised their fists.

Not waiting for a further invitation, Paul vacated his seat and retreated behind one of the partitions that separated the entrance-ways at both ends of the car from the main section of the carriage. Partly hidden from the seated passengers, he waited anxiously for the train to reach the next stop. Knees shaking, he cursed himself for his failure.

The train charged along noisily in the dark tunnel. Flashes and sparks from protesting wheels opened the blackness for a split second and showed rusty pillars, arched, empty corridors. As Paul looked out of the window, he sensed the presence of a woman behind him, close, watching him. He shivered as her warm breath moved down his neck, down his back. Although he looked for her reflection in the dirty window, he could only see his own image in the glass. Yet he could still feel her. Her breath moved on and touched his thighs.

His reflection disappeared as the train pulled into the station. He did not turn around to look at her, but ran up the stairs and out into the street.

*   *   *

The barkeeper, dressed in white, returned a bottle to its proper place, and then raised his arms as if to intercede in the noisy discussion on the public side of the bar. When no one heeded his gesture, he shrugged, a smug smile in his eyes, not strong enough to reach his mouth.

The swinging portals of the establishment opened to the youth's push, then swung closed after him. He crossed to the uncrowded end of the bar and ordered. The barkeeper took his time. He cut open a new bottle, slicing through the plastic seal with one expert twist of his knife, tossed the severed bottle top into a nearby slop pail, inserted a shiny nickle spout, and poured a shot for another customer. Then he made room for the bottle on one of the several glass shelves along the mirror-covered wall behind the bar where whisky bottles stood in long neat rows, their gleaming metal pouring -spouts endlessly reflected by the ingeniously cut glass. Indirect pink lighting cast a soft glow. A hidden mechanical device turned silently, causing the lights to wane and gain in a constant soothing cycle. Imitation leather-covered barstools invited the weary traveler.

Though weary, Paul remained on his feet. When the barkeeper approached, he repeated his request for a beer. The man would not serve him until he had produced his draft card. He scrutinized the card under the light of the cash register, turning it over to read both sides.

General conversation ceased while all eyes turned on the stranger. They watched him drain the glass. The ice cold beer numbed his throat; nevertheless he ordered another. The barkeeper served him and then moved to the far end of the long bar, close to his regular patrons. Gradually, conversation picked up again.

Even though the men in the bar seemed to have accepted the newcomer's presence (at least they no longer stared at him so intently), the barkeeper continued to eye him with suspicion. Dissatisfied, he grunted and wiped the bar top with a quick, vicious gesture.

When the conversation had returned to its normal volume, Paul took a cautious look at the drinkers. Despite superficial differences (some were in their shirt sleeves; others wore wrinkled suit jackets), they all looked alike: pink faces; ruddy necks; protruding, glistening eyes; round clean-shaven chins; prominent ears; freshly trimmed, light brown hair, combed straight back, glued in place by sweet smelling, green hair pomade; stubby fingers, closely bitten fingernails. Their striped silk ties were loosened; the top button of their collars open. Their shoes were highly polished; their pants were worn shiny, especially in the seat and around the knees. Because they were sitting well back on the comfortable, high bar stools, it was difficult to judge their height. They could not have been above average height since their feet did not touch the ground. They barely reached the brass footrail (although, admittedly, the stools were unusually high). They were neither young nor old. Perhaps in their late twenties or early thirties, or forties. Paul would not have been surprised if they had all turned out to be the same age. Even if they had all been born on the same day. The closer he looked, the more resemblance he saw. Actually, he found it impossible to tell them apart. And since their voices were pitched to the same tenor key, and their speech was unmarked by any regional peculiarities, he had just as much trouble in trying to match the snatches of conversation he was able to understand to the appropriate mouths.

One of them said, "Did you ever hear about the dame who was laid in the cemetery?"

"Do you know the one about the cancer patient and the new nurse?"

"Or the man who killed all the cats in the neighborhood?"

"And the father who caught his son in the bathroom . . ."

"Then there were these twins . . ."

"What's the difference between a rooster and Mae West?"

Their heads moved closer together.

"One was good and the other real bad."

"So the moment her husband's out the front door . . ."

"But she wouldn't let him turn the lights off."

"Just a little further, just another little inch. I swear . . ."

"What does a cow have four of and a woman two?"

Loud, knowing laughter.

"Wait! . . . Wait till you hear this one!"

"The bottle has a hole in it, but the woman . . ."

"So she asks again, the teacher, 'Who's Dick Hertz?' "

"He says: 'Cockadoodledoo!' She says . . ."

"Instant pussy!"

"Nine months later she was a mummy."

"Anycokledoo!"

". . . a lovely way to die!"

They shouted the punch lines, rocking wildly on the high stools, nudging one another in the ribs with their elbows.

The barkeeper who had not participated in the exchange of tales, who seemed not to have been listening judging by his expressionless face, now thought it wise to interfere. He stopped polishing the woodwork and addressed himself to the drinkers. He leaned over the bar to make himself heard. He tried to outshout them. He raised his hands in protest. He pointed meaningfully at the semicircle of booths behind the men.

All turned to look. Their words died in mid-sentence. In the abrupt silence, his reproach resounded: "Knock it off, gents! There's a lady here."

It was true. There she was, a latter-day Venus of succulent proportions, sitting by herself in a booth, a drink before her, cigarette in hand.

Everyone was quiet for a minute. Respectful silence. Impressed, they drained their drinks. Subdued, they whispered. When the woman rose, they cautiously turned to take a closer look. She crushed her half smoked cigarette under foot, picked up her handbag, her white gloves, and walked to the ladies' room, her high heels clicking like castanets on the polished barroom floor—perhaps a bit louder than necessary. Conscious of the attention she was attracting, she further exaggerated the swing of her hips. The men ogled her well-filled breech of promise.

"That's the nicest lox-box I've seen today," one thought.

"What a pair of knockers!"

"Who is she?" they asked the barkeeper.

"A visiting whore?"

"You mean a cock-eyed whore!" a wit disagreed.

Soon they were laughing and joking as loudly as before. To add to the aura of camaraderie and well-being, someone farted noisily.

"Hey!"

"Was that you, Tom?"

Tom denied it indignantly.

"Who's responsible?" they questioned each other, accused each other.

"Confess!"

But instead, someone else broke wind and then another.

"The silent ones are worse."

The barkeeper moved away fastidiously and busied himself with his account books.

Paul, who was feeling more and more uncomfortable the longer he stayed, wanted to leave the saloon right then and there. But he thought it best to stay a little longer, sensing that departing now would be misinterpreted as a confession.

"Don't look so innocent!" one of them called out to him.

"I'll bet he's the type that lets one loose in bed and sticks his head under the blankets to get a good whiff."

"Yeah, a sneak."

"A wise guy."

"A sharp shitter."

Paul did not try to defend himself. He pretended not to have heard. Luckily, the conversation turned to another subject.

"The best time to piss is when you're full of beer. Wonderful."

The other agreed. A poem was cited in evidence:

> *The stuff which comes out of the spout*
> *Is nothing but beer with the hops taken out*

Then, the limerick beginning, "There was a young lady from Wheeling . . ."

"What's happened to the lady?" They had remembered.

"I hope she didn't fall in."

"If you keep your boots on . . ."

"And protect your family."

"Another round?"

"All around!" they shouted and insisted on buying the stranger a beer as well, refusing to accept his refusal. Paul lifted his glass in thanks.

"What goes in like a ramrod and comes out like soggy bread?" he was asked, and "Why are chastity belts no protection against Jews?" But no answer was expected it seemed.

The conversation continued.

"We all think that ours is the biggest."

"But it's not the size that counts—as the archbishop told the chorus girl."

"That what?"

More laughter.

"I didn't say it. You thought it!"

"Please. Keep it clean," the barkeeper pleaded. And just in time, for the door to the ladies' room opened. The flushing water roared. The woman, refreshed, smartly groomed, pranced across the tavern, passing close to the drinkers. Her hands smoothed the back of her skirt, pulling it down, patting.

She stopped before the juke box, dug deep into her handbag for a coin, found one, inserted it and then quickly, indiscriminately punched the buttons, A-1, B-2, C-3, D-4, E-5. The record selector moved at her command. The mechanical arm selected her discs with silent efficiency. It was a magnificent machine, all glass and chrome, with multi-colored lights and gold trimmings. Ultramodern. Fully automatic, stocked with a collection of over a thousand and one records, offering its patrons a choice of songs to match every conceivable mood of love (from the sentimental to the cynical, from the platonic to the erotic), every possible kind (asexual, bisexual, heterosexual, homosexual, monosexual, omnisexual, and trisexual), every foreseeable attitude (affected, ambivalent, anatomical, apathetic, benevolent, bilious, callow, comical, desperate, disenchanted, eccentric, ecdysiastic, fearful, frustrated, glaucomatous, glowing, harmless, hard-bitten, hesitant, immoral, inhibited, jealous, joyous, kinetic, knavish, libidinous, lyric, masochistic, melancholic, meretricious, narrow, naughty, negative, niggardly, nugatory, offensive, omnivorous, perverse, petulant, positive, queasy, quiescent, quixotic, repulsive, rhapsodic, romantic, sadistic, stoical, temperate, tenacious, tender, tragic, transient, truculent, ugsome, umbilical, uncouth, violent, vociferous, waspish, whimsical, wholesome, 'xtatic, yielding, zestful), every imagined mode (both sanctioned and forbidden), every feasible situation (love found and love lost), every performable position (face to face, back to back, back to front, cheek to jowl, top to bottom, up to down, in to out), every potential combination and permutation of love (young with old, rich with poor, sick with clean, lame with deaf, blind with dumb, fat with thin, male with female, female with animal, animal with vegetable, or vice versa).

The twin speakers of the music machine filled the barroom with rich, fullbodied notes. Seemingly indifferent to the stirring rhythm as well as to the off-color lyrics, the woman moved to the bar where she chose a stool next to Paul. After neatly pulling her skirt down, she ordered a highball. She disregarded the bold looks of the men clustered at the far end of the bar and played with the swizzle-stick in her drink. Paul looked at her surreptitiously. When their eyes met for an instant, she smiled. He quickly looked away but ordered another beer and finally sat down. The second record dropped to the turntable. The lyrics were even more salacious, the husky voice of the female singer inviting. As she recounted the pleasures her lover-man had given her the night before, her voice sank to an intimate whisper. The drinkers responded with suitable wise cracks and lewd propositions (ostensibly directed at the vocalist).

As if in answer to the men's joint assault, the chanteuse oohed and aahed. First she pleaded with them to stop. Then she begged them not to stop.

"Beat me, Daddy! Beat me!" she cried. "Come one, come all!"

And her words became unintelligible. Just a wild, low, rhythmic gurgle, accompanied by the grunts of her assailants. The record ended with a high scream.

Continuing to toy with her drink, the sole female customer (she had chosen the seat next to the youthful stranger, as far as possible away from the mob of men at the other end of the bar) acted as if she were unaware of the excitement she was causing. She ignored the crude advances. But when the next record proved to be even wilder, she could no longer pretend that she had not heard. Trying to keep her composure, she turned in her seat to face the youth, her back toward the men. Paul could not help but sympathize (the pectoral muscles beneath her satin blouse heaved with indignation), for he knew that she had punched the buttons of the juke box at random.

The records went from bad to worse, from worse to worst, from sly double-entendres to out-and-out obscenities.

Paul did not dare meet his neighbor's glances, even though he now surmised that she was not as shocked as he had first thought. On second thought—perhaps her breasts heaved with excitement rather than with indignation. She swung her crossed leg provocatively. The sheer stockings caught beads of light, highlighting the swell of her calves. Aware of Paul's agitation, she lifted the top leg higher as if she wanted to examine it more closely herself. She sighed, slipped her foot partly out of her tight shoe and wiggled her toes, letting the shoe swing back and forth playfully, in time to the music. She looked directly at Paul; plump, bright red lips parted as if ready to speak.

But he was tongue-tied. He neither knew what to say nor what to do. When she stuck a fresh cigarette in the center of her pursed, wet mouth, he failed to take advantage of the opening. She waited. The unlit cigarette pointed at him, challenging. He could not bring himself to offer her a light, not even when she gave him another chance by pretending to search for a matchbook in her handbag. He watched her grope fruitlessly. Paralyzed, he allowed the opportunity to slip by.

The woman shrugged her shoulders and snapped her purse shut. The barkeeper looked up as if in response to a prearranged signal, matches ready. She tapped the cigarette on the bar top, replaced it between her lips, and accepted the proffered light, lightly touching his cupped hand with her fingertips to steady the flame. They exchanged a knowing smile, and, without another glance at the ineffectual youth, she picked up her half finished highball and joined the noisy drinkers near the juke box. The barkeeper followed, ready to serve as arbitrator.

The men swarmed around her, making her comfortable, pushing each other in a silent but savage struggle to get to the barstools on either side of her, vying for the right to buy her another drink. Ignoring the struggle, the woman sipped from the freshly filled glass, leaving the reckoning in the experienced hands of the barkeeper. Refusing to admit defeat, one of the losers dropped a handful of coins into the juke box, carefully selecting a group of bawdy songs.

The conversation matched the music.

"Get a load of this one!" they said.

"The next one's even better. . . . Worse!" they promised.

"Did you ever . . .?" they wanted to know.

"Well . . ." she admitted.

"Yes?" they urged her on.

"I once saw a movie," she told them. "You know the kind I mean. . . ."

As punishment for his cowardice, Paul forced himself to listen. But the punishment was too painful. After five minutes he called it off and tried to sneak away without being observed.

As he was about to pass by the group of merrymakers, they spotted him. They turned from the center of attraction to jeer. Some stepped forward to block his way.

"Leaving so soon?" they challenged.

"Don't be in such a hurry," they advised.

"That's no way to treat old friends," they warned him.

"That's no way to treat a lady!" they added.

"Ah, let the jerk go." The woman came to his rescue.

Reluctantly, they allowed him to pass through, but before he could reach the door they called him back.

"Careful going out! Watch your step! Don't fall down!" they cautioned him sweetly.

Paul smiled at the good advice. Suspiciously, everyone else smiled also. All smiled. And soon the whole bar was filled with laughter. The drinkers rolled off the stools in their merriment.

"Ho, ho! Ha, ha!" they laughed.

"Come back next year, sonny!" they cried.

"Don't take it so hard," they snickered.

"Losers weepers. Winners keepers," they chanted.

The woman joined in the laughter, her high voice rising above the others.

Paul cautiously skipped away, nodding and smiling while backing out.

The swinging doors snapped shut. The barkeeper sponged the wood of the bar with his white cloth. Drink and food were ordered with renewed appetite, devoured with gusto.

* * *

To forget, Paul sought the shelter of a movie house. The darkness hid him from the mocking looks of the afternoon crowds. They had stared at him as if they could read his thoughts, as if they knew the goal of his aimless wanderings. Had they stopped him and demanded to know what he was up to, he would have had to confess the truth. His eyes would have given him away. It had taken all his courage to face the cashier, to take his ticket and wait for his change, all the while fighting the urge to run home and hide.

When he had passed safely by the ticket taker, he breathed more easily. There was no usher. The darkness was a relief. It was so deep that he could see nothing, although he waited patiently, giving his eyes ample time to adjust to the change. When the visibility did not improve, he inched forward carefully and found a seat by touch. He did not bump into anyone on the way to his seat. Perhaps the theater was completely empty.

The film had already started. Although he was interested, he found it extremely difficult to follow the plot. The scenes were too short, choppy, one pushing into the other, with illogical transitions, sudden, extreme changes in lighting and speed. The pieces of the story did not fit together. The time sequence was all mixed up. Yet, despite the lack of coherence, the film seemed familiar.

It was irritating. At first he thought that he might have seen the picture before. (This was possible because in his hurry to get off the street he had hardly glanced at the display of still photos. Nor had he been able to decipher the title of either of the two films paired in the double feature. He had not bothered to look up at the marquee, and the poster in the lobby had been of no help since its text was obscured by a wide strip of paper pasted diagonally across its face; black background with large white letters proclaiming that the films would be shown *today only!*) But as the film continued he was forced to dismiss this explanation, for, actually, he did not know what was going to happen next; neither could he identify the actors. Instead, the sense of recognition came at the very instant the action took place, at the very moment a word was spoken. It was like remembering the long forgotten words of an old song, being able to join the voice of the singer, keeping up with him, never a note ahead or behind, the two voices blending, becoming one. And for a moment he felt himself being drawn into the life of the film. The doors opened. He rushed through the entranceway, up the circling staircase, along the arch-shaped corridor, into the apartment.

Then, abruptly, the illusion shattered. He was back in the movie house. Someone had bumped against him. A woman's voice whispered an apology. She sat down in the seat next to him.

When their thighs touched, she did not draw back. Without hesitation, she brought her right leg against his left leg and rubbed it up and down against his. He turned his head sideways to look at her, but the dark hid her features. When he put his hand on his own knee, next to hers, she pressed closer. Her hand reached for his, found it, touched it lightly, guided it to her knees and then withdrew.

His hand on her knees slipped between, reaching upwards. Her legs opened, then pressed together. Fingers slid easily upwards, past stocking tops, along garter straps, to smooth skin, to the veil of her brief undergarment. But pressing tightly together, the clasp of her thighs prevented his fingers from slipping under the elasticized border of her panties. Stayed but not rebuked, his fingers caressed the smooth silk-covered, smooth skin. Fingers softly circled the veiled mount, passed over it and returned, circling and recircling, cautiously, patiently.

Soon, though, her thighs weakened. She offered no further resistance to his insistent fingers. Pushing the undergarment aside, he groped for and found the soft, wet-lipped, liquid flesh. His fingers penetrated and stirred.

Her arm fell to his lap. Stirred, she stirred.

But suddenly she slipped away. "No. No. We mustn't here. Wait!" she whispered.

She pushed to the aisle. He followed, stumbling in the dark, chasing her up the aisle. She was just ahead, silhouetted against the doorways of the rest rooms. He could not quite catch up with her, although he was gaining fast. Before he could get to her she had reached the door of the ladies' room. He caught a brief glimpse of her spotlighted by the bright lights of the toilet: blond hair, baby-blue blouse partly unbuttoned, her skirt wrinkled, bunched up, straight, shiny legs, crooked seams, spike heels.

"Wait!" she promised as the door closed behind her.

He waited.

He waited for a long time. He was about to give up when the door of the ladies' room opened. Restored to bloom, washed and powdered, blouse buttoned, skirt smoothed, straps adjusted, seams straightened, she came toward him. Cool and confident, her breasts rising calmly.

"There you are," he said, moving to join her.

"I'm afraid you have made a mistake," she answered.

Stopped cold by her words, he stepped back. She walked past him toward the exit, high heels clicking haughtily, resounding on the marble floor of the theater lobby.

Paul returned to his seat. Soon another woman joined him. Their legs touched. Their hands met, crossed, explored, found, squeezed, stirred. When, inadvertently, his fingernails became entangled in her stockings, she pushed his hand away and pulled her skirt down.

She objected: "Careful! Clumsy fool! I'm not going to have my clothes spoiled," and changed seats.

When another woman took her place, he was more careful. Again, the adventure came to nothing, even though his companion's advances were more overt, her caresses to the point. When she sensed the imminent rush of semen, she quickly removed her hand from his lap. Retreated prudently. Just in time.

As soon as it was possible, Paul buttoned his fly and left the movie house.

*   *   *

Out of the covered dark night bed to sharp cornered daylight. The late afternoon sun at eye level. Clouds of heat drifting, steam rising from the pavement. The street crowded, spilling over.

He is drawn into the maelstrom. The streams mingle and shift, slow to shuffle, then rush between cars, cross in confusion. He lets

himself be carried along, propelled by the current, close to the swirling legs, in lock step, almost colliding but, at the very last, swept by,
now momentarily stopped, now suddenly freed and pushed forward.

Almost touching, but not quite. The hand reaching out. Open-
mouthed. Breath held. But it is too late. Already she is lost among the
other enchantresses. Indistinguishable. Other eyes and lips smile,
promising infinite pleasure. They dance by. Clinging breasts. Deep
cleavages. Skirts flapping display the magnificence of their long legs.
Highly polished metallic cloth gleams. The molded flesh reflecting the
sun. Bodies ablaze. Glorious. Arms, legs, knees, thighs, hips, haunches,
breasts—all moving, rippling, flowing, whirling, encircling him. Flashing whirlpools of beauty spin him, blind him, drown him in a sea of
liquid flesh.

Overcome by an insatiable thirst for all, he wishes to possess them
all at once, to rape their moving flesh in flight. Half the desire is in
the collective movement, in the swirling mass motion of female
limbs.

It is a deadly lust, an unquenchable thirst. For if one were to
stop, if one were to take him, then the others would be lost and the
movement would be lost. In his greed he wants all, not one. And he
wants them on the wing.

The women smile as if they know. They smile with secret satisfaction, breathing deeply, out of breath, taken by their own loveliness.
Their eyes half closed in the contemplation of their glory, walking
somewhat slower, self-consciously, buttocks moving as to a dance
step, tensing against the taut cloth of the skirt, withdrawing, tensing,
withdrawing, tensing, touching, ripe cheek to cheek, one nether lip
kissing the other, full succulent lip glued to lip. They smile self-
satisfied, flouting their joy.

He follows the luring glitter of the tight skirts, the tantalizing
unison of their churning haunches. He follows mesmerized by the
swishing and the whispering of their shifts, the shimmer and shake,
the flowing dip of the buttocks. He walks as if under water, dazed,
his whole body pulsating like a pus-filled wound.

When one of them looks back at him, he thinks that he recognizes
her. The light reflected by her blond hair, the flow of her skirt, the
stride, the sound of her high heels reminds. He hurries after her. She
steps off the sidewalk. Halfway across the avenue, she glances back,
smiles encouragingly. She calls to him. He runs in pursuit, blinded by
the glow of her splendor.

As he reaches the intersection his foot catches in a sewer grating. He trips. The hissing brakes of a truck, the stench from the open mouth of a sewer, steam rising from it, the pain of the impact, laughter, a scream (he does not know whether it is his own or that of an onlooker) merge and press down to choke him. The membrane breaks and warm blood stuffs his nose. He cannot breathe. Thick sweat closes his eyes. Then all melts away and he loses consciousness.

* * *

The nurse bent over her patient, cool in her fresh white uniform. Her starched apron scraped over his bare legs. The crisp hem of the dress cut. His fingers sought for the stiff edge beneath his fingernails, pressed hard. The palm of his hand itched against the firm linen.

The doctor, disappointed, had departed for more serious business. Miss Lydia, the nurse, told her patient how lucky he was. Only a few cuts and scratches which were easily patched up. She closed the office and took him home with her in a taxi.

It was night. A few clouds near the moon broke the monotony of the sky. Fog, rising from the sewers, was covering the city.

She did not waste any time. She slipped her dress off and disappeared into the bathroom to make her preparations. As requested, Paul undressed and lay down on the bed. When she returned, she placed a jar of vaseline by the bed, confidng that she did not do this often.

"Dr. Karp wouldn't approve, you know. He wanted you to get a good night's rest."

She had turned off all the lights except one, a small, pink-shaded night lamp by the side of the bed. "I like to see what you're doing to me," she explained.

She hesitated for a moment before joining him on the bed, posing for his benefit, cupping her naked breasts in her hands.

"Do you like them?"

He reached out for her.

"Easy!" she protested. "Say, this isn't the first time is it, dear?"

Paul shook his head.

"I'm always dry like this after the curse," she admitted when he encountered difficulties in his efforts to broach her.

"Wait. Let me try." She dipped her hand into the vaseline pot and applied the jelly.

"Now, she said. "Like this."

She spread her legs wide and guided him.

"That's better. But slowly, slowly, dear," she cautioned him. "You're so big," she complained. "And so rough."

Suddenly she groaned and held on tight. "Come to me. Come to me!" she implored.

"Now!" she ordered.

She kissed him open-mouthed. Her dry tongue pushed between his lips. It plunged deeper like a thick finger down his throat. Paul gagged. He tried to pull away, but she held him down, clamping her thighs tightly together. She took his hand and brought it back to her cowdung-shaped breasts, placing the other hand beneath her right buttock. Obediently, his fingers played with the proffered wrinkled nipple, rubbing it in a crooked circle.

When he opened his eyes, he found himself looking down at both of them, as if he were removed, standing on the side, an impartial observer, coldly examining the action on the bed. The entanglement of limbs writhed clumsily. The bodies moved laboriously as if they were dragging heavy stones, straining, pushing, groaning, yet getting nowhere. They struggled, thick in each other's arms. Dry groin against dry groin.

"Say you love me. Tell me, sweety. Tell me," she mumbled, mouth to mouth. "Ah," she whimpered with a thick sleepy tongue; her mouth glued to his.

Somewhere in a dark corner of the room, Miss Lydia's dog moaned jealously, chewed itself to pieces, licking its wounds with a wet sloppy tongue, an offensive sound.

*   *   *

Lydia was asleep. Her nude body glistened where the pink light of the bedside lamp touched it. (She had not allowed him to turn the light off.) The flesh seemed flushed, her hair glossy. When pale morning light penetrated between the slats of the Venetian blinds, the glow faded. The color of her flesh changed to grey.

Paul left the apartment without waking her, walking on bare feet. He waited until he had reached the street before putting his shoes on, forcing his feet into the shoes, not stopping to fight the knotted laces. He found a garbage pail and dropped his soiled socks into it.

The fog had thickened to light rain. His clothes were soaked through with the pungent smell of female flesh. When he raised his hands to his face, the odor became stronger. He could taste it, a gamy aftertaste which coated his tongue and which he could not scrape away. His underwear stuck to him. He walked awkwardly, painfully, exasperated by the tickle of the post coital-drip.

11. DISORDER & EARLY SORROW

The raw youth had had his way. That which he had longed for and dreamed of had finally, unexpectedly, come to him. And without any effort by him! True, he had searched for women to gratify his desire, had looked them up and down brazenly, his mouth watering, his hands itching, his private parts aching, but at the moment of showdown he had always backed away, afraid to risk a rebuke. He had been willing to do without, rather than make an outright, up and up attempt. And he would have continued indefinitely, wanting, twitching, but never acting (except for occasional sneaky, cowardly, yet even then half-hearted attempts—anonymous assaults carried out under the cover of the rush hour mob or the equally protecting cover of darkness), waiting for a predatory female to appear miraculously, to lead him by the hand.

"Oh, whores of the alley, please rape me!" he used to pray.

And when none answered his supplication, he blamed them, instead of admitting his own shortcoming.

"Bitches! Tight-lipped bitches!"

He cursed them, yet in the same breath worshiped them. He swooned with admiration. But he could do nothing about it. He hated them. After each defeat he ran home, damned their almond-shaped eyes, their overflowing breast-cups, their pastel colored skirts, their swishing, bouncing strut. He bit his pillow and comforted himself as best he could.

If the nurse had not taken pity on him, his torture would have been prolonged till God knows when.

(His night with Lotte did not count. He had completely forgotten it, or, rather, had erased it from memory along with the other details of his life in the old world. All that was shadowy, almost fictitious. It had happened so long ago, so it seemed, in another life—if it had ever really happened. So little did he believe in the reality of his experience with Lotte that until Lydia had opened herself to his thrusts he had actually doubted the existence of vaginas, had feared that his longings for a soft, warm, moist sheath into which to plunge his stiff tortured organ would never be realized, had feared and half suspected that the depth of the female orifice was greatly exaggerated, had snorted skeptically when one of his school fellows boasted to him about shoving it in all the way up to the hilt and the girl crying for more ("What the hell! Do you think I've got a telephone pole between my legs?" was his supposed reply), wishing that it were true but fearing to surrender himself to the hope of total immersion, suspecting that it was a tall story, a joke to fool the gullible, fearing that when he would finally reach the goal he would find only a shallow trench. It had been the first time as far as he was concerned although he didn't admit it to Lydia.)

Yet on the morning after, he offered no prayers of thanksgiving, no hosannas. He sneaked away while she was still asleep so that he would not have to speak to her. After having first checked to see that the hallway was empty, he closed Lydia's door quietly and ran down the stairs, not wanting her neighbors to see him. Instead of being grateful, he was ashamed.

They had behaved like pigs, he thought, like dogs. Nuzzlng one another, sniffing, licking. They had rolled around in the bed, limbs entwined, tugging, thrusting, legs and arms twisted into a knot, armpit pasted to armpit, crotch to crotch, gaping mouth to gaping mouth, teeth bared, protruding tongues straining to reach farther, to plunge deeper.

He was sickened by the memory of the night, by what he had done, by what he had been forced to say.

"Say: 'I want to do it to you! I want to do it to you!' Say it," she had demanded.

He had repeated it over and over, urged on by her response.

"Yes! Do it to me, sweety. Do it to me!"

Their voices had merged, until demand and response were indistinguishable. And he had done more. Matched her in vile words, in bestial actions, finally outdoing her. Long hoarded obscenities had spilled from him. She no longer needed to egg him on. They had rolled together in filth.

But as soon as it was over, he had regretted it. He had not been able to sleep. When he closed his eyes he relived every fleshy detail of the night. His gorge rose as if he had actually swallowed the flesh he had kissed and squeezed, as if his stomach and intestines were crammed full with greasy raw meat. He had spent the remainder of the night staring at the ceiling in order to avoid looking at Lydia on the bed next to him (she had fallen into a deep sleep, clutching a pillow over her head, feet entangled in the twisted sheets, her torso moving up and down rhythmically, noisily, drops of sweat running together, sagging naked female parts exposed under the light of the bedside lamp) or at her dog who had moved closer when the violent activities had subsided, but who continued to whimper nevertheless.

It made him ill to think of what they had done. He felt as if he had committed a crime, taken part in a vile, degrading act. He had spent the worst part of the night, after Lydia had fallen asleep and before he had dared to leave in the morning, in mortal terror. At any moment, he feared, the door would be broken down and both he and the nurse dragged away. Every sound had seemed ominous. Toward dawn, a wind had sprung up which had shaken the building and caused the doors to rattle as if someone were knocking.

The fear faded in daylight. But the guilt and nausea lingered. Worst of all though, life seemed even uglier than it had before. Somehow he felt cheated.

The morning after, he looked at the women on the subway with suspicion, no longer believing in the resplendent front they presented. From that day on, he suspected even the most beautiful. He who had implicitly believed in the greater glory of female pulchritude had overnight become a confirmed doubter.

No longer trusting appearances, he challenged the firmness of the high-breasted coeds who bent so seductively over their microscopes in the biology class. Beneath every blouse he now saw the danger of disappointment rather than rich promise. And he felt the same uncertainty about other parts of the female anatomy, for he now realized that not only was it possible to dress up the breast in such a way as to disguise its natural form, but that the same trickery could be, and was, applied to hindquarters, thighs, and legs. Just as bras uplifted and held together sagging flaccid breasts, so girdles flattened protruding stomachs, smoothed striated thighs, and rounded drooping buttocks. It was a bitter lesson.

He felt betrayed, yet sensed the fault was basically his. It was he who had assumed that breasts were as firm as they looked, skin beneath its silk covering as sleek, thighs sheathed in tight tapering skinlike skirts as perfectly rounded. In all fairness, the women could not be blamed for his naive assumptions. Inexperience combined with a tainted imagination had led to his begetting and then worshipping a false—worse, an impossible—ideal.

In his mind he had built up an image of a breed of dream women based on a composite picture formed by guarded but frequent trips past the show windows of lingerie shops in which splendidly proportioned manikins in varying degrees of undress were displayed, by stealthily leafing through his foster sister's fashion magazines and feasting hungry eyes on the illustrated brassiere advertisements, by regularly attending movies in which the female protrusions, grooves, and cleavages of Hollywood's many-splendored sirens were highlighted and multiplied by the magic of trick photography, and (perhaps most damaging of all) by persistently reading pulp fiction, mainly murder stories in which detective heroes toyed with heroines and villainesses whose marvelous stone-hard tits cut into space at incredible angles, defying the laws of gravity. No living woman could hope to meet these qualifications. Sooner or later the dreamer was bound to awaken. But because of his timidity, because of his hesitancy and because of his sullen appearance which turned prospective acquaintances away, the awakening had been postponed abnormally long. The little experience he had had with women before Lydia (discounting his dream of Lotte) had been confined to furtive and barely tolerated gropings on park benches or in cellar doorways. The breasts he had touched before Lydia's had been shielded by protective layers of cloth. They had been uplifted and rearranged to conform to the accepted fashion standards of the day. Touched ever so lightly, underhandedly, or slyly brushed up against, they felt firm and satiny. But the deception, if any, was guileless, unintentional; no one had promised him that without artificial support the flesh would stand up to his prodigious expectations.

And of all women, Miss Lydia was surely the least blameworthy. She wore the utilitarian clothes prescribed by her profession: a starched white uniform of the simplest cut. Only the most perverse could have thought of her dress as particularly stimulating as Paul, who found the tailored uniform especially titillating, did—not because he associated it with innocence, not because the thought of soiling it aroused his bestiality, but because the combination of crisp white cloth and slippery round flesh tickled his peculiarly twisted sensuality. His hands ached to feel the cloth, to play with its stiff hem, to rub it against himself, to unbutton it and finger it at the same time as he touched the body of its wearer—just as he had found pleasure as a child in playing with the crisp edges of his freshly laundered bed sheets. Furthermore, Lydia neither padded her bosom nor did her foundation garments hide any deformities. True, when nude, her stomach proved to be not as flat as it might have been, but the flesh was not wrinkled, nor was it scarred. Her pubic hair was not silken, but then it was not wiry either. Her nipples were rather small. Her breasts were of normal size and round, perhaps a bit tired (but not really flabby), admittedly not as well-shaped as they had appeared while encased in their white rayon envelopes, not as high as when supported by the taut shoulder-straps of the brassiere—but who would have expected so much? Who could blame her? There had been no conscious attempt at deception.

Paul did blame her and would not concede that his feeling of being let down was unreasonable, was fatuous, was childish.

And then his expectations suffered as great a blow, if not a greater one, in the midst of the sex act itself—or more precisely, at the moment after the height of the act. While his flesh was still pulsating with the last spasm of pleasure, his mind was already plunging to despair. At the very moment that the hoarded lust broke joyously free, a crushing depression overcame him. Rather than feeling relieved, he felt dissatisfied. He could not accept the sudden end, the abrupt fall. He had not expected it. Somewhere he had heard or read of the mellow glow of contentment which was supposed to follow—not this lameness! Not this fading away, this extinction of life! His flesh like spongy rubber. His spirit crushed.

It was a hard knock. And, as he soon discovered, there was little he could do about it (no matter how much he fretted or grumbled) but to wait patiently for the impotent time between to heal.

* * *

Surprisingly though, he learned to adapt himself to the pattern and to accept the despondency of the moment after as part of the price one paid for the feast. He took comfort in the thought that his burden was shared by others, finally appreciating the wisdom of his textbook of Latin aphorisms: *"omne animale post coitu triste."* He recognized the foolishness of quarreling with his bread and butter. The naked fact was that he would soon be hungry again, would soon need to eat again, no matter what the aftertaste or how painful the digestion.

A healthy vital organ has no memory, knows no scruples.

Ignoring his conscience, dismissing his misgivings, forgetting his past disappointments, doubting his apprehensions, Paul returned to Miss Lydia's bed at the earliest opportunity. She welcomed him, spread her legs wide, breathing deeply, and opened to her sharp shiny white teeth. Eagerly, hot-headed, her young lover slid between her parted thighs.

It was not long before he began to revel in the secret knowledge of his illicit affair. On the way back to the Bronx, he looked boldy and knowingly at the female passengers. Their cool, pretended indifference no longer fooled him. He felt that he could see up their skirts. that he was privy to their innermost parts and deepest secrets. He was an initiate. He knew! The thought excited him. He pressed his hands to his nose and mouth to get the full effect of Lydia's perfume. The smell no longer nauseated him. It reminded him of the long night he had just spent with her. He was proud of his prowess. Lydia had been overwhelmed by his ardor and finally had had to beg him to stop. He had persisted, deliberately, methodically forcing himself to recoup his sexual energy as quickly as possible in order to shorten the dead time between.

It was a victory of sorts, but a hollow one. Although he had for once not allowed his disappointment to destroy everything, had been able to make the best of a bad situation and salvage something useful, to wrest relative satisfaction from the sudden, near catastrophic wreck of his carnal fantasies, there was no real cause for celebration. The successful compromise reached was hardly indicative of a basic change in his sullen character. It was a settlement born of desperation, for he knew that a total defeat in this most sensitive area would make life utterly insupportable. He had had no choice! He had been driven into a corner. He had to come to terms, had to split the difference. He had to go even further than that—to work for the compromise, persistently, doggedly, to force himself not to throw it all up, not to sulk, but for once to accept and to function within the given limitations. Thanks to a basic, to an inborn, though weakened and perhaps even perverted—yet despite all, still tenacious and all-conquering—lust for life (as well as, of course, to Lydia's availability), he had succeeded. In a way, he felt proud of himself.

But the struggle had been a painful one and the compromise

reached had exacted its price. It also had further repercussions. For one, it left him with a general feeling of weariness and cynicism. For another, it led to his becoming further alienated from the bosom of his family—particularly from the bosoms of the mother and sister.

He could no longer look at Mother and especially at Sister without being overcome by a feeling of shame. Martha's breasts (she had developed into a strapping young woman) were now always getting in his way. He tried to avoid them. But where else could he look? He was far too guilty to dare look her in the face; so he cast his eyes downward to her lap and then to her knees—yet these portions of her body were equally disconcerting. Her skirt was continually climbing up her white thighs, and when she made herself comfortable in her favorite easy chair, she bared the rest of her belongings. And not by accident either, Paul thought. There was nothing to do but to bury his face in a book or to keep his eyes closed.

His relationship with the parents was no better. The mother resented his secretiveness. She could not understand the cause of it. And although she no longer expected him to confide in her (he never had), she continued to question him. No matter how quietly Paul approached the apartment, no matter how carefully he inserted the key or how slowly he opened the door, the mother heard and met him with her reproaches, her face tear-streaked, her eyes swollen, her hair matted as if she had been tearing at it in her anxiety.

Then, the flushing toilet thundered ominously and the bathroom door was thrown open. The father, freshly shaven but still in his pajamas, rushed to block Paul's escape and to add his recriminations. He had no illusions about this young man; he suspected the worst.

"Shameless fiend! Viper! Slug-a-bed! Unnatural brute! Masturbator!" the father lashed into the malefactor. "I don't have to hear what you have been doing out all night. I know! You're sick. Depraved! Foul! You smell like a pig. You look like one. Get out of my sight!"

Which Paul did gladly. Not that he particularly minded the questions or the accusations or even the mother's tear-stained face, but he could not stomach the sight of the parents in the morning: the mother in her unbuttoned housecoat with her limp breasts showing through the translucent cloth of her nightgown; the father prudently holding up the pants of his green striped pajamas (the drawstring undone or broken), yet the fly open, exposing low-hanging, doughy testicles.

Paul closed the door of the bedroom. It did not stay shut for long. On his way back to the bathroom, the father kicked it open, furious at the violation of the household rule which stipulated that the door must always remain ajar (especially at night).

Even in bed, hidden from the other members of the family by the paper screen which separated his half of the room from the sister's half, Paul could not be sure of his privacy. Unexpectedly, the father's head might appear, ducking around the side of the screen, checking to see that he was not smoking in bed (hoping to catch him red-handed). Or, without warning, the head of the household's frugal hand might reach out for the light cord and his reading would be abruptly terminated. The bathroom had offered no sanctuary ever since the father had removed the lock. Under the pretext of straightening out after him, the mother examined all his belongings, not only looking through the two drawers which had been apportioned to him in the dresser he shared with Martha, but also turning out the pockets of his clothes, and, despite his protest, thumbing through the pages of his notebooks. What she was looking for he was not sure of—perhaps conclusive evidence of his life of debauchery.

One morning he provided her with this evidence by hiding a soiled pair of Lydia's panties beneath his pillow—one of her scantiest under-garments, pink satin with inserts of lace and black fringes around the bottom edges, which he had bought for her with money stolen from the mother's handbag. The next day he moved away from home. No one objected. The mother returned the panties without a word when Paul demanded them on his way out the front door, holding them up to him at the end of a broomstick in order to avoid soiling her hands.

12. AN OVERWHELMING QUESTION

The tourists in the sightseeing boat took him for a foreigner, a Puerto Rican or Mexican. The guide explained this as the boat passed the old Horatio Street pier, pointing to the group of street Arabs sitting at the end of the dock, their legs dangling over the edge. The interest of the tourists had been awaken by the flute music. The guide, who was quick on his feet, immediately took advantage of the presence of the flute player and his companions. The voice of the flute was sharp, far-reaching, yet not shrill. It was obviously foreign, possibly Oriental or Mideastern. The sound of it floating across the water in the midst of a late summer's day in Manhattan surprised the tourists. They were thrilled. Some stood up to get a better view. The guide pointed to the figures on the abandoned pier, talking excitedly into a microphone. Although electrically amplified, his words could not be understood on shore. The flute player, looking down at the muddy water, continued to play unaware of his audience.

Paul had been sitting alone at the edge of the river, at the far end of the pier, most of the afternoon. The shade provided by the gigantic chimneys of the garbage processing plant cut the heat of the sun. Once he had turned around to take a look at a girl, roused from his siesta by the click of her high heels on the splintered wooden planks. The man with her spat into the river. The girl turned back, walking away rapidly but cautiously, avoiding the cracks between the planks. Her companion followed. The Arabs had come silently. When Paul looked up from the oily water, a group of dark men were sitting next to him talking to each other in a language he could not understand. One of them took out a flute. The others stopped talking and listened to the music, their heads bent.

Although there was no wind, the smell of decomposing vegetable and animal refuse drifted down river from the processing plant at the next pier. This was especially noticeable when the garbage scows unloaded their cargoes. Thick smoke hung low over the chimneys. The river seemed to be stagnant. The sightseeing boat hardly made any ripples as it slowly drifted past the pier.

The guide pointed to the group on the wharf. Paul was accepted as one of them without question, although he had never thought of himself as resembling a Puerto Rican or a North African. Surrounded by Arabs he bacame an Arab. He blended in well with his background and became part of the snapshots the tourists in the boat were hurriedly focusing to take. After the boat had moved on and disappeared beyond the next cluster of docks, the flute player, who had continued to play, impervious to the attention he was attracting, was joined in the music by his comrades. They chanted in counterpoint to the higher pitched melody of the flute. Paul pretended to be singing along with them. The music did not seem foreign to him; neither did his companions. When the next boatload of tourists approached, he eagerly awaited their stares and cameras, enjoying the deception, yet at the same time feeling that it was not really a deception, for it suddenly struck him that he could just as easily have been born an Arab as a Jew or Negro or Swede. Being something, he thought, is very much a matter of chance, a question of who sits down next to one—or rather, and this was much more damning, of who sat down next to one's mother. So much had depended on this, perhaps the whole pattern of his life.

It was amusing to fool the tourists on a Sunday afternoon. But the game lost its savour when the sun went down and the Arabs departed as silently as they had come. He was left alone, disquietingly so. And very much himself, stripped down to the bare wood (not a disguise in reach, not so much as a cigarette to dangle from the corner of his mouth in imitation of a film hero). He tried to explain it to Lydia that evening.

"You see, don't you, how simple it is and how deadly. *Kismet* the Arabs call it. Or is it *Kissmet?* Never mind. . . . I could have been one of them. That's all I mean. Fitting in beautifully, without a ripple, not a seam showing. It's all chance—which spermatozoon gets through first. . . . But even then it was not too late; even after I was born I still had a chance. Yes, I could have been anything. I'm sure of it. Look at my hands! I could have been a first-rate pianist—people have stopped me on the street, perfect strangers, to tell me I have the hands of a concert pianist—and I would have become one too if my mother had only insisted when I was very young. But she didn't. She only asked me once when I was still too ignorant to understand the importance of her question. Maybe she did not want me to accept. Maybe she never really asked me. I only have her word for it. I don't remember being asked. It's possible that she was jealous since she herself played the violin. And then again, I could have been a scientist or a sea-captain had my father been a sailor. Or a painter. Or a mathematician, an explorer, a revolutionary. A boxer. I could have developed into one of the best heavyweights if my father had not suddenly decided that meat was the curse of mankind, and all meat-eaters feedbags for maggots: therefore no meat for his children. And if my mother had not had a weak stomach, a condition gravely aggravated by milk, which—she was convinced of this—upon reaching the digestive apparatus turns to hard, stone-like pot cheese: therefore no milk for her son, even though I was growing weaker day by day. And when help finally came it was already far too late in the day. By the time I came to America and was at last fed decent food, I only threw up all over the good Samaritans' tablecloth because all the red meat and rich milk and cream was too much for me. Damn it! If I had only had the right start. It's as simple as that. But I have never had any luck."

Lydia liked neither the text nor the spirit of his monologue. It upset her. Especially the conclusion which she thought might apply to her.

"Lots of men would consider themselves lucky to be where you are right now!" she wanted him to know.

When he failed to respond, she mellowed, sensing that he was genuinely disturbed by his afternoon's experience.

"Forget it, sweetie," she begged him. "Why would you want to be an Arab anyway?"

Paul did not want to forget it. He left as soon as he could disengage himself from her comforting arms, annoyed with himself for having tried to explain his feelings to her. He resolved at least to try to limit future visits.

"See you soon, honey," she called after him, already half asleep, her dog curled up next to her, making himself comfortable in the place his mistress's lover had vacated, licking himself smugly, but keeping one eye on his rival, wary of a sudden attack.

"Stupid cunt-hound!" Paul hissed at him as he closed the door.

During the next month he kept away from Lydia as he had

promised himself, devoting all his time to his writing. The afternoon with the Arabs had renewed his enthusiasm for work. He thought of nothing else and spent his days in the 42nd Street Library doing research. He studied the confessions of St. Augustine, Rousseau, Nat Turner, Tolstoy, Charles Lamb, Fanny Hill, a Young Man, and an English Opium Eater; the autobiographies of Cellini, Mill, Harris, Wright, Yeats, a Flea, an Ex-Colored Man, Madeleine, Trollope, and Hooker; the memoirs of Casanova, Brantôme, Martinus Scriblerus, Moll Flanders, a Midget, Wanda and Severin, Defoe, Mr. Badman, and a Lady of Pleasure; the diaries of Franz K, Virginia Woolf, Pepys, a Coxcomb, and a Chambermaid. He thumbed the *Index Librorum Prohibitorum* and cracked *The Book of the Dead* as well as Gower's *Confessio Amantis*, Burton's *Perfumed Garden*, Moore's *Memoirs of My Dead Life*, Wilde's *De Profundis*, Gorky's *My Childhood*, Hogg's *Confessions of a Justified Sinner*, Lord George's *A Night in a Moorish Harem*, Newman's *Apologia Pro Vita Sua*, Bunyan's *Grace Abounding*, Gide's *If It Die*, Anonymous's *My Secret Life*, and Strindberg's *The Confession of a Fool*. Nor did he neglect the thinly fictionalized autobiographical novels of the once so popular "confession" school of writing, from Butler's *The Way of All Flesh* through Sacher-Masoch's *Venus in Furs* to Proust's *Remembrance of Things Past*.

At night he applied what he had learned from his diurnal research to his own pencraft. By the end of the month he was exhausted. He had produced over two hundred pages.

He thought of himself as part of the great tradition. Sitting in judgment upon himself, he felt an intimate kinship to his literary forebears. He considered them his blood relatives, his physical as well as spiritual brothers, his bedfellows, his doubles who like himself had fearlessly cut and dissected, probed and squeezed, performing vivisections upon themselves without recourse to anesthetics. And not unlike many of his predecessors, through the detailed analysis of every quirk and flaw, he soon found himself employing writing as a means of self-flagellation, strewing salt on his open ulcers, picking at his scabs, forcing old wounds to bleed again, never allowing the smallest scratch to heal, reporting every failure, every shortcoming; and then becoming fascinated by the color and shape of the abscesses and the lumps of pus which he squeezed out, fondling the boogers he pulled from his nose, captivated, proud, doting on them, cherishing them as his very own. As the constipated father said when after nine painful days he finally found relief and looked into the bedpan, "It may stink like hell, but it's mine and I love it!"

The analogy was too close for comfort. Although he was still fascinated with what he had brought forth, he found the stench overpowering. When (after a deep restorative sleep) he attempted to return to his labors, he could not, no matter how hard he tried. Even to reread what he had written turned his stomach. He saw no possibility of continuing. And the more time that passed, the more foul the work seemed.

The very existence of it, locked away in a suitcase and hidden under his bed, troubled him. He did not want to be in the same room with it. Yet when he was away from the room, he was more keenly aware of it. He rushed back terrified lest his landlady had, during his absence, opened the suitcase and discovered his secret.

He became abnormally fearful of the possibility of sudden, accidental death, for then his belongings would be ransacked by his step-parents who would ferret out and pry into every hole and corner of his room until they had stripped it bare, who would not desist from their search until they had sifted every crumb of his private life. Neither his dirty laundry nor his personal papers would escape their scrutiny. And without doubt, his novel would become the principal morsel of evidence in the autopsy. His appeal, "TO BE DESTROYED IN CASE OF DEATH!!!" which he had printed in red crayon on the first and last pages of his work, would, of course, be disregarded. If anything, it would serve to attract their attention. The sole solution was to destroy it before it fell into their hands.

Then he thought of one other alternative: to expose himself voluntarily while he was still alive, to visit the old couple and force them to listen as he read his confession out loud.

"Father," he said on the telephone," I have something extremely important to tell you and Mother. I'll have to come and see you tomorrow evening."

When he opened the suitcase, he lost his nerve. He simply couldn't face the trip up to the Bronx. And what was much more serious—he now came to the devastating conclusion that the writing was juvenile, the style overblown, the ideas simple-minded, the tone sentimental. It was a whining complaint, full of self-pity, rather than the cutting exposé he had thought it to be.

It would have to be destroyed.

Carefully tearing the pages into small pieces (he did not want to stuff the toilet), he flushed them down. The water roared on its way into the sewer. The empty tank took a long time to refill. In his fervor to be rid of the hated foolscaps, he pulled the chain too soon, before the tank was filled; the mechanism rattled, it wheezed, the water pressure was insufficient. Torn fragments of paper slowly circled, dipped, disappearing for a moment around the bend of the bowl's gorge, but then popped to the surface again. After a while he caught on to the trick. When the water reached the top of the tank, the shut-off valve emitted a tell-tale whistle. Now it was safe to flush.

(Since the process was slow, Paul, despite his abhorrence for his work, found himself glancing over the pages as he dropped them into the bowl. Here and there a sentence or phrase struck his fancy. He fished them out and later copied them into a new notebook. Besides shoring these fragments (there were not many), he also preserved the chapter titles, listing them for possible future use: "Childless Pain-birth, The Bedrock of Dry Dreams, A Mighty Trauma is Our Beginning, Father Noon & Mother Midnight, Son of Tantalus, Coupling Couples Uncoupled (or the Wrecked Tangle), Outskirts & Inskirts, Growing Pains, The Assend of Mt. Venus, Through the First Gate, Coitus in Absentia, The Devil's Tattoo, Softboiled Eggs, Leeches & Suppositories, In the Market Place, An Invitation to a Succuba, Hindsight Seen from the Side, Lapsus Lingam, A Bed of Thorns, The Scream of Consciousness, Play Dead, A Cerebral Hemorrhoid, Dildo & Anas, Lemmings' Way, The Walls of Deceit. A Short Guide to the Long of Marriage, From Romance to Ritual to Habit, Through the Anals of History, The Transfer, Killing Time, The Last Day of Winter, The Armpits of Death, An Eyewitness Report from the Execution Pit, Petering Out." In all he did not rescue more than six or seven pages worth. He labelled the notebook "Fragments from an Abandoned Work" and put it away in his suitcase.)

When the last scrap of paper had been disposed of, Paul washed his socks and underwear. It was dawn when he finished. The cleaning operation had taken all night. He felt relieved and very tired.

Although he knew that he should consider himself fortunate in having recognized the true worthlessness of his novel and having had the strength to destroy it before it could cause him any serious embarrassment, he was not as thankful as he might have been. He tried to avoid thinking about the full implications of his distressing discovery. For a while he considered beginning work on a new novel. But his flesh revolted at the idea. When he tried to put pencil to paper, his hand failed to function properly. The writers' itch was routed by the writers' cramp. And if, by sheer stubbornness and perseverance, he managed to squeeze out a page or two, he was sure to destroy it when he re-examined it the morning after. (A similar attitude was perhaps reflected in his method of dealing with his soiled body linen. He no longer allowed any dirty laundry to accumulate, but scrubbed his underwear religiously every night before retiring.)

Thereafter he put away all hope of becoming a novelist, although (for the time being) he continued to cling to some lesser literary ambitions. He had never liked poetry, but had always been interested in diaries and even more in collections of aphorisms. In that form, he thought, his literary cravings might find an outlet. And possibly the need for brevity might prevent the recurrence of the faults which had ruined his novel. The rigid frame of the epigram would keep him from digressing, would force him to rip the factitious padding away, to strip down to the naked bone.

He liked the idea. Even the method of composiion was a healthier one. No long hours of research, no need to lock himself up alone in his room. On the contrary, the aphorism hunter functions best in the midst of activity, on crowded subways, on buses, in the park, in the zoo, in department stores, in the Automat. He could gather material while attending lectures, while at work or at a party, while standing on line, while going for a walk, or while drying his hands in a public washroom.

One of the best places for this work, Paul discovered, was a park bench in Central Park or Washington Square, and on rainy or cold days in museums. To disguise his activities (for he did not want to be spotted as a writer) he bought himself a medium sized sketch pad and a charcoal pencil. Thus he could sit for as long as he wanted before a painting on one of the backless stone benches in the Metropolitan Museum masquerading as an art student, pretending to be sketching but actually listening to the comments of the passers-by and jotting down those snatches of their talk which struck him as significant.

All went smoothly for a while. Although he did meet with one minor setback when he returned to the pier. The Arabs had disappeared. He waited for them all day long, but they did not return. The sightseeing boats passed the wharf at full speed. The tourists did not look in his direction. He had no better success the next Sunday and when he asked about them, no one seemed to know anything. They did not remember ever having seen them. When he insisted, they turned belligerent and threatened to break his nose. After that,

he kept away from the pier. Otherwise all went well. Better than he
had expected. He severed the relationship with Miss Lydia amicably
by sending her a lavish funeral wreath with a formal note attached
giving thanks for past services rendered. So that was that. He felt
pleased with his strength and display of will power.

His new writing project was coming along nicely. It had not taken
him long to find the format that best suited his needs. He hit upon it
by chance. One overpoweringly hot afternoon in mid September, not
long after he had put an end to his novel, while sitting before a
medieval reliquary at the Cloisters, he overheard a fragment of
conversation between two rabbinical students.

One asked the other, "Do you find it hard getting up in the
morning?"

Paul could not hear the answer. They had moved to the next
display case, out of earshot. But there it was—the perfect formula he
had been searching for. What better way to present enigmatic
problems than as questions? The form fitted the content as snugly as
the gold glove covered the martyr's severed hand. The question and
answer pattern (although in most instances the question by itself
would do) was the natural offspring, the modern version of the
traditional aphorism whose roots reached back to the riddles of the
Middle Ages, if not further back to the sacred books and before.

Paul was enthusiastic about his discovery. Before long he had
compiled a tentative list of crucial, all-important, leading questions in
his sketch pad:

1.

Question: Do you find it hard getting up in the morning?

2.

Question: If heat rises, why is it cooler in the mountains?

3.

Question: Do sunburned corpses lose their tan?
Answer: No. (That is, provided they don't sweat.)

4.

Question: Is the second coming ever as good as the first?

5.

Question: What goes in like a ramrod and comes out like soggy bread?

6.

Question: Suppose, I turned the page and read that which I had already read before. Suppose, I turned the corner and saw the beast which had devoured me the night before?—What is the disease I am suffering from?

Answer: *Déjà vu* or glossolalia or echolalia or metempsychosis. (In any case, we advise you to see your family physician immediately—unless the symptoms disappear by tomorrow morning.)

7.

Question: Through the anamorphoscope "dog" becomes "God." What is TIT spelled backwards?

8.

Question: What was Narcissus's motto? (Please translate into clean English.)

Answer: "Love yourself tonight. Hate yourself tomorrow."

9.

Question: What is your favorite German maxim? (Please do *not* translate.)

Answer: *"Mädchen die sich nieder bücken*
Kann man gut von hinten ficken."

10.

Question: What can good God-fearing children chant when troubled?

Answer: "Christ, Christ, he's our man
If He can't do it, no one can!"

11.

Question: What did the sinner say to the Celestial Railroad Conductor?

Answer: "O Lack, O Wanna
                 O Eerie, O Central
                 O choo-choo, O straight track!
                 Is there room for one more?"

12.

Question: Do you believe in a Supreme Being?
Answer: It's not easy to deny Providence when you live on Rod
                 Island.

13.

Question: Speaking of human beings, what is the universal
                 divisor?
Answer: Everyone, even the most enlightened, has his private
                 parts.

14.

Question: Whom should a nice girl be more afraid of—a unicorn
                 or an anteater?

15.

Question: What was the pregnant clown doing when you last saw
                 him?
Answer: Jestating.

16.

Question: If you could be metamorphosed into any piece of
                 apparel your coy true-love may be wearing at the
                 moment, which garment would you choose to become?
                 (Warning: Think before jumping! You may only
                 choose one.)
Answer: *D-e-l-e-t-e-d.*
Comment: Foul! No play! A tampax is not a garment, clothing,
                 apparel, or attire, not even by the most liberal stretch-
                 ing of the term. You are, therefore, disqualified. Please
                 leave the room at once.

17.

Question: Is it proper for a gentleman to ride a mare?
Answer: Only at night.

18.

Question: What did the lady in the subway say to the masher?
Answer: "Please! You are squeezing my prosthetic *nubrest.* Would you kindly mind moving to the other side?"

19.

Question: Why does it rain harder in courtyards than on the streets?

20.

Question: Why did the father, the mother, and their two children all make water into the same glass jar?
Answer: For a family urinalysis. (It's cheaper.)

21.

Question: Why did the woman in the bar, next to the juke box, encourage her dog to masturbate against her extended leg? (Notice that she first kicked her high-heeled pump off. Also notice the sheerness of her stockings.)

22.

Question: In what way is the brain "female to the soul"?
Answer: In the same way that the hand is female to the penis and male to the pudendum.

23.

Question: Charlemagne's war cry was "Mountjoy!" What was the battle cry of the Pubic Wars?
Answer: "If you won't spread, I shall divide!"

24.

Question: Oh whores of the alley, I've been in the promised land (front) and back; what can you offer me—Jerusalem?

25.

Question: Why are chastity belts ineffective against Jews?
Answer: They eat lox.

26.

Question: Is love's labour ever done?

Answer: the bakers can't
                 the lovers won't
                 on their day off
                 let stale bread lie cold
                 nor warm beds mould

                          27.
Question: Do expectant fathers suffer? If yes, of what?
Answer: Some do. They choke in deathsweat of childless painbirth.

                          28.
Question: Who died first: Adam or Eve? Why?

                          29.
Question: Is it only a coincidence that both religious fanatics and
                 perverts write on toilet walls?

                          30.
Question: What would make for a good oxymoron?
Answer: The mixture of Salt Peter and Spanish Fly.

                          31.
Question: If a man, living by himself in a neat studio apartment,
                 had locked himself out while taking a bag filled with
                 garbage to the incinerator and were foolish enough to
                 knock on his own door (although knowing full well
                 that no one could be there), who might answer his
                 knock and open the door?

                          32.
Question: Why do men have the urge to expectorate while
                 urinating?

                          33.
Question: What is more painful than horseshit through a pigeon's
                 asshole?

                          34.
Question: What determines the position of the yoke in a hard-
                 boiled egg?

35.

Question: Can constipation be cured?
Answer: The best laxative of all is fear.

36.

Question: "In the beginning was the word." What was it?
Answer: mum

37.

Question: Why do you feel so ill at ease when the lights are turned on between shows in the movie theater?

38.

Question: What are you thinking as you climb the stairs?

39.

Question: What are you thinking of as you wait for the elevator?

39 bis.

Question: What shall we do in the meantime?

But after a while he became disenchanted. The questions no longer amused him. They depressed him. Although he had easily filled the sketch-book from cover to cover, he put off starting a second collection. When he tried to rearrange his questions by subject matter, he saw what was wrong: basically, the questions were all the same; basically, although their forms differed somewhat, they dealt with the same thing, the same ultimate situation. At bottom, allowing for the attempts at humor (slapstick or gallows, effective or not), they were monotonous variations on the same dismal theme. By blowing the fluff away, by peeling the coat of bright paint off, by cutting away the fat, one could all too easily find the common denominator and reduce them to one unanswerable, unsolvable query, or, if one preferred, to one unsatisfying answer. They all led to the one overwhelming question.

Once he saw this, it was all up with him as a writer. He threw the pad into the nearest refuse can, not even bothering to destroy the evidence. If someone wanted to dig it out of the garbage, they were welcome. He couldn't care less.

13. DIE HEART & AND LIVE EASY

He had overslept again. The wind-up alarm clock had rung itself out; the clamor had not awakened him. The metal clapper of the clock simply moved him from one level of sleep to another.

He had slept late into the afternoon every day for the past two or three months. Perhaps he had forgotten that he was asleep.

The flames of the gas stove jump and sputter with a slapping sound, slurp at the cold air, greedily. The stocky metal stove stands near the foot of the bed (in which a young man lies fast asleep although it is mid-afternoon), partially jutting out past the archway that separates the combination living and sleeping area of the flat from the kitchen. The two windows in the wall behind the head of the bed (a three-quarter mattress on a low wooden platform) are shut and locked, their paper shades pulled half way down. Brown felt weather stripping has been forced into the cracks of the window frames. Despite this, a cold draft can be felt. A thick layer of soot covers the sills, the table between the windows, the telephone, radio, and old-fashioned, round-faced, wind-up alarm clock on the table, the red lacquered chest of drawers, the homemade wood and brick bookcase, the plywood seats of the ice cream parlor chairs.

Someone has again pulled the chain in the hall toilet. But instead of the sound of rushing water, a hollow asthmatic wheeze is heard. The metal pull chain rattles against the tank. Then the sound of the hook and eye lock being thrown open, the door falling shut, shuffling footsteps, unidentifiable, sexless, ageless. Then silence.

All at once, the refrigerator motor which has been laboring noisily shuts itself off. In the sudden silence, the lapping of the gas flames seems extremely loud, out of all proportion.

Perhaps he had forgotten that he was asleep. On the other hand he may have been aware of being asleep, but either unwilling or incapable of arousing himself from the stupor. Since he neither worked nor studied, the need for sleep could not have been a physical one. If anything, the long hours of sleep seemed to make him more tired; the longer he slept the more difficult it was for him to wake up. His sleep was not restful, not tranquil. It was not even deep. He moved about uneasily, turning over, crawling from one corner of the bed to the other, thumping the pillow, kicking at the blankets, arms folded over his eyes and ears in an attempt to shut out all light and sound (despite this, he must have heard the shrill noises from the street and from the adjacent apartments).

He forced himself to stay asleep. He had no reason to get up, no plans, no direction, no ambition, no obligations, no commitments, no involvements. When he did get out of bed and out of the apartment, he wandered from bar to cafeteria, and when they closed to the indistinguishable cold water flats of casual acquaintances, foraging aimlessly, neither hungry nor interested. Or possibly intentionally (so it seemed) wasting his goods with other ne'er-do-wells and drifters—intentionally, because he could not find a cure for the weariness and dejection which had overtaken him. He was not sure of the cause nor whom to put the blame on, although he felt that it was not his fault alone. Obstinate and resentful, he would not lift one finger to save himself, even though he clearly saw himself being pulled under, sinking into the quicksand.

The telephone must have been ringing a long time before it woke him. When he finally reached it, the ringing had already stopped (yet he could still hear the bell long after the final ring, echoing, distant but continuous). He lifted the receiver to his ear anyway and listened to the steady hum of the dial-tone and then, when that was cut off, to the faint vacant whistling which replaced it, whispering hollowly through the dead wires.

He puts his hands over his ears. The sound continues. Interminably, drawn out. He waits for another sound to break the thread. But the room is silent. No one dares to move. He has put both hands over his ears, elbows resting on the table, head bent over. His eyes are open but he does not look around, neither at the other occupants of the room nor at the heavy ornate furniture beyond the table. The high-backed chairs which are lined up in two straight rows on either side of the long table are reflected in its highly polished mahogany surface. The table top is bare, free of any dust, as if it has recently been cleared and wiped. A soiled linen napkin lies on the boy's lap.

The room has become darker. It is late afternoon. The corners of the large room are lost in the dusk. The last of the weak winter light barely reaches the large dining table at which the boy sits, elbow on the table, one arm raised to support his head, the hand covering his ear; the other arm has dropped to his lap where it plays with the crisp edge of the soiled white linen napkin, pushing it back and forth between his fingers. Otherwise the room seems to be empty.

The winter light was deceptive. The ringing of the telephone awakened him earlier than usual. The clock showed that it was only a few minutes after two.

When his eyes begin to close again, he rouses himself from his lethargy with a sudden effort. Dropping his hands from his ears, he rubs his eyes hard, pushing both palms into the eye cavities, kneading the eyeballs into life.

The cold air helped. The fine rain which had been falling when he left his room was steadily becoming thicker. Water soaked through his hair and ran down into his collar. He entered a large, almost empty, self-service cafeteria, bought a cup of coffee and sat down at a table near the entrance to the right of the revolving door, next to the steamed-over plate glass window. He rubbed the steam from the window with the sleeve of his coat, clearing a circular area the size of a head through which a portion of the street could be seen.

It is not raining quite as hard as before, but it is still raining. The rain falls in dotted, perpendicular lines, not at an angle but straight, with a certain force, the individual drops seemingly penetrating the concrete ground. The surface of the shallow puddles is pierced by the drops, punctured by the sharp stabs of the falling water. The deeper puddle on the flat roof of the one-story building across the way does not appear to be attacked with the same ferocity. The depth of the water softens the blows. The water gives. It opens with ease, swallowing the falling water. Its pockmarked surface resembles a lake whose calmness is roiled by the bobbing heads of water bugs.

The cafeteria has filled up gradually. He now shares his table for four with two others, a man and a young girl (or, rather, a young woman). The girl arrived soon after him along with two friends who left when they finished their coffee. She has remained behind. She also looks through the window at the rain-smeared street. To keep the patch of glass clear, he is forced to wipe the window continually. Because of this, a wet stain has formed on the right sleeve of his coat. The third person at the table has only recently taken his seat.

Unlike his table companions, he has brought back a full tray from the steam table. He does not remove the dishes from the speckled brown tray, but puts the tray down in front of him and begins to eat immediately, not looking at his tablemates or at the steam-covered window. The tray contains: (one) a large plate on which are piled a double helping of baked beans, two frankfurters, and a smear of mustard, (two) a smaller plate with two slices of white bread and one pat of butter on a square of wax paper, (three) another small plate, the same size as the bread plate, on which a piece of apple pie rests, a fair-sized slice, (four) a cup of extra light coffee.

The coffee cups before the other two occupants of the table no longer contain any coffee. They are filled with cigarette butts. The girl's cup holds more butts than his. No one seems to have bothered to enforce the *no smoking* sign which hangs, framed like a diploma and covered by glass, on the wall between the doors of the ladies' room and the men's room.

The girl spoke to him first, after her friends had left.

"Let me help you with the window," she said.

He declined her offer, and enlarged the area of the cleared patch to give her a better view of the street. After a while, he asked her if she wanted another cup of coffee. He lit her cigarette for her whenever she took one from the pack that she had placed before her on the table. The red and white package had been torn open at the wrong end. He smoked also, although not as much as she.

When the cafeteria began to fill up with the dinner crowd, a bus boy asked them to leave.

He walked across the street to the subway entrance with the girl and followed her down the stairs. When he asked her whether he could come with her, she mumbled a reply, shrugging her shoulders. The roar of a subway train drowned out the young woman's answer. Her lips moved but the sound was lost.

A glass-roofed shopping arcade connects the two side streets. The stores on both sides are closed. Some are sealed by corrugated metal shutters on which the names of the owners have been painted with great skill. The letters only seem distorted when seen from close up; at a normal walking distance the names stand up straight despite their wavy background. Although the stores are dark, the arcade is dimly lit by overhead lights. These lights are placed at infrequent intervals above the polyangular glass roof in an unsuccessful attempt to simulate sunlight (or moonlight). The geometric skeleton of the black metal framework is clearly outlined. The lights also spot what at first appears to be a nest of squirming bugs on top of the glass. A closer look shows that the vermin are dried up and dead. Past its midpoint, the arcade veers sharply to the right, running almost parallel to the side streets before it twists back to the left and opens onto the next street. The smell of urine is particularly pungent in the middle section of the arcade, in that part of the passage which runs parallel to the side streets and which (because of the Z-like course of the tunnel) cannot be seen from either entrance.

The parlour floor of the brownstone had been converted into a furniture repair shop. They had to pass through it to reach the apartment. The store was filled with broken chairs. An old man with a skull cap was mending the seat of a cane chair. He did not look up from his work as they walked by him, although the bell above the entranceway had tinkled as they pushed the door open.

The apartment resembles the furniture store below, but it is even more crowded. Old furniture is piled to the ceiling, one piece on top of the other, chairs, beds, bureaus, tables, mirrors, clothes trees, cradles, hutches, sofas, wardrobes, and a grand piano that has been propped up on its side, its legs removed. It is impossible to know where one room ends and the next begins. The girl leads him up another flight of stairs to a bedroom.

The bed was so high that they had to step on a chair to reach it. Mattresses had been heaped on top of mattresses, leaving just enough space on top to enable them to sit up without banging their head against the ceiling. The view from the top of the mountain of bedding was excellent.

Someone had pinned a corner of the drapes back far enough so that a broad slice of the street was visible through the otherwise covered window. The angle of view was deceptive. The street seemed far away, even though the bedroom could not have been any higher up than the third or fourth story.

The apartment houses are pasted together in rows. They vary only slightly in height and shape. Their flat roofs tend to accentuate their likeness to mausoleums. They look unoccupied. The files of oblong windows are dark, light brown paper shades pulled half way down to the point at which the upper and lower window panes meet. The clasps of the window locks are clearly silhouetted against the lighter colored shades, just above the pullstrings of the blinds which hang straight as a plumb line, not swaying but fixed in position as if glued, the circular rings at the bottom end of the strings flush against the window panes. The black tarred roofs are wet, their flat surfaces broken here and there by air shafts, ventilators, and uniformly rectangular brick chimneys. Neither these shapes nor the zigzagging fire escapes noticeably lessen the box-like appearance of the buildings. Behind the parallel lines of apartment houses, some of the structures of the business district can be seen, warehouses, loft buildings, and factories. An illusion of variety is given by the variously shaped water towers on top of these buildings which otherwise are elongated replicas of the apartment houses. One water tower looks like an Italian bell tower, another like the Parthenon, a third has been faced with bricks and looks like a miniature rectangular house (complete with dark windows in which the shades have been neatly pulled halfway down) duplicating the house on whose roof it stands. Most of the water tanks, though, have not been disguised. The squat cylindrical tanks stand on steel stilts, their sides covered with weathered brown shingles, their roofs pointed like the hat of a Chinese coolie. After a winter storm when the roofs are covered with snow (while the snow has already turned to black slush on the streets) a visitor to the city looking out of a window from the upper floor of a skyscraper might understandably mistake the panoramic view for that of a graveyard, dotted by thousands of white marble tombstones.

After having made her guest comfortable, the girl jumped down from the bed, slipping easily out of his grasp.

"Stay here. I'll see if I can find us something to drink," she said and was gone.

He did not try to follow her. The sea of furniture around the bed seemed bottomless and he doubted that he could find his way through it by himself. Besides, he felt warm and comfortable. The rain pounded on the roof over his head. He thought that he heard the girl moving about in another room. When he sat up to listen more carefully the footsteps stopped. Occasionally a piece of furniture creaked or made a sudden popping noise as if a spring had snapped. He lay back on the pillows, closed his eyes and listened to the rain. Pleasant, like a summer rainstorm drumming on the canvas top of a tent.

He has forgotten that he is asleep, and it is not until the telephone rings that he realizes it has happened again.

"Hello?"

"Yes?"

It is a woman's voice. He does not recognize it although he knows that he should.

"What?"

"Isn't there something you want to tell me?"

"No."

"Are you sure?"

"Yes. . . . No."

She has hung up before he can tell her that she has the wrong number. The same woman (or another woman who has asked a similar question) has called him two or three times before. Each time he has been too dazed by sleep to answer her clearly or to ask her what she wants or who she is. Before he has a chance to think, to be fully awake, she has hung up.

He had fallen asleep. When he opened his eyes it was almost completely dark, so that for a moment he was not sure where he was.

He looks around trying to find a familiar landmark, but the clumps of furniture are so tightly pressed together that their distinguishing shapes are lost. What appears to be the back of an armchair sprouts a round table leg that pierces the glass door of a china closet in which dirty dinner plates are piled as in an overflowing sink. Then again the plates could be glass-covered, oval photographs in ornately carved wooden frames; and the armchair the upside down padded headboard of a four poster bed. It is hopeless to attempt to unravel the piles in the dark, especially since he has lost all sense of direction, as if the walls have turned around. He cannot even locate the exposed corner of the window.

Rather than risk losing his way completely, he decided against leaving the bed. He would wait until she returned or until morning. Just then he heard the girl's voice from a nearby room.

"Are you awake?"

A light threaded its way through the furniture. She held a kerosene lantern above her head.

"The lights aren't working up here."

He climbed down cautiously from the bed and followed her. In the room to which she led him, the furniture had been partially cleared away (or perhaps the furniture had as yet not been allowed to pile up). The windows were covered with wine colored drapery. Floor to ceiling bookcases lined two walls of the room; a faded tapestry on the fourth wall (depicting what appears to be the after-math of an orgy, a classical garden scene of flowing fountains, green, shade-giving trees, sweet smelling flowers and fragrant herbs, thick grape vines, swollen melons, bending fruit trees, their bough laden with overripe apples and peaches and nectarines, moss covered banks whereon lie plump, pink fleshed nude women, some with suckling, open-mouthed babes at their breasts, and muscular, thick-lipped men sleeping ensnared in each other's arms, limbs and heads twisted grotesquely) hid the door through which they had entered, falling into place behind them with a cloud of dust. The floor was padded with so many layers of flowered Persian rugs that he thought that he was walking on a soft mattress. A crystal chandelier hung from the high ceiling, bathing the room in light.

"Go ahead, sit down. Don't let the mess bother you. Just shove those things aside. We can move to another room tomorrow." She pointed to a leather couch which, like the other pieces of furniture, was buried beneath a heap of soiled clothes and dust-encrusted bric-a-brac.

The girl lowered the flame of the lantern and put the lantern down on the marble coffee table in front of the couch, not bothering to find a clear space for it, but setting it down in the middle of a dinner plate which was smeared with the remains of a meal.

"There's nothing to eat, but I've found some beer and a jar of bennies."

The congealed beans give under the weight of the lantern. Next to the plate lie two paper twists of mustard (one still unopened, the other half empty, its contents crusted), another soiled plate, its edges smeared with mustard, an open can of pork and beans, gold-rimmed drinking glasses, six demi-tasse coffee cups, the saucers filled with cigarette butts, stale ends of bread, a dead rubber plant in a copper pot, a glossy greyish slab of Swiss cheese, a leather-bound book, face down, a framed photograph also turned face down, its paper backing spotted with the blood or excrement of bedbugs, two tarnished silver coffee spoons, an onyx ashtray, more plates (but from a different set), an empty half gallon jug of California burgundy, a bent can opener, half an orange, the cut edge moldy, a torn brown paper bag, a grease stained pot holder, an open jar of instant coffee, a pack of cigarettes that has been ripped open at the wrong end, a coke bottle lying on its side, a pink garter belt, a sealed package of soup crackers, a ceramic candleholder in the shape of a fish, a cardboard box of

sleeping pills, a paper coffee container in which float the dis-
integrating remnants of dinched cigarettes, a key ring, a pair of
patent leather spike-heeled shoes, a cracked pickle jar, an unopened
bottle of curdled milk, loose potato chips, a roll of purple postage
stamps, another ashtray, more cigarette butts.

Although the room is sparsely furnished it appears to be crammed
because of the piles of refuse that have gathered everywhere. Even
the bookcases, which line two of the walls from floor to ceiling, have
been used for this purpose. The lower shelves, the ones that are
within arm's reach, are covered with remnants of food, dirty dishes,
unopened letters, and soiled clothes. The highly polished mahogany
table top is scarred with cigarette burns. Overflowing glasses have left
sticky ring-shaped marks on the endtables.

The curtains are drawn, but dust has seeped in. (Although the grey
dirt that covers the surface of the furnishings may be mostly cigarette
ashes). Behind the drapes a window must be open since the hangings
billow and shudder with uneasy animation. The chandelier sways. It
tinkles softly.

The ringing of the telephone did not arouse him as it once had.
The spring which powered the alarm clock's bell had snapped. The
butterfly shaped wind-up lever, which had required effort to turn,
now spun freely in either direction at the lightest touch. The loud
persistent ticking of the clock indicated that it could still be used to
tell time, even though it could no longer serve to waken sleepers. The
sleeper had not moved.

Often he slept until evening. His dreams were as long and silent as
the winter night.

Only on rare occasions, perhaps toward the end of the night when
the silence is suddenly broken by the approach of a freight train,
would a sleeper be reminded of the proximity of the railroad tracks.
Wheels screech on the metal tracks. Couplings rattle. Window panes
vibrate. In the daytime the noise of the trains is buried beneath the
rumbling of heavy traffic, the clatter of streetcars, the moan of
garbage trucks, the honking horns of irritated drivers, the nagging
voices of mothers calling to their straying children, the blaring organ
music from kitchen radios introducing the daily chapters of soap
opera serials, the singsong cry of the junk man.

The winter sky is expressionless, uniformly white; absolutely no
gradation of color, blank (not even a glare at the horizon) like a vast
exhibition hall expertly lit by indirect lighting.

Rows of red brick tenements present an uninterrupted front. The houses form rectangular blocks. At regular intervals, grey asphalt paths divide one oblong from another. The brick rectangles seem to shrink in the distance. Way down the avenue, the grey interstices disappear. It looks as if the brick walls are no longer chopped into blocks; but this has to be an optical illusion.

Although the building had a self-service elevator, they walked up the stairs. They stopped half a flight above her apartment (rather, her aunt's apartment, as she had explained she lived in the suburbs but stayed with her aunt during the week in order to avoid the long train trip back and forth).

They stand on a small landing between the fourth and fifth floor, a spot at which the stairs twist to allow for a steep climb in a rather narrow stairwell. They have moved into the deepest corner of the landing. She leans against the wall, facing her escort. They have just kissed, but now his head is lowered to the right side of her neck; his lips touch the inside of her coat collar. His eyes, which are within an inch of the two-toned green wall behind her, are open. He shifts position. Now his head is on the left side of her neck; his lips force their way between the collar of her coat and the strands of hair which have slipped out of place from her upswept hairdo. Behind her left shoulder is a closed double-hung window. Its glass panes are frosted, double sheets of glass with a wire mesh (diamond pattern) in between. His eyes are open, almost touching the window. At this close distance, the diamond shaped wire within the glass stands out clearly.

Her eyes are also open. She is looking at the wooden railing of the stairs and at the segment of the fourth floor hallway which can be seen from her angle. Probably she is worried that one of her aunt's neighbors will pass by, look up, and see her in a compromising position. In any case, she takes a small step to her left, away from the apex of the corner.

"Don't."

Their coats are unbuttoned. His hands are inside her coat, behind her, under her plaid wool skirt which has been pulled up. The skirt is bunched up about her thighs; the coat hides her stocking encased legs and the narrow strips of bare flesh between the stocking tops and the white rubberized material of her foundation garment. His groin is pressed against her. His coat is also open, but his fly remains buttoned. Legs bent forward, he tries to maneuver himself into the best possible position, stooping over, pushing at the same time.

The young woman's cardigan has been pulled out of her skirt; its top three buttons are undone. The hands which partially unbuttoned the sweater are no longer pulling at the cloth cups that support the twin conical shaped mounds of flesh. (In the struggle, one shoulder strap, which was possibly too taut in the first place, broke; consequently, the right mound is lower than the left.) The hands are pushing the plaid skirt upwards. The process is slow since she does not help him. She hinders him by leaning hard against the window sill in back of her; thus, the front of her skirt is pulled up higher than the back. One of his hands is underneath the wool skirt touching the rounded hump of her girdle. The other is outside the skirt, fingers pulling at the accordian-like horizontal folds of the skirt. As she bends backwards from the waist down, he crouches forward trying to keep his groin in position. His knees are bent forward. One hand attempts to push her upward and forward, while the other clutches at the folds of the thick material of her skirt.

"Don't."

Her hands are also behind her, one beneath the coat on top of the skirt holding his right hand back, the other under her skirt pulling at the fingers of his left hand which have worked their way under the bottom edge of her girdle.

Her eyes were open, fixed on the fourth floor landing, half a flight below them, where the elevator had stopped.

"Wait! There's someone coming."

Neither moves. He is looking at the diamond design in the window. She stares past the wooden banister at the hallway. But the elevator starts up again with a sudden loud click.

When he stepped back, away from her, to open his fly, she quickly moved out of the corner.

"Don't!" she said. "We can't do it out here. Let me check to see if my aunt is asleep. If it's o.k., I'll let you in."

She already had her keys out. The door opened only a few inches, just barely enough to let her squeeze past the fox lock which guarded the apartment against burglars.

"Wait," she said and closed the door.

He has returned to the small landing between the fourth and fifth floor where he leans, half sits, against the frosted window in the corner. His eyes are fixed on the section of the hallway of the fourth floor which is visible past the wooden banister of the stairs. The elevator has returned to the fourth floor; no one has opened the door. The hallway remains empty. His coat is now buttoned, its collar raised against the cold. The rough material of the collar grates against his lips. He turns his head slightly, but the coat still touches his lips. Suddenly the elevator starts up with a loud click. Someone has probably pushed the button on the ground floor.

It was snowing lightly. The dry crystals did not stick to the asphalt. They were driven by the wind, swept away as if by a straw broom. The snow did not even stick to the window ledges (nor would it have stuck to the branches of trees if they existed).

The bus struggles up the hill, away from the railroad station. It roars as it pulls its load along, straining its bowels, protesting.

Once over the crest of the hill, it lurches forward. It slides downhill, freewheeling, backfiring, now tearing at the intestines of the passengers, then grinding into gear, braking with a hiss of released air.

The passengers cannot disentangle themselves. And the bus is off again, accelerating, its wheels spinning, taking hold, tightening its grip. The passengers have become a part of its machinery, their innards enmeshed, connected to the driveshaft, conscious only of the jolting motion, unaware that cobblestones have replaced asphalt, that the city's buildings are fading into the night like a pen and ink drawing washed away by the rain.

The sharp sounds of footsteps from the apartment above do not awaken the sleeper although he must hear them. He has pulled the blanket over his ears. He does not respond when the clatter of high heels resounds on the stone staircase approaching his flat, nor when someone knocks repeatedly at the door. The room is dimly lit, one window-shade pulled halfway down, pale winter light barely penetrating; the other, the shade of the window at the head of the bed, is pulled all the way down, its pull string dangling below the window sill, not quite touching the head of the sleeper.

"Are you finished?"

He shook his head and strained to finish, pumping rhythmically, but then his thrusts slowed down.

"I'm all dry," she said. "You'll have to get off for a while."

He dismounted and lay down on his stomach next to her. Her eyes were closed, eyelids forming two narrow folds of flesh as if she were squeezing them tightly shut.

"Don't you like it?" he asked.

"It doesn't bother me. It's only that I get sore easily."

She felt for the cigarettes on the endtable next to the bed, lit two, and handed him one. "Sure I do. Why would I let you do it otherwise? But I'm all dry down there. Wait a while and then we can get started again."

The room has become cold. Most likely, the steam heat has been shut off for the night. Her eyes are closed. She has pulled the blankets up to her waist. Her breasts are partially exposed. They are big and white, well-formed but doughy. His left arm lies across them, his fingers pulling at her right nipple. The fingers sink into the breast. The flesh gives like soft butter.

The pounding on the door has stopped. The room is almost completely dark. It is late afternoon or early morning. The boy sitting at the long table has raised his head to look at the old-fashioned clock. Just then the large hand of the clock jumps forward with a nervous twitch. Somewhere nearby, perhaps out in the street or in another room or in the next-door apartment, a baby wails, but it could be a cat.

The ice in the courtyard is thick and lumpy, the grey color and texture of blisters. The flames of the gas stove flap loudly. Ice flowers have formed on the windows.

Despite his half-hearted efforts to remain awake, he sank deeper, down into the thick cream-of-wheat drowsiness. The grains swelled; overflowing, they covered him, shutting the light out. He turned against the pushing numbness. But his eyes were stuck together, closed, eyelids glued to eyes. His hands groped for the pillow above his head. It broke and smothered him in its feathers.

14. THE PROMISED LAND

When spring came, Paul recovered. The change in season was only partly responsible for his reawakening; the principal inspiration, the prime mover, was female—a young up-and-coming prostitute named Lola whom he had met at a May Day cocktail party.

He had always been fascinated by whores, both the high-class ones and the streetwalkers. He had read about them, the magnificently beautiful courtesans, fatal women of the town, cruel and seemingly heartless creatures, who, after betraying and destroying their admirers, suffer a sudden, mysterious change of heart, repent and end up as faithful, loving wives, nursing the skeletal bodies of their lovers back to health through the zeal of their reformation, by the animal strength of their rich, vibrant flesh. He had watched the hookers near the markets at night and followed them through the streets, sat next to them in bars. The sight of their glittering breasts inspired him, although he had never dared to approach them, fearing to shatter the burning fever dreams he had about them by the cold commercial arrangements which would then have to be concluded.

Yet neither the recognition of the silliness of such romantic stories nor his sqeamishness prevented Paul from pursuing Lola with a vigor, a tenacity, foreign to his basic reticent, perhaps even lackadaisical, personality.

The fury of his pursuit overpowered Lola.

At first she thought nothing of it, for she had in the past allowed herself an occasional lapse from her strict business routine. She even told him so after the party.

"About once a month I feel like this and then I need to have the devil driven out of me. Now turn me around and do it to me again, lover!"

Which he did. But then he turned her around again and again and again, and before she was fully aware of it he had all but moved in.

When she woke up to what was happening it was already the beginning of June. She looked at the bills which had been piling up and saw that her bank account would barely cover them. She had not entertained a client since the day Paul had taken her home from the party. The one night stand, which she could readily afford, had turned into a month-long affair that threatened to ruin her career.

"Now look," she said, running her hands through her wheat-colored hair. She jumped out of bed. "This has gone too far!"

But she did not cut him off completely, partly because she could not bring herself to do it and partly because Paul resisted, obstinately clinging to her skirt like a bedbug.

"I've got to get back to work," she insisted, pacing impatiently back and forth, her stiletto-heeled slippers clicking angrily. "And you've got to get out," her polished fingernails drumming on her dresser top in a fast devil's tattoo. "Go find yourself another hobby-horse! I'm all worn out. I've had it! Look, you're giving me bed-sores."

She tried to shake him off, but he would not be dislodged so easily. Finally she tricked him by sending him out on an errand. By the time he came back, she had given orders to the burly uniformed doorman to slam the door in his face. For a week she refused to answer the telephone. Then, despite her better judgment, she talked to him again and proposed a compromise: he could visit her after-noons if he got out by sundown and if he promised not to make any jealous scenes.

He promised, but did not keep to the agreement. He could not hide his resentment and wasted much of the allotted time sulking. Once he bit her so hard that he drew blood. Even this did not prevent her from meeting her date that evening.

She promptly repaired her damaged breast. "If you were a paying customer, this would cost you extra."

The next afternoon she would not take her brassiere off. 'I've got to protect my assets, lover."

Despite such put-downs, Paul continued to visit Lola regularly. His love for her had become more intense. Although he tried to keep away for as long as he could, he invariably arrived at her front door a few minutes after noon.

The doorman looked right through him, not bothering to open the door, but not stopping him. The elevator operator showed his disdain openly, deliberately jerking the elevator to a rough stop. Paul leaped out of the car quickly to avoid being caught between the slamming doors.

He found Lola seated at an open window, looking out. She did not answer his greeting or turn around. Nevertheless she allowed him to have his way with her; sullenly, yet offering no resistance, languidly, she let herself fall back into his arms. He slipped the short silk robe off her shoulders and slid in between her thighs without stopping to undress. Her buttocks were so smooth and round, so slippery, that he had to hold on with both hands. Her hard, bullet-shaped breasts seemed unusually swollen, their sharp points scratching his chest through the cloth of his shirt. But her soft-lipped temple of love soothed his flesh, cooling the blood-hot tip within its liquid center.

Afterwards, as she was dressing, she voiced her anger, accusing him of being impossibly jealous and of interfering with her work, taking up too much of her time, waking her up too early and staying too late. She was physically and emotionally worn out by the time her clients arrived. It would be best, she insisted, if he would not come to see her every day. He would have to be satisfied with once or twice a week like the others. And if that did not suit him, then he did not have to come back at all.

He was too rough, taking her with his pants on as if she were a streetwalker. She pushed her bra strap aside and slipped her right breast out of its cup to show him a fresh bruise. She had other complaints. He did not shave every day. He was surly and insulting to her friends. Even the elevator operator had complained of his rudeness. She threatened to have the doorman throw him out bodily if he did not stop bothering her. And besides, she wanted to be alone for a while.

Paul held his tongue and managed to control his hand which longed to slap her exposed breast. Instead, he plucked the cigarette from her mouth and flung it out of the window. Cursing her beneath his breath, he walked away from her and sat down in the middle of the satin-covered kingsize bed. She told him to get out. He did not answer, but turned his back and gnashed his teeth, biting her foam-rubber pillow.

When she picked up the telephone to call the doorman for help, his tantrum was nipped in the bud. The resoluteness, the threat in her voice worried him.

He left the bed and sat down on the floor near her to plead his case. He begged her to let him stay, rolling his sheep's eyes up at her, moaning like a moonstruck calf. When she refused to respond, he changed tactics. He told her a new joke, and, although she didn't laugh, he sensed that she was softening. At least, she took her hand off the phone.

Hoping to please her further, he offered to recite some of her favorite stories. Not giving her a chance to say no, he quickly began by telling her the one about Leonardo da Vinci who, for kicks, threaded the bones of a corpse on a string and played with it as if it were a puppet. He related the fable of the anteater and the unfortunate virgin, the parable of the misused love philter, a necrology of the children's crusade, an eyewitness account of the great Cairo fire (spread by pigeons acting as flying torches), the romance of Ahab and Jezebel, an excerpt from the memoirs of an executioner's assistant, an exposé of prenatal fratricide, a short history of the relationship between autos-da-fé and suburban orgies, an anthropological report on the quarterly public hangings of witches, warlocks, and their offspring, the tragedy of the distraught lover in the coal bin, the old limerick describing the frugal necrophilism of an old hermit (named Dave), and an original love poem entitled "My Bestiary." He told her how he had gone to the zoo that morning and what he had seen. He described the animals, their strange habits, their silly tricks. In his anxiety to amuse her, he exaggerated and embellished, changing the bison into a unicorn, telling her that the chimp now smoked a clay pipe instead of his customary cigar, describing the incredible erotic gymnastics of a chesty platinum blond mother of newborn twins with the bull elephant's gigantic proboscis.

Lola listened closely, frequently interrupting to ask further details. Slowly, her anger faded. Soothed by the flow of words, her eyes began to close as if she were slipping into a trance.

"Go on!" she said when he paused to pull her down to him on the floor.

She no longer offered any resistance. She did not push his hand away. She allowed him to take her again (with his pants on), pushing her half slip out of the way, guiding him, staying his thrusts whenever he threatened to end his recital.

Only when she was exhausted did she allow him to conclude the story telling. She sighed with satisfaction, kissed him, and then relenting, said that he could stay after all.

"Better than that," she continued. "Listen! I have a crazy idea. How would you like to come and live with me?"

Yet the proposal was neither as wild nor as romantic as he had in the first flush of wonder thought it might be. Basically, the new arrangement was to be a practical one. He would not share her bedroom, instead could have the maid's room which was unused anyway. (Lola could not tolerate the smell of female servants.) In return he was to perform certain menial tasks (as well as acting as a sort of minstrel or storyteller in residence). When called for, he would mix drinks, serve tea, answer the door, run to the store, put out clean towels, change the sheets, wash the dishes, and in general keep the apartment neat. (The heavy work was done by a charman who came three mornings a week.)

Paul accepted her offer without hesitation.

From then on, time had no meaning for him. He remained in her apartment, never went out on the streets. When Lola asked him to fetch something for her from the outside, he always found an excuse. Fortunately she did not ask him often. He hoped that she was unaware of his resolve not to leave the premises, not even for a moment.

Although he broke many of her dishes, especially on the days when men came to visit her, Lola did not object to his carelessness. She did not seem to notice the piles of broken crockery. Yet she must have been aware of it, since he made sure to order different colored dishes to replace the broken ones. Her guests were undoubtedly surprised to have tea served in cups which did not match their saucers (and on bad days, in paper cups); but they gallantly overlooked this oddity. Perhaps they were afraid of displeasing Lola. Or were they simply amused? At any rate, they seemed satisfied enough to give Paul dirty looks. He retaliated with chipped cups.

What bothered him most, though, was being asked to change phonograph records while Lola was entertaining her admirers. This did not happen often since he carefully prepared the automatic changer before a visitor arrived. He soon caught on to their individual likes and dislikes, arranging the tempo of the music to keep pace with their activities: a sultry torch song to begin with, then a wilder jazz piece (a Louis Armstrong solo seemed the most effective), and finally a soft sentimental ballad. Most of them preferred popular or light classical music (the Boston Pops for example) to make love by. A Latin selection seemed to amuse them for a change, but was not liked as a steady diet. Only a few tolerated a Bach fugue. One elderly corpulent gentleman, given to an inordinate amount of grunting and snorting, a very unfriendly type who would not give his name (it was Dr. Karp as Paul later discovered)—contrary to the ways of Lola's other steady callers who were not in the least bashful or apprehensive, who positively took pleasure in being welcomed at the door by their proper names and titles: Dr. Heissmeyer, Dr. Winkelmann, Dr. Korbel, Dr. Schildausky, Major Becker, Captain Schwartzhuber, Professor Krankenman, Willy Dreimann, Ph.D., Baron Trzebinski, Sir Kitt, General Hochmut, Father Knochlein, Director Rauff, Fritz Suhren, Christian Wirth, Max Kulpa, Ernst Lustig, Alfred Metzner, C. S. Schwantz, Jr., Pani Palitsch, Monsieur Rascher, Herr Jauch, Mr. Waldeck, Mr. Binder, Jack Armstrong, and just plain Robinson—brought his own album and insisted on beating time to Wagner's *Die Walküre*. Lola was unexplainably, violently annoyed by this (even though she usually, as a matter of good business relations, was willing to do anything within reason to please her customers, true to the hand embroidered sampler above her bed which advertised her philosophy, "Our Motto: A Trip Around the World, Not Just a Cunt Tour"—the plaque being a souvenir from the war days which she had spent in an officers' brothel, having turned professional, she explained, not out of preference but necessity as a result of having been seduced by her employer's son—). She did not encourage the opera lover to return.

"God only knows what he'll bring next!" she complained to Paul.

"So?"

"Have you ever tried to suck a cock while listening to Mahler's *Kindertotenlieder*?"

Paul was not sympathetic.

Occasionally clients were not satisfied with the background music Paul had selected and would demand a different tune right then and there. Perhaps they did it on purpose, sensing the houseboy's distress.

Although he did not want to look at the naked bodies on the bed, he could not avoid it, being drawn to them, despite his loathing. For a moment he did not recognize the distorted features straining in torsion, the voluted limbs welded together.

He knew that he should have killed them. Yet he didn't and consoled himself by remembering that if these visitors enjoyed the pleasure of his mistress for fifteen minutes at most (she was very skilled in dispatching their desires promptly), he lay with her for hours. To be able to make love for an exceptionally long time was one of the few talents he possessed, and with Lola, who also wanted these long hours of pleasure, his small ability grew to extremes. There were times (especially during her menstrual period when for four or five days she preferred not to accept clients) when they would stay in her bedroom forever, completely unaware of the change in the sky outside or of the earth's revolving orbit. The shutters closed, the drapes sealed, touching the floor, heavy eyelids closing over the eye of the day, muffling the noise of life but heightening the sound of bare flesh on cool sheets. And then (for a while) the long-suffering lover could forget his humiliation, the envy and bitterness, forget the fluorescent day and live in pneumatic twilight.

15. THE BOOT

In the beginning the unicorn is made much of. A gold-leafed cage is hung from the bar that spans the two stone posts at the main entrance of the park. The prize captive is proudly displayed in the aerial cage. A dozen maidens bathe it. And twelve others, young and beautiful with wild flowers in their hair, hand-feed it fresh green acorns. They hang wreaths of multicolored flowers around its neck. And the unicorn growls softly, very softly, so as not to frighten them.

The crowd gapes with wonder. Never before has the zoo been so popular. The capture of the unicorn is held to be of the highest significance. The people watch expectantly. They wait through the night. The gates of the park which have always been shut at sunset and locked for the night remain wide open. In the morning, other maidens, even lovelier, even younger and more seductively innocent, freshly washed and perfumed, come to the cage and offer ripe flowers, riper dark green acorns.

But nothing happens. The lethargy of the beast surprises everyone. It does not attack the virgins (who have competed for the honor of the sacrifice), but meekly eats the proffered acorns, absentmindedly licking with a large moist tongue the cool soft hands that feed it. It shows no passion, no hatred, not even toward the woman who has betrayed it. Perhaps it has forgotten.

Time passes softly. The wreaths of flowers woven of bright summer blossoms fade and dry. They seem to hang heavier from the haunches of the beast.

A cold wind slowly rocks the cage. The people have gone home. The animal keeper feeds the unicorn brown acorns, and at night peels the gold-leaf from the bars of the cage. Winter visitors to the park pass the cage by, neither afraid nor interested.

Then someone complains to the authorities. A petition is passed around. The stench of the animal is unendurable, its shabby hair matted and full of thorns, the cage rusty, creaking from neglected chains. Perhaps the droppings infuriate the people the most. Or it may be that the unicorn's silence is the main cause of its fall from favor. The spectators expected much.

It is therefore decided to move the offender as soon as feasible. And when, a few weeks later, the wild boar dies, the move is made. The cage is toward the end of the zoo, next to that of the goats. The keeper has forgotten to clean away the old droppings of the boar and to change the water. But this does not matter. The unicorn does not seem to notice or care. As before, it makes no effort to clean itself or to move away from the piles of filth which cover the floor of the cage. The pigeons walk around the beast unperturbed or sit on its back, taking their meal from its dung, picking at the bits of hay and grain that hang from its long hair.

The unicorn is forgotten. No one seems to resent it anymore. It hardly moves. Its dark eyes are cloudy, far away.

When the ice cracks and the sun gathers and burns the snow, visitors again come to the park in large numbers. Occasionally, a couple leans against the cage, but the smell or the animal's dull groans soon make them move on toward the shelter of a tree or a park bench. The goats in the next cage sense the coming spring and move about with sharp, short steps.

The unicorn also seems disturbed. The pull of spring awakens its senses. Or it may be the sound of music from a parade in the streets near the zoo, the beat of drums which makes it lift its head and sniff the air. Then another sound penetrates—the sharp, exciting heelbeat of female flesh, not passing by, but approaching and stopping before the cage. And standing there, not turning away, high heels scraping against the asphalt-paved walk as with impatience, as if she has come expressly to see the prisoner and is now waiting for him to make the next move, shifting her weight from one leg to the other.

The beast opens its eyes and recognizes her at once.

He rises, shakes his head against a wall of air, steam hissing from nostrils. He roars as if in pain. Stamping feet shatter the music in the street; they press on the air as on the breath of sudden silence. (With one flap of clumsy wings, the pigeons scatter for the top of the fence. Two birds lie dead, trampled to death at the moment of waking from slow sleep, their naked pink feet reaching stiffly upward. The goats turn, back away, hoofs beating wildly, clawing at the cement ground in panic.)

Suddenly, in the moment when the stench of excrement mixes with that of blood, the proportion of the beast and cage is upset. The unicorn at full height is enormous. The stable in which he has been chained appears to have shrunk. And for a moment it seems as if he will charge and crash through the flimsy iron and stone barrier which separates him from the woman.

But his rage subsides as suddenly as it has erupted. The eye of the storm closes; the winds die down. He stands motionless, staring at the woman before him.

She is still beautiful but no longer in full bloom. The white spring flower in her hair is dying. Somehow, the year has changed her also. She seems weary. The only reminders of her past arrogance are her outthrust breasts.

After a while she sits down on the green painted wooden bench before the cage. The afternoon passes slowly. One after the other, the pigeons return from their retreat and are soon calmly pecking at the odd pieces of straw as is their custom, carefully avoiding the two dead birds. The goats, once again brave, approach and stick their bearded faces between the bars, looking about with hard, inquisitive eyes. The unicorn, tired of standing, lowers his bulk, resting his head on the ground. His eyes remain open, fixed on the woman who crosses her legs and lights a cigarette.

When the afternoon sun falls out of sight behind the tall hotels at the edge of the park (huge red brick buildings which look as if the skin has been pulled off them, their bleeding flesh exposed), and the gatekeeper blows his whistle as a warning to the visitors that the gates are about to be shut for the night, the woman rises from the bench, crushes out her cigarette, straightens her skirt, and walks away from the cage toward the grand boulevards, spike heels sounding in the dusk, swinging her bogus alligator bag with a certain professional dexterity. In the distance, the gatekeeper's shrill warning whistle sounds again.

*   *   *

Lola was no longer entertained by such stories. Not only had she heard them before, she also recognized them for what they were: sly, cowardly, facetious digs.

Pushing a fluffy pillow under her blond head, she stretched, sighed deeply (as if with relief in having reached a decision), the tips of her unbelievably firm breasts (not round, but plush, conical shaped, slightly wall-eyed, leaning outwards, one pitched to the left, the other rising to the right) quivering, and, suppressing a yawn, said, "Kiss my sweet ass!"

She did not mean it literally. (Paul did this without a verbal invitation whenever he could, grabbing her from behind, pushing his face into the cool tautness of her silk slip, pushing the sleek material up to kiss her thighs, nuzzling the cool between, working his way slowly upwards, lingering at the deliciously tantalizing crease in the flesh which marked the sudden, steep ascent of the perfectly rounded hillocks.) She meant, "Get out!"

And this time she was determined to put her foot down. She was not willing to put up with any more of his tricks.

"Kiss my foot!" she cried.

Lately he had been breaking vases and lamps as well as dishes, bumping into tables, tripping over extension cords, slipping on the rugs as if he were drunk. Lola suspected that it was done more than half deliberately. Out of frustrated malice. Rather than attack her openly, he sneakily attacked her belongings. Not that she grudged the expense of replacing the ruined furnishings, she minded the motives behind these accidents—especially when she discerned that his rages were not solely motivated by jealousy as she had first thought. His belligerence was more devious, more despicable than that. And she was only beginning to fathom the depth.

Noticing that he no longer begged her to stop receiving her numerous clients as he used to, she began to wonder. She smelled a rat. Had he only pretended to be jealous? When, to verify her theory, she spoke of retiring or at least curtailing her activities by accepting the exclusive protection of one of her wealthy admirers (she had many such offers), he did not respond as he once would have or as she thought he should have.

"A perineal whore never changes her stripes," he grumbled skeptically.

She saw through the flip answer, sensing that he feared that perhaps she was in earnest. To test him further, she kept up the pretense for a while longer. He became unbearable, pacing back and forth through the large apartment as if he were looking for something, stopping before the dead telephone which she had deliberately (and with a dramatic flourish) disconnected, peering through the Judas window into the empty hallway, opening and closing the refrigerator, raising and lowering the blinds, fiddling with the radio, and then marching off to his room, slamming the door.

Making believe that she had misunderstood, she followed and reassured him, "Don't be so childish, darling. My becoming a kept woman won't change our relationship. Dr. Karp is very understanding. I've made it perfectly clear to him that you'll stay on. I have no intention of pushing you out."

Paul looked away, avoiding her.

"Silly! Isn't this what you have always wanted?"

He could do nothing else but agree. Yet his lovemaking was not as convincing, not as frenzied as it had been on the days she had given herself to her clients. Then he could hardly wait, already pawing her while she was closing the door on the last customer, taking her— unwashed, still damp with sweat, still warm from the preceding occupant—on the floor of the foyer.

When Lola guessed that Paul was sexually aroused by aiding and abetting her in her trade, that he was titillated by the grunts and sighs, the musky smell of the flesh exchange, that he was secretly thrilled with his lowly role, that he might actually derive pleasure from being humiliated, from being stepped on, enjoy writhing beneath her silken whip (just as much as she had enjoyed forcing him—or at least she had thought that she was forcing him—to witness her being handled by other men), when she realized how she had been fooled, she really lost her temper.

"Kiss my shoe!" she screamed as she kicked him in the ribs.

She now suspected that he was in love with her, mad for her, not despite her being a whore, but because of it! Her conclusion was confirmed when she asked him to assist in a special performance one of her most generous patrons wanted her to put on for a group of visiting business executives he was entertaining. Although Paul rejected the invitation, she sensed that he hesitated, that the temptation was there despite his professed disgust. When she returned from the party, he was waiting up for her and did not refuse to listen to her blow by blow account.

The morning after, not one breakable object in the house escaped unscathed. Yet he had the place cleaned up in time for her evening callers.

After that outburst, his destructive fits subsided (though he still knocked over an occasional chair or spilled a drink on the carpet). He became quieter, morose, doing whatever she asked without a word of dissent. But beneath the docility Lola smelled a basic, though passive, tenacity.

Given enough time, she was sure, she could have driven this out of him. But he was not to have the time. Things came to a head sooner than she had expected.

First of all it dawned on her that he was taking advantage of her in yet another, even more cowardly way, simply by hibernating in her apartment. She realized that he had never, not even once, left her suite since the day she had allowed him to move into the maid's room. He was using her bed as a retreat, as a snug nest, as a sanctuary. He was using her to provide him with free food and lodgings. And in addition getting all the sex he could handle. While she, like the proverbial story-book whore with the golden hair and the soft, golden heart, had given him a free ride. No wonder he was willing to lick her shoes!

Feigning sleep, Lola lay on her back, nude, one pillow over her face, arms raised, encircling the pillow, a second pillow under her rump, legs spread, the pubic mount raised.

"Great merciful God!" Paul cried in mock veneration. "Like the golden fleece tied to the altar—prepared for the sacrifice!" and he knelt down on the bed to pay homage, his weapon rising to attention.

But just as he was about to mount her, she rolled over to the far side of the bed and turned her back to him.

"Kiss my ass!" she said.

When he tried to force himself on her, she did not respond. She lay stiff and motionless, her lips pressed together, eyes cold.

"I'm going to fix you, but properly!" she promised him. "You'll see. I'll get my pound of flesh and some blood too, and I know just the place where I'll start chopping."

Then to make things worse, the elevator operators, who had never before dared to look at her sideways, began to make veiled but nevertheless obscene remarks about her boarder. And, though, she quickly squelched this impudence, she chalked it up against Paul's account.

Hardly had she dealt with this minor annoyance when some of her important clients made it clear that they would be happier if Paul were to disappear. By now he was getting on their nerves, as well as in their way.

That did it. Although there was an added impetus which helped Lola make up her mind to kick Paul out immediately. His name was H. Grabner.

Lola's new lover, who sported a thick, reddish yellow beard, cut uniformly short to follow the strong outline of his jaw, grown, he confided to Lola in a stage whisper, to hide an old duelling scar, was an ex-army officer turned business man. (Among other interests he owned a piece of a supper club, a private investigations firm, a chain of employment agencies, sat on the board of directors of a major railway line, and had many valuable connections in high-society circles.) He and Lola wasted no time coming to an agreement. Although no contract was signed they understood each other, joining forces effortlessly, smoothly, by instinct. The timing was perfect.

When he heard about the trouble Paul was causing her, he as her manager (for that was the position he had assumed), wanted to take care of the intruder himself, but did not insist because Lola thought that she would enjoy doing it herself.

Nevertheless he warned her, raising his voice to make sure that Paul, who was sitting in the kitchen, could hear, "Get rid of your fucking towel-boy by tonight. If I so much as smell him in your place again, I'll squash him like a worm!" and he stomped on the floor with his leather boot to emphasize the point.

16. CERBERUS

Before he realized it, Paul was out on the street, rudely thrown out of the soft bed in which he had basked for more than three months. The lock clicked shut. The doorman, arms folded across his chest, blocked the way back, a grin on his ruddy face (glistening as if after shaving that morning he had smeared his cheeks with vaseline). The shove he had given Paul to help him through the front door had really not been necessary. It was done for the effect, a cheap way to show off.

The display of force was appreciated by the onlookers. Lola, for one, applauded. Of course it might have been someone else, though Paul thought that he could distinguish Lola's shout of approval, her voice recognizable despite its ten-story drop from her window. He did not pause to verify his suspicion, but picked himself up from the sidewalk and backed out of range as fast as he could to avoid further trouble and disgrace.

Dispossessed from what to him was the hot center of life, Paul could not reconcile himself to his loss. Lola had struck suddenly, viciously. Yet he should have been prepared for the blow. Now that he reconsidered her behavior, the obvious portents of her turning against him stood out all too clearly. Even a fool would have expected it and tried to defend himself. He had not wanted to see. He had ignored the ringing telephone, refused to recognize Grabner's voice. He had not watched the door. When it lay splintered, he had stepped over it, closing his eyes to the fact that it had been Grabner who had beaten at the door, who had broken through and entered. He had relied on the power of an outdated, secondhand love potion, a drop of which he secretly added to Lola's orange juice every morning—all the while knowing that the love potion he had dreamed of does not exist, that the liquid in the amber-colored vial has long evaporated, that it is part of a fairy tale for children, a story told by the court jester to the bored, giggling women of the castle (while their men are away fighting)—all the while knowing that the only potent love philter is the strong right arm which shatters and takes, which does not hestitate. He should have realized that Lola was waiting for this, open-mouthed, her blood rising to the call, her eyes eager. She wanted to be conquered and carried off.

Grabner's appearance was no accident. He had been expected all along.

Despite his fear of the doorman and of Grabner, despite comprehending the futility of trying to regain his place, Paul stealthily returned to the scene of his ordeal after dark. Standing diagonally across the street from her building, shielded from the sharp eyes of the doorman by the darkness and by the archway in which he crouched, he kept his night-long vigil.

It had been a close, humid night. Toward dawn a hot wind sprang up and scattered the night clouds, lifted the curtain. Protesting, creaking, the night shutter rolled up. The street lights died one after the other, leaving uneasy shadows. A sharp splintered moon cut through the quilted sky, but was soon chased out of sight by the wind. The only sound on the deserted streets came from a swarm of flies that had gathered to rummage in the loose entrails of a split melon which lay discarded in the gutter.

He should not have been out so late at night, but because he did not want to concede that he had waited in vain again he had ignored the speed with which the night was passing. Dawn surprised him, coming silently over the roof tops, pushing through the teeth-like gaps of the fretted cornices.

As before, he had not had any luck. Despite it, he knew that he would try once more the next evening. Since his expulsion he had waited opposite her apartment each night, hoping to catch Lola by herself. And this time it would be different. He knew now that he must overpower her. He would no longer be afraid. He would not hesitate. He would take her by force if he had to.

As yet he had been unable to see her or talk to her. A telephone conversation would not have been right. It would be awkward and filled with moments of stupid silence. It would be hard enough to stand next to her and explain how he felt, or perhaps not explain (that would be better), rather show her, without apologies or a word about his past failings, that it was all different now and that he was ready to carry her off.

He would be wise to wait for the right moment and not to spoil his chances with a premature attempt. Most likely, he wouldn't get more than one chance. It would be much better to catch her off guard, to wait until she leaned out of the window (to shake her feather duster or, more likely, to get a breath of fresh air after an evening of heavy drinking) and then to call up to her ("Pssst, pssst, love! Here I am. Come on down for a minute. I've got a surprise for you."), or to wait silently until she came out for a midnight walk (she liked to look at the stars) and to follow her and suddenly, without warning, slip his arms around her from behind and drag her off before she knew what was happening. All this could, of course, only happen late at night when the streets are dark and empty and everything seems unreal and even dramatic.

Usually he did not lie in wait for her all night, yet this time he had been so lost in his thoughts that he did not notice how late it had gotten. It was dangerously close to dawn.

He hurried away from her house, not looking back. It would be senseless to meet her now. The sky was already turning light around the edges.

The streets were deserted. He walked fast. As always, the walk seemed like one long continuous street. Houses matched each other in endless boring rows. He was tired. His eyes burned with lack of sleep. The smoke from his cigarette irritated. A gust of wind tore the cigarette out of his mouth. He chased the butt, caught it, then threw it away and lit a fresh one.

The cigarette did not help to dispel his apprehension. All seemed ominous—the long, straight, treeless avenue, the dilated sky, the dark buildings, the even darker doorways and alleys. And when he heard a sharp noise from somewhere behind him, he was swept to the edge of panic. He wanted to look back, yet he didn't dare. He hurried on, faster than before. The cigarette burned his lips. He threw it away; still each breath tasted of hot dry ashes.

Nothing moved on the street ahead of him. Yet he knew that he was no longer alone. The back of his head ached with fear. Finally, unable to bear the uncertainty any longer, he turned to look back. The rows of buildings watched with grave stone silence.

Then he spotted it. A thick shadow leaped from the black mouth of an alleyway.

It was only a dog. Yet on second look his fear returned, for the animal was huge, certainly the largest dog he had ever seen, and, judging by its savage expression, bloodthirsty. It growled and then snapped its mouth shut, gnashing ferocious teeth as if in anticipation.

Paul tried to whistle. The brute would not be charmed. It snarled and came toward him. There was nothing else to do but run. He ran as fast as he could, the dog close behind and gaining with every giant step. He reached the entrance of his rooming house a moment ahead of his pursuer and slammed the door shut. The beast hurled itself against the door, but the lock held.

It was frightening, yet it could have been worse. At that he had been fortunate: the dog had not caught him. Even more important: Lola had not seen his defeat.

17. FULL STOP

Having locked and bolted the door, Paul leaned against it to catch his breath, squeezed in the narrow space between the chest of drawers and the door. The room was so small that if the door had not opened outward there would have been no place for a chest of drawers. The bottom two drawers could not be opened because the head of the bed was pushed up against the round knobs. Only the drawers above the metal frame of the bed were usable. The foot of the bed touched the wall opposite the door. In place of a closet, a wooden clothes rod, approximately the length of a broom handle, spanned the width of the room over the foot of the bed. Presumably a previous tenant had improvised a room divider to cover the clothing area; all that remained of this attempt was an uneven row of thumbtacks on the ceiling. A few shreds of the oilcloth used for this curtain adhered to the plaster, caught beneath the tacks. A wooden shelf affixed to the wall above the bed, running almost the full length of the bed from the chest of drawers to the clothing rod, served as a bookcase (though it could just as well have been intended for storage or the display of souvenirs and other knicknacks). Fortunately, it was placed at a sufficient height above the bed so that the occupant could sit up without banging his head. Opposite the bed stood a straight chair and a narrow drop-leaf table with both of its leaves folded down permanently, making use of the table extremely awkward since the dropped leaves prevented anyone from putting his legs under the table. This became more annoying when one realized that the table could never be opened in such a small room, for, closed, the table, as skinny as it was (it looked more like a plank than a table), already took up all the space between the side of the bed and the window. A person sitting on the chair facing the knife-edge thin length of the table, his back to the door, could not fit his legs under the table top. At best he could force one leg between the dropped leaves, but then his foot would become entangled in the grooved, round table legs. (For some reason, perhaps to steady the table when it was opened, there were eight such spidery limbs, four touching the floor, the others dangling.) The bed was the only place to stretch one's legs. In many respects, the room was more of a sleeping alcove than a room, although unlike an alcove it was completely self-contained with four walls to separate it from the adjacent chambers. In addition, the niche was sealed off by a solid door.

Paul strained against it as if he were forcing it shut against an assailant. He put his ear to the wood, but could hear no menacing sound or movement from the corridor on the other side of the door, only the usual creaking, deep night sounds of the old building settling, chips of cement dropping, ricocheting in the hollow spaces between the walls.

He did not move away from the door. He found this position the most comfortable, or just as comfortable as lying down on the bed. Certainly it was more satisfying than sitting on the straight kitchen chair, for then he would have had no place to stretch his legs.

After work he had usually stretched out on the bed, glad to get off his feet. But since he lost his job he found lying down for an extended period of time as tiring as standing on his feet all day. Instead of feeling the strain in his feet and calves, he felt the fatigue in his back and kidneys, a dull steady painful pressure. When the pain became worse, he got up from the bed and stood against the door, forcing his body into the narrow slot between the dresser and the door. There, tightly wedged between the hard immovable objects, he seemed to find the most relief. Not that the pain in his back disappeared completely, but he no longer felt, as he had while lying on the bed, that somehow he was wasting away, slipping away ... shriveling ... shrinking ...

He had tried holding on to the vertical bars of the bedstead, but this did not help much. The bed was too large. The longer he lay on it the larger it became—though when he had first seen the room he had hesitated to rent it because he thought that the bed, which took up the largest area of the minute cubicle, would be too narrow and too short for him.

The landlady had shrugged her shoulders at his concern. "It's big enough. You'll soon get used to it. I've never had any complaints before. Of course, this is ·a single room. If it's a double you want, it will cost you extra. . . . Well, what do you say, young man?"

When he had handed her the first week's rent in advance she added, as if she now felt sorry that she had bested him so easily, "The bathroom is right next door. There's an extra convenience for you!"

After a while he became accustomed to sleeping with his legs drawn up (rather than stretched out to his full length, the way he had, as a child, been taught was the only proper way to sleep if one wanted to grow up tall and straight). After a while he also began to appreciate the small size of the room. It was neater than a large room. It just fitted him. It seemed tight and secure, especially with the door shut.

Lately, though, he had discovered that far from being too small the bed was, on the contrary, too large. Even though he lay sprawled across it, more than half of it was empty. This disturbed him. He changed positions continually, rolling from one side to the other in an attempt to fill all the corners of the bed at once. But there was always an empty space next to him, either to the right or the left. (When he remembered the conversation he had had about the bed with his landlady, he began to suspect that she had switched beds. Yet this was highly unlikely since the room could not hold a larger bed. Moreover an experienced and hardened rooming house owner would hardly make such a change in accommodations without charging her tenant for it, whether she felt ashamed of the high-pressure sales job with which she had originally hooked him or not. She never mentioned the size of the bed or the proximity of the toilet again and did not show any undue concern for his comfort when on the first of every week she came by to collect the rent. She did not even look into the room, for which Paul was grateful because the dirt had been piling up, especially lately, after the loss of his last job.)

Whatever the explanation, the bed was no longer comfortable. He rattled around in it, tossing up and down, slipping, fading . . . (He seriously considered lashing himself down with a rope.)

Pressed against the door, Paul felt safer. He constructed a headrest for himself by piling books on top of the dresser so that he could remain wedged snugly in the corner between the back of the chest of drawers and the door for as long as he wanted. Thus propped up, with his back to the closed door, face toward the bed, resting his chin on the books, he could doze off.

*   *   *

It was as if the bottom had fallen out of his bottle and with it all hope and all desire for revenge. While at first he thought of himself as having been sold and betrayed, he gradually began to understand that he was unworthy of such melodramatic reactions. Rather, he had been forsaken or, even more precisely, discarded—left by the side of the road as not worth any further consideration or anger. (At most he had been a minor irritant. He posed no serious threat. The doorman easily protected Lola from any overt attack, and, if needed, Grabner could always pay him a personal visit—although it seemed as if this would hardly be necessary. To be sure, in the beginning, Paul had pursued Lola by writing her long, daily letters in which he pleaded for his reinstatement. But these attempts could not have been very annoying since Lola enjoyed showing the letters to her new lover. The ineffectual, adolescent appeals offered them a good laugh.)

Although Paul's deterioration had become physically noticeable, he did not seem to care. It was as if he deliberately fostered it, seeking to debase himself even further. This may have been part of his tortuous scheme of revenge. Perhaps he hoped to shock Lola by his rapid decline, dreaming that his fall would make her feel sorry for him and for what she had done. His choice of work bore out such an explanation.

Granted that decent employment was hard to come by, especially for someone with little experience and no skill or trade, nevertheless the disappointed lover made no effort to better his lot. Instead he sought the lowliest work possible. (Not that there is anything wrong with cleaning toilets; someone has to do it. Urinals don't rinse themselves!)

He gave up his more or less tolerable job as a dishwasher in a small, lower East Side luncheonette when he saw an ad seeking porters for the night shift in the public toilets of the central Hoboken bus terminal. The pay was no better, nor were meals included as they had been in the luncheonette. The hours were long, the work tiring and dirty, the working conditions abominable, but Paul seemed pleased with the change.

Out of the corner of his eye he could see dirty water dripping from an overflowing sink, shiny, slippery as saliva, drooling onto the tile floor. The booths were empty. He strove to finish before the next bus load arrived. Then every stall would be occupied and the high-ceilinged room would resound with the straining breaths of the constipated, the relieved sighs of those who had diarrhea, the moans of those who suffered from piles, the rumbling and groaning, swishing, swirling, the gurgling of the rust- and acid-eaten plumbing. Paul threw the long-handled brush aside and plunged his arms into the bowl, using a rag and his fingernails to get at the deeply encrusted slime and finish the the job properly. He still had to take care of the urinals; they were in almost constant use even during the dead hours of the night.

The men at the urinals enjoyed making obscene gestures and cracking jokes at his expense. The bus drivers were the worst, leading the others on. They cursed him: "Out of my way, you stupid s.o.b." They called him names: "Skinny runt!" They jeered: "Say boy, do you have a minute? Then wipe my motherfucking ass!" They found fault with the way he handled his broom: "Hey doc, a little more elbow grease!" They threatened to lodge a complaint: "Fish out that cigarette butt, sonny, or I'll call the manager." They badgered him with immoral propositions: "I've got a nickle. Do you wanna come into the pay-toilet with me for five minutes?" They cast aspersions on his manhood: "Cocksucking fairy!" They threatened him. They crowded around and pushed him aside before his work was completed. They deliberately kicked his pail and mop over. They urinated all over the floor, right after he had wiped it clean.

If Paul had selected the job expressly to degrade and punish himself, he could not have hoped to be more successful. Not only did the work disgust him (he had been terrified of toilets since childhood), but the patrons, sensing his vulnerability, obligingly added to his torture.

Yet he had miscalculated his stamina. At the end of the first week he had taken all he could and was forced to resign from the job. He retreated to his room and bolted the door.

* * *

Secure in the tight cleft between the door frame and the chest of drawers—he had worked his way deeper into the recess—he held on.

By twisting his neck to the left he could see the stone ledge of the bricked-up window in the opposite wall of the airshaft into which the room's only window opened. No one, of this he was certain, could look into his room. Alternate windows had been sealed. The remaining windows facing the shaft were so arranged along the octangular sides of the pit, the angle of descent so steep, the shaft so narrow, that one could not distinguish between the bricked-up and open windows. Additional protection was provided by the closely spaced vertical iron bars that sealed his window.

However, the room was not as well protected against intrusion as it first appeared. The shaft acted like an echo-chamber, multiplying and amplifying the bedlam of his neighbors' lives. Smells rose like boiling milk and poured into his room as if through a funnel. The city's heat crawled down the airshaft, through the open window, through the walls. The whole building seemed to be sinking into a river of sweat.

He did not try to escape. It had been futile to run in the first place. There had never been a possibility of escape. Once he had tried to run away (or at least thought of it) but the menacing grey walls of deceit surrounded the whole city, and the walls were swelling, growing, spreading in a closing circle. They rose high above him. He felt himself going under, rudely pushed down, away from ...

*   *   *

Lola leaned against the open door, nudging the top of the bureau with her breasts. The papillae showed dark and bristling through the pastel-colored material of her blouse. Her visit did not raise Paul's hopes. He had not even wanted to open the door for her.

He had recognized her footsteps in the corridor, but only pulled back the bolt after she had insistently pounded on the door, warning him that she would get the landlady to break the door down if he did not let her in.

"Did you think I was a dog," she enquired when he at last opened up, "to be kept waiting out here in this miserable hallway? ... Good Lord, what a pigsty!" she screamed when she saw the condition of the room.

She jumped back. "I'm not going to set foot in there. The place must be crawling with roaches. You were never too clean, you know, but this is unbelievable! ... What's wrong with you?"

Paul did not respond.

"But never mind that now," she suddenly smiled, patting his arm. "I haven't come here to scold you—although you deserve a good tongue lashing—not even for those dirty letters you wrote me or for blockading my apartment. You don't know how lucky you are that I defended you. Grabner was going to go after you, but I held him back. I did. I don't really know why, but I did. After all the trouble you made for me, I stood up for you. ... Look at me! Aren't you glad to see me?"

She tried to pull him out of his corner. "Don't you have anything to say for yourself?"

Before he could answer her, she had resumed her lecture, "What's the sense of locking yourself up in this disgusting hole? If you are trying to hurt me, it won't work—you know? I'm no longer responsible for you. I never was. I know you're doing this to annoy me. You pretend to be oh so innocent. And stupid. But you're not. I see through it. Because you're too yellow to come out in the open, you thought that you could embarrass me by making yourself out to be a martyr. Coward! Did you really think anyone would believe you? Why, if I were to tell my friends the whole story, if I told them how you treated me, how you took advantage, how you wormed your way in and lived off me, sucking my blood like a tick, they would tear you to pieces. Grabner was ready to, and I hadn't told him the half of it. I couldn't. I was too ashamed to."

She took a step back, straddling the doorsill, one foot in his room, one foot in the hall. "Don't look so smug! I'm not ashamed of what I did, you know! I'm ashamed of you. Just looking at you makes me sick. I can't stand a whiner. You never even tried. All you can do is complain, blame others, and feel sorry for yourself. ... Act your age and stop sniveling!"

She opened her purse and handed him her handkerchief. "Here!"

Although he had not been crying, Paul accepted the lace handkerchief and wiped the sweat from his face.

"Go on, blow your nose."

Tapping her foot impatiently, she waited until he had done as she bid. "Sweet Jesus! I must be mad to want to help you. ... How long do you intend to go on living like this? making a pest of yourself, brooding, scheming, polluting the air ..."

"It's all one to me," Paul finally admitted. "I don't care what happens."

Lola brushed this off, "Don't talk sentimental rot! Now listen, one thing is clear: you can't stay here any longer." She spoke slowly and calmly to make sure that he would understand her. "I talked it over with my friend and persuaded him to help you. He is willing, if only you'll cooperate. We agreed that the best thing for you is to take a job out of town somewhere, down South or out West, anywhere as long as it's not near the city."

She paused to give Paul an opportunity to think about it.

"Actually, it's all arranged," Lola explained. "Unless you spoil it. And you better not, my pet! It took a lot of doing to get Grabner to give you this break. ... Anyway, he wants you to come down to his employment agency today to sign the contract. By tomorrow you can be on your way. The train leaves early in the morning. So you'd better get started if you don't want to mess everything up."

Paul nodded, but made no move to get himself ready.

"Don't you want the job?"

"Yes, but I'd rather look after myself," he said and took a step back into the corner.

"You haven't done too well up to now."

He had to admit that this was true.

"Then don't be a fool! You'll never get another chance like it. Everything has been taken care of," she insisted. "I don't remember all the details, but Grabner will explain it to you when you see him. It's a good job, with an important organization. A new life. They have factories and warehouses all over the country. And it's all so simple for you. They'll put you up in a dormitory until you find a place of your own. Usually they recruit directly from the universities, but the manager is an old buddy of Grabner's who is willing to let you try out as a special favor to him. ... You can send me a postcard when you get there. ... Be a dear and don't make such a big deal out of it."

"I'm not."

"Then let's get going." She had managed to drag him out of the corner by his shirt-tails. "Don't you have a clean shirt? You little stinker! ... Oh, never mind. Let's just get out of here. I can't bear this room for another minute! ... What a pigsty! You really stink! Don't come so close. I should have you disinfected first. ... What's holding you up now?"

He had come around to the front of the bureau where he was dutifully searching for a clean shirt.

"So you've finally decided to listen to me, have you? Or do you think you're doing me a favor? Don't be so sure. I didn't have to come and get you. You know? My friend offered to take care of you himself. And if he had come after you, you wouldn't have that stupid grin on your face now. ... Hurry up! I can still call him. He'll know how to get you out of my hair once and for all. . . . Another thing, my little man! I think you should know that our meeting was no accident. It was all arranged by the good doctor. Can you guess which one I mean?"

"Dr. Karp?"

"Right the first time! He put me on to you. We had just about given up on you when you walked into his office."

Paul frowned, "But you weren't there. And I didn't get to know you till the year after."

"I like to take my own sweet time. It's men who are always in a hurry."

"But you did try to call me on the phone, didn't you?"

Lola shrugged.

"Did you ever work as a nurse?"

"No. But will a masseuse do? or a manicurist, or a nursemaid, or a receptionist in a dentist's office? . . . Anyway, I didn't come here to answer questions."

"Why did you come?"

"To finish this whole stupid business! Why else? To settle old scores."

"I don't know what you mean."

"You don't?" she laughed in his face. "You will soon enough. But if you don't, then you don't. It doesn't really matter. Not to me, it doesn't. . . . Come on! Get moving. We're wasting time with all this silly talk."

Paul held on tight.

"Don't be such a baby, Paul. Are you still afraid of going to the doctor? I'll hold your hand if you want me to. Then it won't hurt, not even a teenie-weenie bit."

Paul held on tightly to the chest of drawers with one hand and to the bedstead with the other.

Lola's voice softened, "Oh come on, don't look so grave. I was kidding around. Playing a game."

Lola reached out a hand. "Look, I was only joking. Really and truly. Cross my heart. . . . Look, would I have told you if it were true? It makes no sense. I don't like Dr. Karp any more than you do. Don't you remember? The time he came I didn't even want to service him. He gives me the creeps. With his kooky tastes in music and his nasal congestion, the old wheezer. I've been with freaks in my days, but never one like that. Once was enough with that fat tub of guts, believe me! All right? ... Be sweet and get yourself ready so that we can get out of here." She blew him a slow, fat kiss.

Paul hesitated. "I don't know."

"Don't be such a goose. I only want to help you. But you're so headstrong that you make me lose my temper. Don't make me angry again; I'd rather ..." she put her lips against his ear. "Do you remember the fun we used to have together in the maid's room? ... What did you call it? 'A turn in bed,' and 'back stairs work,' and 'fitting it in,' and 'taking it down,' and 'sticky work'. ... You had all sorts of cute nicknames for it. My 'kicky-wicky,' ... my 'privy parts'—remember? Oh, you were a dirty little rat, all right! But a sweet one!"

Alternately cajoling and threatening, Lola worked to persuade Paul of the advisability of the move. Gradually he weakened, began to see the futility of resistance. The senseless, ludicrous tug of war was exhausting him. All the fuss was not worth it. After another round he was ready to promise anything to calm her down (and even more to please her). Believing that she meant no worse than to get him out of town (obviously she could not forget him so easily after all), and recognizing that he had little to lose (he might have become ill and succumbed in this god-forsaken hovel without anyone caring or knowing), and thinking that he could always change his mind if he found the job unsuitable (no one could compel him to stay if he wanted to quit), he finally agreed to cooperate and to go peaceably without any further fuss. He acquiesced silently, nodding his head, almost with a sense of relief.

18. THE FINAL SOLUTION

She led the way. Through what appeared to be the freight entrance of a loft building, along a cobblestone driveway which opened into a courtyard, across the yard to a covered passageway lined with small shops. He followed close behind.

"Hurry up," she said. "We're late as it is."

She walked rapidly through the narrow streets. The streets appeared narrower and deeper than they actually were because of the thick complex of office buildings which rose high above the sidewalks in that section of the city, their corniced roofs projecting and shutting off a view of the sky, forming elongated archways. Yet here and there a narrow strip of the sky could be seen. It was almost dark out. The sun had dropped behind the buildings, but there was no relief from the stifling heat. The approaching darkness was not accompanied by a cooling breeze. Instead, a damp mist settled. Steam rose from the sewers.

Despite her high heels and narrow skirt, she walked so rapidly that her companion was out of breath trying to keep up. He followed a few steps behind, but not too far as he was not familiar with the neighborhood. He doubted that he could have found the way without her, and was glad that he had accepted her offer to help him. He had wanted to go by himself, but she had insisted. She knew the way, walking quickly, determinedly, without looking at the street-signs, cutting through back streets, leading him on a zigzagging course.

The streets were empty of traffic and pedestrians. This was to be expected in that part of the city which was solely a business and financial area. Because of the lack of movement and because of the long arcade which the identical façades of the buildings formed, it seemed later than it was. The woman moved quickly, without looking back at the young man who followed her. When she sensed that he

had fallen too far behind, she stopped and grudgingly waited for him
to catch up.

The mist seemed thickest in the yard. It clung to the cobblestones.
They crossed the court and entered a glass-roofed passage. The
business establishments which lined its way were already closed for
the night, except one small antique shop next to the entranceway of
the building; its shutter was raised half way, revealing a display
window lit by a single naked bulb, crammed full with faded objets
d'art, trinkets, and other bric-a-brac. An old woman, probably an
unexpected customer, had just entered the shop. The back of her
head, her white hair braided in a bun, was visible for a moment
before the door closed. At the same time, the light in the window
went out.

He would have walked right past the entranceway, his attention
distracted by the sound of the closing door, if his guide had not
caught his sleeve and pulled him into the building. The elevator was
standing on the ground floor, its brass safety-gate pulled shut and
padlocked. She had forseen this and led him to the staircase.

"It's only one flight up."

An old-fashioned sign in the shape of a severed hand pointed the
way. The stairs were so steep (or else he was so out of condition)
that he was out of breath before he was half way up and had to stop
for a rest twice more before he reached the top. Grabner's name was
painted in gold letters on the frosted glass pane of the door at the
head of the stairs.

The waiting room was crowded. Paul had not expected it. He
thought that Lola's friend (or "fiancé" as she now called him) had
deliberately arranged an evening appointment so that the three of
them would be all alone in the dark fortress-like edifice. This was
obviously not the case, for every seat in the large hiring hall was
taken. It seemed that Paul was to be treated like any other applicant.

The man sitting in the end seat of the first row of benches jumped
up to offer Lola his place. She ignored him and walked past the
railing which separated the waiting area from a raised section of the
room where four male clerks sat on backless stools behind unusually
high desks. She nodded in answer to their greeting, and, with one
graceful movement, vaulted to the top of the second desk in from
the door. Sitting sideways, she paid no further attention to the clerks
or to the waiting men on the other side of the wooden railing which
divided the room in half. The clerk whose desk she had chosen

continued with his work as if nothing unusual had occurred. Yet since she obstructed his view of a large portion of the hall, he was forced to crane his neck whenever he needed to look at the employment seekers.

Paul was obliged to wait standing up. The six long benches were completely filled although, if they had wanted to, the occupants might have moved closer together to make room for him. The clerk closest to the door raised his eyes from his work to look at the latecomer. He tapped the pad of paper before him twice with the top of his pen. Paul thought he understood and moved away from the door. He found a suitable spot in the back corner of the hall next to an empty clothes tree. There, he leaned against the wall and waited for his name to be called.

Although the wait was long, everything proceeded in a well-regulated way. The prospective employees waited their turn without fidgeting and promptly, when their time came, entered the inner office, the door to which was cut out of the center of the wall behind the clerks. One after the other. No one tried to push ahead. Even though they were not seated in the order of their turn to be interviewed, they seemed to know whose turn it was. At the very moment the door to Grabner's private office opened, the next supplicant in line was already climbing the three steps to the clerks' platform, opening the catch which released the gate in the middle of the railing, and moving along the carpeted passageway between the second and third desk. Then he slipped into the inner room while the applicant who was coming out held the door open and softly closed it behind his replacement. The procedure worked smoothly, as if the men in line had rehearsed their movements beforehand.

The clerks need never have looked up to supervise the orderly procession. But every time the door opened, they raised their heads and watched sternly, pens poised over the papers before them, as if they were waiting for one of the petitioners to make a false move, hoping to apprehend the felon in the act. They made no secret of their watchdog function. A more hostile quartet of examiners would have been difficult to find.

The atmosphere of the office, Paul thought, resembled that of a schoolroom rather than an employment agency; only the office was much better organized and the waiting men were much better behaved.

"Next!" The chief clerk tapped the edge of his desk with the top of his pen.

Paul's turn had finally come, but despite his resolve to match the clocklike precision of his predecessors, he had failed to time himself correctly. He was far too late getting started, and was not even half way to the railing when the clerk's impatient voice cried out.

Not to be completely outdone, Paul took the three steps up to the platform with one leap. The ever-alert clerks observed him closely. Lola did not look up from her fashion magazine as he hurried by her. Obviously, she intended to remain in the antechamber while he was being interviewed.

*   *   *

I thought I recognized him, although it had been a long time. His pink face leaped at me, shiny and smooth as if he had recently shaved his beard off. A scar. A smirk of welcome. The outstretched arms.

"You!" The word was out of my mouth before I could swallow it down. I turned back to the door, but it had already clicked shut. There was no knob on the inside.

"Sit down, my friend." He took me by the elbow and led me to a chair.

"Get hold of yourself. I won't bite." He settled himself in the leather-covered executive armchair behind his desk, elbows on the armrests, hands clasped.

I tried to get out of the chair, but the legs wouldn't move. I wanted to protest, but I couldn't open the mouth.

"What's all this nonsense about?" he kneaded his hands vigorously as if he were rolling a pencil between them. "Well? ... I haven't got all night. ... And stop flapping your arms about like a hysterical bird!"

Perhaps I was flaying the arms without knowing it like a non-swimmer beating at the water to keep from drowning, but I don't think so. I was paralyzed. If I had been able to move I would have been out of the chair running.

"Out with it! Speak up! I can't hear you."

I heard him only too well. Not only his voice, but his labored breathing, the sound becoming heavier as his irritation increased.

"Are you going to explain yourself or not?" he wheezed, fixing me with an unyielding stare. "I'm a busy man. Do you want the job or no?"

"No. ... Yes. ... No." The voice came from my mouth, but I couldn't feel the lips moving. "I don't know."

"What kind of stupidity is this?" He shook his head in disbelief. "Lola has been telling me about you, but I didn't really believe her till now. I thought she was exaggerating."

I opened my mouth to answer, but he jumped down my throat.

"Just shut up and listen! Think carefully before you say something you'll regret." The pencil in his hands (there was one there after all!) snapped in two with a loud crack that made me flinch as if I had been shot at. He hurled the pieces across the room.

"Take it easy. Wipe your mouth and flush the toilet!—as they say in the army." He held up his hand as a signal. Then, as if heeding his own advice, he smiled and selected a fat cigar from the humidor on his desk, rolled it between thumb and forefinger, held it to his ear, smelled it, licked it, and finally put its tip to the flame of a Zippo, lighting it with leisurely care. He drew deeply before looking at me again.

"Now, what's all this fuss about? Wait!" he cautioned me against speaking prematurely. "Hear me out first. I see dozens of young men like you every day of the week. College graduates, dropouts, street-corner hang-abouts. All at loose ends, all dissatisfied, all ready to blame others for their botched lives."

He paused to blow a mouthful of smoke at the ceiling.

"Of course, you're a special case in one sense. You're a two-time loser. You failed twice, not just once." He leaned across the table toward me to make sure that I couldn't wriggle away. "Don't even think of arguing with me. It's all in the records. I'm sure you don't want me to waste time rehashing past history. ... Do you admit it? No need to say anything. I'm not interested in confessions. Just a nod if you agree."

I nodded.

"O-kay. That's a start at least." He looked down at some papers on his desk as if to refresh his memory. "As I was saying ... ordinarily, people are given only one go at it. You were given two! An unheard of chance to start all over again. And then you have the nerve to lay the blame on others! Your parents, your teachers, your benefactress, all of womankind, even your old wet-nurse! To blame heredity, the climate, the times, the stars, the political situation, the capitalist system, humanity. Or whatever. Damn it, if that doesn't take the cake for ungratefulness!" He pounded his right fist into his left palm with such ferocity that I could feel the pain.

"And let me tell you something else," he continued. "You would fail three times too if you were given a third chance! Your case is a clear illustration of the law of permanence. You're the living proof of it."

He raised his cigar and shook it at me like a fat brown finger: "If the goodies of the world were to be redistributed today so that every mother's son and daughter of us had an equal share, no one more, no one less, by tomorrow the picture would look just like it did yesterday—the same haves (the same half) would have; the same have-nots would be going begging. And whining that they were not given a square deal to boot! Your kind is always ready to blame others for the mess they got themselves into."

He rolled the armchair back a bit and swung his feet up on the desk. I was not surprised to see that he wore old-fashioned high shoes.

"Call it the law of stagnation. Do you follow me?"

Not really. I suppose that I heard the whole speech, but only one phrase registered—*a third chance*.

"Yes," I lied, realizing that it was now my turn to speak and that I had better be convincing if I wanted to salvage what was surely my last chance. "I'm beginning to understand. But is it really too late? . . . Couldn't you—" I stopped myself barely in time. "I mean, wouldn't it be possible for *me* to make something of myself if I had the opportunity to start fresh? From scratch. . . . I realize it's hard to believe, but I know that things will be different from now on. I swear it. If I could somehow do it all over. Now that I know. . . . The other times didn't really count. It's only now that I really appreciate what the new job could mean. I didn't listen to Lola when she tried to tell me. But didn't she say that everything was already settled? . . . Why let it go to waste? Couldn't you forget the way I acted before? Please. I promise. I've changed. You'll see. I swear. If only you'll reconsider. You won't be disappointed again. It makes no sense to have been shown the truth and then to have no chance to use it. Won't you reconsider? Three has always been my lucky number."

Grabner scowled. He puffed out his cheeks till the scar stood out like a shiny zipper (I could count the stitches). But he was weakening, so I continued to plead as sincerely as I could.

"All right. All right! I'll probably regret it, but I believe you," he finally gave in. "But this is absolutely the last time."

"Agreed!" I leaped at the opening. "One more chance is all I ask, all I need."

From then on, all things considered, the session went smoothly. As it turned out, Grabner had already taken care of the formalities. My traveling papers were prepared, waiting in my folder.

Grabner did all the talking. This time I listened attentively and the more I heard the happier I became. What at first had been no more than a desperate grab at a straw, any straw, to escape from sure doom, became transformed into a genuine belief. The clouds of gloom lifted and I saw the hope of a fair future. A whole new way of life—unspoiled country, fresh air, unrestricted living space, clear running brooks, green hills, fragrant hay fields, dew-wet grass, wild songbirds, virgin forests, skyscraper-high evergreens, snow-tipped mountains, warm fires at night, songfests, tranquility, new people friendly and spontaneous, love without guilt, open, free relationships, no more lies or fear, away from the past, out of the prison, escape, liberation, old sins forgiven, old mistakes forgotten, no parents or family, no teachers, no one to remind me of my childhood clumsinesses, no witness to my past humiliations, nothing to hide, no one to avoid, everything fresh and clean, reborn, free and joyous, and the opportunity to work hand in hand with others like me, hard work followed by well-deserved leisure, earned rewards, a cooperative, a new youth movement, a collective, to belong to a community, to want to belong, to be needed, to be accepted . . .

I was even to have a new name—Peter Sun!

Grabner handed me my passport, a beautifully printed document with my name inscribed in Gothic letters, the visa stamped with red sealing wax and a tricolor ribbon, the cover made of what appeared to be hand-embroidered gold silk; my one-way ticket (seat reservation and berth booked, prepaid); and a pocket-size timetable which listed the itinerary of the special train (non-stop till the frontier): "Pleasantville, Garden City, Youngstown, Nova Newfoundland, South Thule, Outer Topia, Inner Harmony, Lotophagia, Schlaraffenland, Whispering Glades, Bide-a-Wee Township, Centreville, Lower Lapland, Venusberg, Green Acres, Cedar Grove, Welcome Inn, New Beeland, Sugarloaf Mountain, Lemondrop Falls, Happy Hunting Grounds, Wonderland Springs, Camp-Freedom-Through-Labor, Forest Lawn, Eden Valley, Heartsease County, Resurgam, Paradise Junction, and points West—Sy Barite, Fireman, I. Kutcherkakov, chief engineer, W.B. Cooke, head conductor, Lucy Lockett and Kitty Fischer, Hostesses, Harry Krishner, tour director."

By this point my head was swimming. I could no longer pay attention to all the other exciting details although I wanted to. Grabner had to shake me out of the trance into which I had fallen. He waved the contract in front of my face like a fan and lent me his pen for my signature.

"Make it snappy," he warned me, winking to show his good will. "We don't want to miss the boat, do we? The train leaves on time, on the dot, of that you can be sure."

After I had signed the contract in triplicate, Grabner invited me to come around to his side of the desk to take a closer look at a picture of the new-town of which I was to become a citizen.

Without realizing, I had been staring at it thoughout the interrogation. I now gathered that the country scene depicted on the large wall calendar behind the desk, which had caught my eye from the beginning, was actually a colored painting of the hamlet to which I was being sent. The picture, done in the childlike style of the primitive school of landscape painters, showed a winter scene of a small valley town nestled among snow-covered hills. It is evening—warm, orange colored lights glowing in the windows of the cottages; behind the cluster of cottages a large building, the factory, dark smoke rising from its chimneys, a flock of sparrows circling, warming themselves in the smoke, and then other sprawling structures, more smoke stacks and outbuildings, and in the background a towering warehouse, bricked-up windows, partially hidden by giant fir trees. The fat, black birds on the telegraph poles have settled themselves for the night; the stream which follows the road to the village is frozen over; falling snow obliterates the road. In the left foreground, an open van struggles to reach shelter before it also is overtaken by nightfall. The reclining figures of a dozen or so youths in the back of the wagon can be clearly seen, leaning against each other, shoulder ιο shoulder, arms linked, hands in pockets, bareheaded, mouths wide open, their identical wooden faces red from the wind and cold. The driver is bent over, his featureless face wrapped in a white scarf, black stovepipe hat pulled over his ears. Yet despite the storm, the entire setting suggests the warmth and tranquility children associate with long winter evenings in the country.

19. UPPER BERTH

thedarknessbroke open andtrumpetingaroundthebend thesunrolledout
ofthenighttunnel rising betweenapartmenthousesrushinginto thesky
spinningwheels grindingalongtimegroovedtracks teetering almost
overturning butthen rightingitself slowingdown crimsonstreamers trail
inglimplythroughswirlingcloudsof steam

Awakened by the sparks of the oncoming sun, the pigeons on the
roof of the central railroad station stumbled from their hiding places
deep in the niches of the ornamental stone molding. They plunged
clumsily into the air, falling. Then, flapping their wings noisily, they
regained their balance and swooped up, gliding far above the roof-
tops.

As the minute hands of the four synchronized clocks, one on each
side of the mammoth, glass-domed station, touch the hour hands,
covering them so that it appears that the clocks have only one hand,
the arrow pointing down to the Roman numeral at the nadir of the
circle, the train slides out of its quay. Without any further warning,
before anyone is aware of it, the train slips out of the station. The
dispatcher raises his flag. Automatic switching devices click into
action; rails move into place beneath the locomotive's wheels, steering
the long train smoothly away from the platform at a sharply oblique
angle, so that the wagons seems to be moving away sideways. Disappearing around a curve, the train plunges into a tunnel. Soon it is
travelling at a break-neck speed. First the station, then the city fade
from sight. Rocking across open country, the train speeds to deliver
its cargo. The steady motion calms the passengers. Many of them
have fallen asleep.

Even though they arrived a full half hour before the scheduled
departure, the train was filled. The youth carried a heavy suitcase

which scraped against his leg with every step. He hobbled between his escorts, progressing at an erratic pace, now shooting forward, now falling behind. His companions urged him to walk faster. The woman pulled, the man pushed. When he switched hands, transferring the suitcase from right to left, it bumped against his escorts. The man became angry. He had not expected that the train would be so crowded. They had come early, purposely to avoid the crush, but all the seats seemed to have already been taken. The cars were so overstuffed with rowdy, shouting youngsters that they could not even fight their way into the train. The mob blocked their access, perhaps deliberately. When they reached the locomotive without having found an empty space, they turned back, slowly retracing their steps, carefully looking into each window. To add to the confusion, parents, relatives, friends, well-wishers, and perhaps idle sightseers jammed the aisles. The guards tried to restore order by requesting those who were not passengers to leave the loading area.

The minute hands of the four round-faced clocks inch forward in unison. A warning bell rings. The guards at the entrance to the track pull the iron gate closed. But the train remains motionless. After warning the visitors, the conductors secure the doors. They walk along both sides of the long train testing the doors to see that they are locked. The bystanders waiting on the platform have become impatient. They keep looking up at the clocks. The faces of the passengers are pressed against the sealed windows of the wagons. Those who have come to see them off have grown tired of waiting. They no longer wave their hands. They pocket their handerchiefs or use them to wipe the sweat from their faces. The sun has broken through the early morning haze. It seems to have ignited the glass-domed roof, smothering the station beneath a quilt of heat.

Walking back from the locomotive toward the rear end of the train, the trio moved slower, stopping frequently to peer into the wagons. The young man between the woman and her male associate struggled with his heavy suitcase. He shifted it from one side to the other, opening and closing his free hand to relieve the bruised flesh. When he bumped against the woman, his free hand accidentally touching her skirt, she jabbed him in the ribs with her elbow. Resolutely pushing a way through the throng on the steps and in the aisles, she helped him find a place. Her colleague remained on the platform. The youth followed, dragging his suitcase behind him. A warning blast from the locomotive momentarily quieted the brawling passengers. Before leaving, she bent over him, so close that their heads touched, but he could not hear her. The conductors slammed the doors shut. The train jerked forward and then back.

When the public address system warns the spectators that the doors are about to be sealed, she struggles to free her hand from his clutching fingers. Seeing her difficulty, a porter comes to her assistance, helps pull her hand free. Yet the sealed train remains in the station. The crowd on the platform has thinned out. Most of them have been forced back behind the iron gate leading to the loading platform. However, the youth's escorts are allowed to stay. The man is talking to the railroad officials. They stand by and smile when he lifts his young female companion up to the level of the window. His powerful hands encircle her waist. The white straps of her brassiere show through the thin material of her pastel blue blouse, most noticeably at the top of her shoulders where they cut into the flesh.

The conductor opened the door just wide enough to enable her to squeeze through, bracing himself to prevent the travelers from tumbling out after her. Even then he had trouble in getting the door shut again. She jumped into the arms of her fiancé who had been waiting for her on the platform. The platform had in the meantime been cleared of all visitors. But the train did not move out of its slot although the engineer had already released the brakes and given three short blasts on his whistle. The cars jerked forward and then bounced back, couplings clanging, steam rising from wheels. Conductors ran up and down both sides of the train, double-checking the doors. As her lover lowered her to the ground, the rounded outline of her buttocks attracted the attention of the guards who were now standing around without anything further to do. Although her skirt was not excessively tight, the material clung, especially to the cleft. There the skirt seemed to be of a darker color. The young men at the windows of the carriages fought to get a better view.

Seen from the platform, the train seems unusually crowded. The students have moved to the windows, their heads pressed against the glass. Even though the doors have been bolted and no additional passengers are being admitted, they continue their struggle, not for seats, but for a chance to look out of the windows. The windows are sealed and the platform empty of relatives and friends. Besides the railroad officials, only two observers have been permitted to remain on the quay. They no longer seem interested (perhaps because it is almost impossible to distinguish among the faces; pressed to the glass, the features of the emigrants appear distorted, noses and foreheads discolored by the pressure). Backed up against one of the supporting pillars, they kiss. Although the woman's eyes remain open, she may no longer be able to pick out the face of her friend from among those pressed to the window pane. The faces—seen from the platform, looked at through the dusty, rain-scarred windows—resemble one another so much that even a close relative could not know one from the other.

Facing the motionless train, her back against the steel girder, she kept her arms tightly wound around his neck. The voyagers seemed to be cheering the lovers on. They opened their mouths even wider and beat against the windows with their fists. She winked and waved to them in response. The train jerked forward, steamrising, wheelsprotesting. But soon it moved gently, almost silently, sliding out of the station precisely on schedule, just as the large hands of the clocks covered the hour hands, the black pointers past the middle of the dial, a little past the Roman numeral, starting to inch upward again.

Moving away from the platform on a sharp tangent the train quickly picks up speed. Suddenly the quay is empty. The polished steel rails gleam, reflecting the burning sun with blinding intensity.

About the Author

Although whelped and weaned in central Europe, rescued from the natives by distant, humanitarian relatives and brought to the USA to grow up absurd under the name of Peter Sun (Spielberg being an allonym), the author insists that the anti-hero of TWIDDLEDUM TWADDLEDUM is purely a figment of his imagination and bears no resemblance to his character, living or dead. "The artist, be he born or made, is a pathological liar," he writes. "This is particularly true of the authors of so-called autobiographical novels. The closer to the self, the higher the degree of distortion. No harm intended. As a matter of fact, each lie brings the writer nearer to poetic truths, to universal verities."

Peter Spielberg, whose principal domicile is New York City where he teaches modern literature and creative writing at a major municipal university, has published a book on James Joyce's manuscripts. Stories and poems, fragments and shards of his longer works have been included in many literary magazines and Philip Rahv's anthology, *Modern Occasions*. BEDROCK: A WORK OF FICTION COMPOSED OF FIFTEEN SCENES FROM MY LIFE was released last year. He is currently completing a new novel, *Play Dead*, a jocoserious palindromic fiction dealing with modern family life, sexual games and domestic murder.

FICTION COLLECTIVE

Books in print:

> *Reruns* by Jonathan Baumbach

> *Museum* by B. H. Friedman

> *Twiddledum Twaddledum* by Peter Spielberg

Forthcoming works by:

> Jerome Charyn
> Leslie Epstein
> Raymond Federman
> Jack Gelber
> Steve Katz
> Jascha Kessler
> Barton Midwood
> Mark Mirsky
> Ronald Sukenick